Wandering On The Treadmill

WENDY OGILVIE

Copyright © 2015 Wendy Ogilvie

All rights reserved.

ISBN:1512074071

ISBN-13:978-1512074079

Dedication

For my mum who taught me the importance of dreams
And for Carl who allows me to follow them
And for my Nan, who told me I would write a book one day.

Acknowledgements

I would like to say thank you to everyone who has helped in my quest to publish my book. Annie Farmer, for being an excellent beta reader and sounding board; fellow author, Jenny Conrad, for her advice, Chrissy Hobbs, for providing the cover, Kardy Laguda for helping me with marketing, Valerie, my editor, for pointing out the story flaws, and my amazing boyfriend, Carl Baldry, who gave me my very own office to work in.

I love you all!

Chapter One

Saturday 16th June

Today, I am officially 'Wanda Mikos - Personal Trainer' and I have the T-shirt to prove it! Smiling, I examine my reflection in the mirror. Oh dear. My tummy — which could once have been described as washboard — is now a muffin top over my new black training bottoms. Wisps of unruly hair are escaping from my ponytail and I'm beginning to regret giving in to Jared's homemade curry last night. I know that as a Personal Trainer, I should be lithe, lean and drinking a wheatgrass shot, but the university social scene has left me with some bad habits. However, all is about to change; I am a woman with ambitions. One of which, is to become a fitness trainer for movie stars in Los Angeles. It's a big dream, but I have a career pathway worked out and it starts this year.

Unfortunately, I still need to fulfil the slightly smaller ambition of obtaining some clients to help pay off my student loan and keep up with the rent. I pull on my gym shirt, have a last look in the mirror and start my day with a positive mantra. "Wanda girl, this is the year your dreams come true. And you're going to have to work your butt off...literally!"

"Great stuff, there'll be more room on the sofa," Jared says, poking his head round the door.

"You're so funny, Jared."

"Just thought you may want to know that it's 9.40 a.m. precisely, so you had better get that wobbly arse to work."

"Oh shit, is it that late already?" I re-check my hair for the third time, grab my sports bag and head out of the bedroom. As I reach the front door, I notice a large white envelope on the mat. My tummy does a cartwheel and I stop and look along the hallway. Jared is in the lounge eating toast. I keep my eye on him as slowly, hands shaking, I pick up the envelope and slide it inside my bag.

***

Three weeks ago, the Phoenix Gym in Briford gave me my first job as a Class Instructor and now Personal Trainer. So far, I have put up posters advertising my services, taken four spinning classes and beginners' yoga. Today however, the gym is inviting anyone who is not a member to come along and try the facilities for free. I'm relying on my sparkling personality to convince someone that they desperately need my expertise. Fingers crossed.

As I pull into the car park, I notice a large banner declaring 'Phoenix Gym Open Day' rippling in the morning breeze. Kerry and Marcus, our aerobics instructors, have set up a matted area in front of the entrance and are taking some of the regulars through their paces. "Now grapevine to the left, let's see some energy people!" Marcus shouts. He loves the sound of his own voice, but luckily nobody seems to mind. Passers-by stop to watch when they hear the *whohoos* as the class increase their pace.

The gym is situated on the first floor up three flights of stairs. I have worked out that running up and down them thirty times, could burn off nearly three hundred calories. Entering the gym, I look to my left and spy Karen, the gym manager, exiting the lift with a tall, gorgeous blond bloke. I notice, rather begrudgingly how good they look together; her 5ft 8' lean figure complimenting his tall athletic frame. She strides towards me with the fake smile she saves for those she loathes. I prepare myself for an introduction but she wafts past me as the hot guy turns to give me a cursory glance. Karen notices and clamps a power-grip on his arm dragging him off cave- woman style towards the gym office.

Karen Lester is a woman who thrives on being the boss. We call her Miss Hitler as we reckon she was going to join the Russian Women's Wrestling team but thought they were far too light and fluffy. I think Hitler would have liked her work ethic.

I shake my head and laugh before starting my floor check with a general sweep of the free-weight section looking for stray barbells and plates. Men are much worse for making a mess in the gym as is usual in the home. My brother Jared is gay so you think he may have more feminine instincts for household chores but he hasn't.

I notice Karen and her 'attachment' moving quickly from the office to the stairs. I am busy picking up weight plates and don't bother to look up.

The gym is filling up with new members who are enthusiastically prodding the buttons on the machines and picking up dumbbells. These are the 'New Year Trainers'. I know it isn't New Year but it works the same. They join because they realise their beach holiday is four weeks away and they are in no fit state to be seen in swimwear. They will be on an exercise-high until their holiday arrives and then won't move their wobbly arses again until they declare 'getting fit' on their list of New Year resolutions.

I am taking a yoga class later so I decide to pop down to reception to check how many are booked in. As I jog down the stairs, I find myself looking around for the sexy guy Karen was hauling around.

"Hi Annie," I call to the receptionist, "can I have the class schedule?"

"Yes here you go my love."

I check what time my yoga session is then walk across to Karen's office but I'm called back by Annie.

"Wanda, this lady has just joined and wants some advice on training. I told her you were providing free consultations today."

The plump woman standing at the counter is fidgeting and pulling on her hair.

"Yes, of course. Hello, I'm Wanda, what's your name?"

"Vanessa," she says offering me her hand.

"Good to meet you Vanessa. If you want to come up to the gym, we can have a quick chat and I'll show you around."

She definitely perks up once I have shown her around the gym and explained the process of working with a trainer. I think I may have my first client.

"So Vanessa, do you think one-to-one sessions might be what you're looking for?"

"I think that sounds just what I need at the moment," she says, with a determined nod of her head.

"OK, let's sit and sort out prices and find out what your training goals are."

I indicate the way to the office. I can tell there's a story behind her visit to the gym today and I am interested to find out more. Karen arrives at the office doorway just as we sit down.

"Wanda, this is Mrs Clamp and her daughter Fiona," Karen puts her arms around Mrs Clamp and her daughter — not very successfully, they are rather large — "they want to have a look around and talk about their fitness goals."

"I was just going to finalise some details with this lady actually."

"OK, I'll get Zoe to show them around the gym and bring them back to you in five minutes." Fortunately for me, I am the only qualified PT in the gym at the moment. I want the opportunity to gain two more clients, so I give Vanessa a quick guide to cost and make her an appointment for next week.

One hour later, I have also managed to convince Mrs Clamp and her daughter that they need my services. This is definitely one of my better days. I grab my folder and make my way to reception. I have no real reason for going other than hoping for another look at the hot guy if I'm honest. I reach reception but there is no sign of him so I divert slightly towards Karen's office on my way back to the gym. Unfortunately he's not there either but as I cast my eye around the office I spot a large white envelope sitting on the desk. It looks exactly the same as the one in my bag. I was going to wait until the end of my shift to open mine, but I have a sudden need to know its exact contents.

Chapter Two

I'm sitting in the car park staring at the, now slightly crumpled, envelope, which has been in my bag since this morning. Squeezing my shoulders to my ears, I release some tension and slowly pull out the contents. I can hardly bare to read it.

Dear Miss Mikos

We are delighted to inform you that your application for entry into The Main Event competition has been accepted. Please familiarise yourself with the rules and regulations on page two.

We look forward to meeting you.

Kind regards

Patsy Cosby & Rae Flynn

Whoopee! I can't believe it. Step one of my career plan is underway.

I'll read the rules and regulations later.

***

As I enter our flat, the garrulous squawking of Jared and Megan fighting for supremacy on the latest Wii game hits my ears. Meg is my other flatmate and oldest friend. They look up as I enter the lounge.

"Well?" says Meg, pressing the pause button, "how did it go today?"

"Fantastic! I have so much to tell you, I don't know where to start."

"From the beginning and don't miss out a thing," Meg says tucking her feet under herself on the sofa."

"Firstly, the big news is that I have my first clients, a lady who wants me to train her three times a week and a couple of fat women who have booked in but I'm not sure they'll turn up."

"Wanda, that's great."

"The bigger news is —" I pause for effect, "I was accepted as a contestant in The Main Event competition!" I jump up and down on the spot and fling my head around in jubilation.

"Oh my God Wanda that's fantastic!" Meg says rushing up to give me a hug.

"Is that what the envelope was you sloped off with this morning?" Jared asks.

"Yes, I didn't want anyone to know until I found out if I'd been accepted. They only take a certain number of contestants."

"Well done, babe that's great. When is it?"

"Not until the end of August, so that gives me ten weeks."

"Is this that aerobic thingy you were going on about?" Jared asks, as he grabs a bottle of water off the coffee table.

"You make it sound like an aerobics class, Jared. It actually involves taking one of the examiners for a PT session, and then you have to pass an interview and a written test. The final part is to perform a routine in front of an audience, which must demonstrate: strength, balance, flexibility and power. All of which I have of course."

"What do you win?"

"The company take the winner to Los Angeles for three months to work with them and their clients. If they think you're good enough they offer you a permanent job."

"Yeah right, good luck with that Sis."

"And there's more, I think we might have a new Health & Fitness manager and he's gorgeous."

"What do you mean you think?" asks Meg.

"Karen was carrying him around like a rucksack all day but never introduced him to anyone."

"That woman's like a limpet. Anyway, I think we need to celebrate. Mojitos at Povkas Bar anyone?"

***

Povkas Bar is just six minutes walking distance from our flat. We know this because we timed it the first time we went there. It is owned by a rotund Turkish man called Manny. He speaks perfect

English and is on first name terms with most of his customers.

As we push through the door, I notice it is rather empty except for a few people who look like they came for lunch and haven't left yet. We make our way to the bar, which is a dark wood semi-circle surrounded by tall tables and stools. Almost every wall in the bar is adorned with sepia mirrors and along one side there are booths, which seat six at a squeeze. Meg and I slide into a booth and signal to Jared who has gone to get some drinks.

"Here we go," Jared says, placing the tray of cocktails on the table and lifting one in the air. "Congratulations Wanda on getting what you want, and hopefully getting a fit boss today."

We chink glasses.

"Right," says Megan, pushing her Mojito to one side. "Let's start with the hot guy; just how gorgeous are we talking here?"

"Well, if you take Brad Pitt's dimples, Richard Gere's eyes and Robert Pattinson's jaw line, add broad shoulders and wavy blond hair, that would describe him perfectly I think."

"*Mondieu*, but he sounds *tre fantastic!*"

"Jared, you do realise that if you want to speak French, you can't fill in words you don't know with English words spoken in a French accent."

"*Oh ferme la bouche.*"

Jared has been learning French. He is a flight attendant and fell in love with the South of France last year. His aim is to live there with his handsome boyfriend — no sign of one yet — and to own a boat. Dreaming big obviously runs in the family.

"Anyway," I announce, as I bang both palms on the table, "are you both going to help me win this competition or not?"

Megan and Jared pull their glasses away from their lips and look at me.

"Yes, yes of course we will," they chorus whilst each squeezing one of my hands.

"How can we help?"

"Well Meg, as you teach gymnastics, I thought you could help me with the strength and balance stuff."

"Wanda, I assist someone who teaches five-year-olds."

"That's OK. Plus you were a great gymnast at school."

Megan pulls her long naturally blonde hair away from the back of the chair and nods. "OK, should be fun. I might even be able to get the hall at the leisure centre so you can practise."

"That's great. Thanks, Meg. There is a slight fly in the ointment though," I say, screwing up my face and tapping my fingers on the table.

"And that fly would be what?"

"I have a suspicion that Karen has entered too."

"Oh my God, why would crapface enter, she's not even a Personal Trainer."

"Technically, she is. I know she didn't finish her degree but she does have other course certificates that qualify her. I think she only took the manager job because she couldn't hack it at Uni."

"Is that why she hates you?" asks Jared, getting up to get another round of drinks.

"Yeah, she hates the fact that I stuck it out. But she has entered the competition before, two years ago I think. She didn't win but apparently her routine was fantastic."

"Poop, she ruins everything." Megan sighs, sliding out of her seat to let Jared pass.

"Poop?"

"Yes poop! Shut up Jared. You know I hate to swear."

I stifle a laugh as Jared makes a face and navigates his way to the bar.

It's great to watch my 6ft, olive-skinned brother, smile sweetly as every girl tries to catch his eye. His athletic physique brushing past actually stops them mid conversation. Many a girl has been left red-faced after trying her best flirting techniques on him. It makes for quality entertainment.

"Can we get back to discussing my dilemma?" I suggest, as we start on our second cocktail.

"Sorry, Wand', carry on."

"The thing is, Meg, even if she doesn't win but gets placed higher than me, I'll never be able to stay at the gym. She'll make my life hell and remind me of it every bloody day."

"Never say never Wanda my girl; we will think of something."

The three of us spend the next hour or so discussing various ways of sabotaging Karen's attempts to win the competition. With each passing cocktail, the ideas become increasingly outrageous, ending with an idea Jared has to put itching powder inside her leotard and leg warmers. I think he's been watching Mum's Jane Fonda videos again.

By 10.00 p.m., we move to the bar and check out the songs in the karaoke book. Manny thinks that karaoke is the latest thing and nobody has told him otherwise. It is funny though and he only does it once a month. I'm trying to persuade Meg to join me in a chorus of *'It's Raining Men,'* when a guy taps me on the shoulder and offers his singing services if I pick a different song. Megan is too shy to sing in front of people, plus she's tone deaf, so I take him up on his offer.

"My name's Gary by the way," he says and holds out his hand. Gary is about 5ft 10inches with brown hair that flops across his eyes. He is wearing cool jeans and a red checked shirt.

"Wanda," I respond, shaking his hand. "And this is Megan."

Meg smiles and shakes his hand. "Thank you for rescuing me."

Gary and I choose the classic *'I've Got You Babe'* by Sonny and Cher. Arm in arm we wow the crowd with our incredible talent. Well they cheered anyway.

Gary turns out to be a giggle and one of his friends, Luke, has taken to dancing with Meg around the bar. She looks a little awkward but he seems really nice. I think when we changed from cocktails to shots, we should have gone home but alas we did not. Jared spent most of the night talking to his two best friends and singing power ballads on the tiny stage. Megan got Luke's phone number and I think I kissed Gary goodbye but I'm not one hundred percent sure. Oops.

I wake Sunday morning and leap out of bed. Oh, who am I kidding? I'm not even sure it's my bed. No, it's OK, I can see my Tuesday knickers on the floor over by my wicker chair. They haven't been on the floor since Tuesday, they just have *'Tuesday'* embroidered on the front. The other days of the week have been gone for some time. Not really sure why *'Tuesday'* survived. Perhaps I went commando for a while so they didn't get much wear.

We drank about four cocktails and who knows how many shots last night before Jared had the most excellent idea of grabbing a very healthy chicken kebab on the way home. To which I commented. *"Jared darlin' we've probably jus' drunk 'bout five thousand calories. Do you fink it's going to make one soddin' bit of difference whether our kebab is chicken or not?"* I don't remember much after that or actually eating a kebab which really pisses me off as if I hadn't drunk so much, I wouldn't have eaten anything and I wouldn't feel like death was closing in this morning.

***

Smacking my lips together, my tongue feels void of all moisture. I think a dental nurse has been at the inside of my mouth with her suction thingy. I try to sit up but someone — probably the same nurse — has implanted a heavy plate into the back of my head forcing it back to my pillow. I take a swinging motion and finally approach a seated position. Oh dear; the plate in my head just dropped to my stomach. I need the loo or maybe a bucket; my head is about to explode and — WHAT THE HELL IS THAT SMELL? Gingerly, I lean over the side of my bed as the stench of a half-eaten donor kebab with chilli sauce hits my nostrils. I can't hold onto the other half any longer and sprint to the bathroom.

I'm so glad that my training for the competition starts tomorrow. Why can't I ever remember how bad this feels when I'm ordering my fourth cocktail? Seriously, that would be so helpful. I wonder if there is an app for that.

I throw up just the once and instantly feel better, which is good because I really need a shower. I turn the shower on and wait for the water to pass freezing point whilst hopping about the bathroom trying to pull off my pyjama bottoms. Gently, I step into the shower cubicle. The warm stream of water running over my skin is a relief but I can't close my eyes without holding on to the wall. Never again— and I mean it this time.

***

We spend most of our afternoon on the sofa watching the *Twilight* box set and gulping down gallons of water and left over pastries. Meg brings them home from The Coffee Snob where she works part-time. It's perfect for her really as she actually is a coffee snob. By 6.00 p.m., we manage to shuffle to the kitchen to make something to eat and I grab a pen and paper.

"What are you doing, Wand'?" asks Meg as she sits at the table picking at her pizza.

"Working out my training plan for the next ten weeks; I need to set myself goals and we need to work out when you can help me with the gymnastic stuff."

"I'll ask Trevor at the leisure centre if we can use the hall this week."

"That would be great. Jared, are you joining Phoenix this week as I could use a little push in the gym as well?"

"Count me in," Jared says yawning and laying his head in his hands.

"I need someone to choose the music with me too. Actually, I need to read the competition rules before I do anything. I'll get the paperwork."

I start reading the information sheets and realise it may not be as easy as I first thought. They provide a list of typical questions, which could be asked during the interview:

- *What exercise would you avoid giving to someone who has just been diagnosed with a glenoid cavity injury?*
- *Who should you not give heavy leg training to?*
- *What type of training involves peripheral heart action?*

I don't have a problem with these questions as I know the answers but I don't do well under pressure. On the other hand, they are quite technical and I think Karen will struggle as her training was pretty basic. I can feel myself grinning as I continue to read. The next page of the competition notes are too boring for someone with a hangover and I realise that I've been repeating *blah, blah, blah* in my head for the last five minutes. I'll read the rest tomorrow. I'm going to go in before my shift in the morning, so I can get my training done first. Actually, I can't wait to get started.

Chapter Three

Monday 18th June

I'm feeling decidedly perky this morning as I get ready for the gym. I need coffee first though. Actually, I might have a Liquorice and Fennel tea. Unfortunately, as I reach the kitchen, the wonderful aroma of French roast hits my nose; courtesy of The Coffee Snob, I mean the café *not* Megan.

"Did you make enough for me?" I ask. I'll have the Liquorice and Fennel tea tomorrow. It's only the first day after all.

"I will make you one in a sec but I need to ask Jared a question first. What the hell are you wearing?" Meg holds her hand to her mouth to hide a giggle.

"Don't you laugh; these pants were white last week! One of you must have put them in with your pink washing."

"There you go poofy-pants." Meg hands him a coffee.

I cannot help but laugh at Jared who looks so indignant. "Mum always says you look good in anything. Let's take a picture for her."

"Don't you dare. Anyway, Wand' I'm going to join the gym today but then I'm off to work. I won't be back 'til tomorrow as I have a layover."

"*Ooh* you lucky thing, with anyone nice?"

Jared sighs as he leaves the kitchen. "Honestly, Wanda that wasn't even funny when I started this job six months ago."

***

I'm still feeling good as I arrive at the gym. Saturday's cocktails and kebab were just a celebration I tell myself; today I start thinking like a competitor. I arrive an hour early to get some training done before work and bump into Elliot who has been in since 6.30 a.m. Elliot has been at The Phoenix since it opened two years ago. He is nineteen with strawberry-blond hair, which he moulds into a weird shape. He looks rather like a fish, but is funny and sweet. Actually, I think he might be gay. This assumption I must admit is based purely on the way he bounces around the gym like Tigger-on-crack. He is also quite effeminate and certainly not afraid to wear pink. Because my brother Jared is gay, I assume to be an expert in gay detection but I've been known to be wrong before.

"Morning Elliot, have a good weekend?"

"Yeah, man it was madness. Went to a crazy party in town on Saturday and ended up on the beach with someone 'til five o'clock in the morning."

I want to ask male or female, but can't bring myself to. "Sounds great, is it love?" I ask, giving him a nudge.

"Nah, Sam's cool but love? Don't make me sick."

Sam! I can't believe it. Couldn't have been a Mark or Lisa so I could tell which gender we were talking about. I'm determined not to ask anyone at the gym, especially as I've been here a month already. Jared is joining today so I'll get him to find out for me by using his 'gaydar'.

"Is Karen in?" I ask.

"She was in the studio earlier but I think she's back in her office."

I knew it! She has been accepted as a contestant in The Main Event competition, which is why she was using the studio instead of running outside or on the treadmill as usual.

"By the way, Mike was asking questions about you yesterday," Elliot says, raising his eyebrows.

"Who's Mike?"

"The new Health & Fitness manager, haven't you met him yet?"

"No, but Karen hasn't introduced him to me."

"Well, he knows who you are."

Yes! Right, stay calm I tell myself. "What sort of questions did he ask?"

"Just things like, how long have you worked here, what classes do you teach *et cetera*."

"Oh, that's boring. Didn't he ask if I have a boyfriend?"

"Nah sorry, perhaps he'll ask you himself." Elliot winks as he walks away.

After a quick chat with Pat Moorcroft, our other receptionist, about her ailing cat Rufus, I grab a protein shake and head for the gym and notice Karen clip clopping towards me with her long blonde hair swishing back and forth. I pull myself up to my full height – 5ft 5 inches – and smile broadly. "Morning, Karen. I hear you were in the studio this morning; training for anything special?" I know this is not particularly discreet but I couldn't think of anything else and not knowing is killing me.

"No, just doing some yoga before work. Did you manage to get anyone to sign up for personal training?"

Talk about change the subject. "Yes, I have a client who is going to train with me three times a week for the next six weeks and Mrs Clamp and her daughter are coming back to see me this week."

"Well done, Wanda I'm so pleased for you. Let me know how you get on." Karen places her arm around my shoulder and squeezes. At 5ft 8 inches and wearing 3-inch heels she towers over me like an alpha male dog. Just as I'm about to say something cutting, I notice Mike in the mirror. Ah, the reason for Karen's sudden appreciation of my efforts. I unravel myself from her grip.

"Morning, Wanda," Mike calls from behind me. "I don't believe we have met yet?"

I stop and turn to face him as Karen puts her body between us.

"Wanda, yes I forgot about you, can I introduce Mike Diamond, he's the new Health and Fitness Manager?"

"Hi, Mike Diamond, a girl's best friend," I say smiling and instantly regret every word except maybe hi. I do have a tendency to blurt out the most stupid things when under pressure or embarrassed.

"It's nice to meet you Wanda. You're a Personal Trainer I see," Mike says, nodding towards the logo on my top and politely ignoring my stupid remark.

"Wanda has only taught a few classes and been gym instructor so far as she's quite new too," Karen announces.

"Oh I meant to tell you Karen, I have been accepted for the Main Event competition."

I look into her large eyes to check her reaction. She flinches slightly as though she has just been pinched.

"Oh Wanda that's fantastic, what great news, maybe we can get together and I can give you a few tips as it is your first time."

I am just about to ask her if she is competing when she practically shoves me to one side and grabs hold of Mike's elbow. He looks stunned but smiles tightly. "Well I look forward to working with you Wanda." He says revealing the sexiest dimples I have ever seen.

"You too," I say casually as I walk away. I can't believe how cool I'm being. Give it a few more weeks and he won't be able to resist me. That's the plan anyway."

I am annoyed with Karen for not telling me whether she has been accepted for the competition when it hits me — perhaps she hasn't been accepted. Perhaps the contents of her envelope had REJECT stamped across it. That must be it! Poor thing must be so embarrassed I almost feel sorry for her.

I decide to really push myself on press-ups and lunges making a good start to my routine. I'm about to time how long I can hold a plank for, when I notice Mike walking towards me.

"Sorry, didn't mean to stop you. Shall I go away?" He says looking down at me on the floor.

"No it's fine; gives me more time to recover from the last exercise," I reply, tucking a stray hair behind my ear. "How are you getting on?"

"Good thanks. Wanda, could I ask you something?"

Oh my goodness, this is it! He's going to ask if I have a boyfriend. "Yes of course, anything."

"Is Elliot gay?"

"Oh, erm, I don't actually know. I have tried to find out but no luck so far."

"OK, don't worry, I'm sure Karen will tell me soon enough. Just didn't want to put my foot in it. Sorry to interrupt your workout."

"No problem," I say feeling a little disappointed. Oh, who am I kidding, I'm gutted.

"Hey, Wanda what did Mike want with you?" Zoe asks, running up to me and plonking herself on the mat.

"Nothing really," I sigh. Now could be a good time to ask Zoe about Elliot. She's been working with him for a year and is really cool but I can't bring myself to.

"Don't worry girl just give him time. I'm sure he will see you in a new light when you turn up at the summer party all glam and gorgeous."

"Party, what party?"

"The members and staff Summer Ball. Didn't Karen tell you?"

"No she bloody didn't; probably had no intention of telling me either, cow!"

"It's not until next month so you have time to prepare. And may I suggest you make the most of the girls, I certainly would." She winks, gives me a thumbs-up and bounces away. I realise that my face is screwed up as I watch her leave. What girls? I wonder if she meant taking advantage of Meg and Jared. I know he's gay but calling him one of the girls is a bit harsh. Oh well.

I decide to have a jog on the treadmill before I finish and set my earphones up so I can watch the television. My run begins with a gentle jog, which is when I realise I'm not wearing my sports bra. My boobs start bouncing around like a shirt in a washing machine. Oh the 'girls' I've just got what Zoe meant. Bit cheeky, but she has a point. My lady-lumps are rather fabulous if I say so myself. Bringing the treadmill to a stop I discreetly tighten my bra straps and get back to it. No more excuses.

I increase speed so my jog becomes more of a sprint but have to tuck my arms in close to keep any boob bobbing to a minimum. I keep it up for the next five minutes, puffing and sprinting. Once I reduce the speed a little, I glance across at the gym desk. Mike is talking to one of the instructors. He turns, looks across at me and waves. I turn slightly to wave back but my right foot clips the edge of the treadmill forcing me into a Bambi-style recovery as I grab the safety bar. How embarrassing!

My first training session has me sweating but I know that I will need to up my game for the competition. After eating the bagel and peanut butter I brought from home, I shower and run back up to the gym — 13 calories — to meet with my very first client.

"Hi, Vanessa." I hold out my hand to the nervous-looking woman by the office. "Are you looking forward to your first training session?"

"Yes, bit nervous but excited," she says, pulling at her oversized grey T-shirt.

Vanessa is thirty-five, 5ft 5 inches and about two stone overweight. We chat as I take her blood pressure and measurements. I hadn't found out much about her at the open day so I was looking forward to finding out what had prompted her gym visit.

"So, Vanessa, can you tell me what your fitness goals are?"

The standard reply to this question is *to lose weight and tone-up*, so I was not prepared for the answer that came.

"I want to look so fucking fantastic that my cheating bastard husband will spend the rest of his life regretting the day he let me go!" She takes a breath, looks up and bursts into tears.

"Oh dear." I don't know what else to say. I have never been very good at dealing with heartache, not even my own. "Well, at least you have a specific goal," I manage. "Let's not waste that healthy rage; we'll use it to get you into the best shape of your life. I promise he will regret losing you." I hand her a tissue.

"Sorry, I promised myself I wouldn't cry today."

"Don't worry, happens all the time. When did your marriage break-up?"

"Months ago, but our divorce came through today."

"Well, no wonder your eyes are now the same shade of red as your hair!"

Vanessa manages a smile. She looks pretty when she smiles; her teeth are perfect and her green eyes sparkle, just a little. Although her thick red hair is pulled into a bun, she definitely has potential. I suddenly realise I'm about to become her trainer, agony aunt and best friend all rolled into one. Helping her gain back some self-esteem is going to be a challenge, but one I am looking forward to.

Friday 22nd June

I've spent all this week trying to find out if Karen has been accepted for The Main Event without success. However, I have just noticed her go into one of the studios again. She is rehearsing her fitness routine, I just know it. I decide to ask Pat on reception if she knows anything. Nothing gets past her.

"Hi, Pat, have you seen Karen?"

"I think she's in one of the studios," Pat replies, tilting her head toward the studio.

"I won't bother her then if she is training. How's your cat?" I hate cats but I don't want to ask her for the gossip outright.

"Doing better thanks, his poo is more solid since he's been on the tablets."

"Great," I say feeling slightly sick. "By the way has Karen told you anything about entering a competition?"

"What competition?"

"I think she may have entered The Main Event but she won't tell me."

"Hasn't said anything to me, but I'll let you know if she does."

"OK thanks. Love to Rufus, glad he's better."

Now I know it would be wrong to peep through the studio window to check out what Karen is doing, but this is a life changing competition for me. If I win, I realise my dream of living and working in Los Angeles where I'll transform celebrities and stars to skeleton-like proportions. Losing of course could mean having to put up with Karen's gloating whilst I work my notice at the gym then go and teach Thai Chi to the over 60s in a school hall.

I run to the studio, quickly check to see if anyone is around and slowly slide up to the window at the top of the door, just in time to see Karen perform a handstand with splits. I can't do that. She spins around towards the door as I pull away from the window. I don't think she saw me. A few seconds later I peer into the studio again armed with the video on my phone. Karen jumps, kicks and spins around the floor, finishing with a one-legged balance pose which she holds perfectly still for a whole five seconds. Oh poop.

Wandering back to the gym I check the video. Karen's legs look even longer when she is flinging them around and her balance is incredible.

"Wanda, did you want to see me?"

Crap, it's Karen.

"Erm no don't think so," I mumble, whilst trying to turn off my phone.

"Oh, I just saw Pat as she was leaving and she said you were looking for me."

"Yes, yes I was. I forgot." Oh my God think Wanda, what did I want to see her about?

She looks at me with her perfect eyebrows raised waiting for a response.

"One of the members was asking me about the party next month but I said I hadn't been told about it but would find out."

"Oh, well, it's only just been decided so I'll get some posters up this week," she says looking flustered.

"Great, I'll let them know."

Karen turns to leave and spins around with such force her hair narrowly misses my right eye. What a bitch! I must remember to swing around her sometime soon and poke my wax-laden ponytail in her peepers.

***

I'm waiting for Jared to join me for a training session and I ponder on what I can wear to the Summer Ball. Parties are a great way to get to know everyone much better. Plus, I'm a pretty good dancer and I brush up well. Watch out Mike Diamond!

I hear the gym door open and in walks Jared dressed in white shorts, a turquoise vest and turquoise trainers. I can't decide if he looks really stylish or just really gay.

"I think I'm going to need sunglasses to train with you today," I call out shielding my eyes.

"Very funny, do you want me to train with you or not?"

"Sorry, of course I do. I hate doing strength training on my own."

Strength training with Jared is great as we are very competitive and I know there will be no slacking.

"Come on let's start with some press-ups. Have you warmed up?" I ask.

"I cycled here if that counts."

We place our hands down on the mat and start counting off repetitions.

"...18, 19, 20, 21," I glance across at Jared who is not struggling at all.

"Come on Sis; keep going, 25, 26, 27, 28."

"Wow, that's impressive," Mike comments as he walks past us wearing a grey suit with the trousers tucked into a pair of green wellies. Grateful for the interruption, I flop onto the floor.

"Just our warm-up set," I tell him, puffing and pushing myself off the floor whilst trying not to look like my 70-year-old Greek grandmother.

"You can do more than me," Mike says as he strides towards the door.

Not wanting him to think that Jared is my boyfriend, I shout. "This is my brother Jared. And by the way, why are you wearing wellies with a suit?"

Mike turns and smiles the biggest smile. Oh my God he's so gorgeous.

"There's a flood in the men's showers again. Got to go, see you later. Nice to meet you Jared.," He raises his hand as he walks out of the gym.

"See what you mean about those dimples," Jared says as he stares after Mike.

We finish our training in one of the studios with some Proprioceptive Neuromuscular Facilitation. This involves the 'stretchee' getting into position whilst the 'stretcher' pushes them, in stages, beyond the point they can reach on their own. I'm sure it was used as torture in the old days. Today however, it's considered extremely effective for elite athletes. Still feels like torture to me though.

Finishing our workout, Jared wanders off to have a shower. I grab my towel and I'm about to shut the studio door when I see Karen heading my way. I smile weakly hoping she will walk straight past but no such luck.

"Were you rehearsing your routine?" she asks.

"No just stretching," I reply before turning towards the changing room. I bet she had her big fat nose up against the window when I was practising earlier.

"How's the routine going?"

"Good, thanks. I'm having trouble with my handstands but the rest is good."

"Seriously, Wanda, you're not intending to do a handstand are you?" she says sarcastically before looking over my right shoulder as if I've just disappeared.

"No of course not I…"

"Oh, Mike there you are," she calls out, "can we hook up for coffee later?"

"No problem," Mike replies. "I just need to finish in the men's changing room."

Karen throws him her sweetest smile, which resembles the grimace my mum had when she was constipated: an unfortunate consequence of the boiled egg diet.

"OK, bye-bye, see you then." Karen sighs and stares after him until he disappears. When I watch her watching him, I realise The Main Event isn't the only thing we might be competing for.

Chapter Four

Friday 22nd June - Weight 10st 1Ib

Megan, Jared and I gather around our large pine table in our kitchen to view the video of Karen's routine. Although I'm feeling guilty about it, I remind myself that it's a competition and I need to know what I'm up against.

"OK, here it is." I press play. There is a period of silence whilst we all watch the video.

"I hate to say it but she's really good. Can you do that?" Jared asks pointing to the shot of Karen performing a handstand with splits.

"Not at present, no, but I am confident I can do anything she can...and with more grace."

"If you say so, Wand'," Jared says and pats me on the shoulder.

"Why is she so far ahead with her routine?" asks Meg. "You haven't really started yours, have you?"

"She is further ahead because she's just rehashing her routine from two years ago!"

"That's cheating surely, anyway, don't worry Wanda, you're gonna be great."

"I hope you're right, Meg. Come on, you need to take my body fat percentage and measurements so I can check my progress each week."

"Right, you get the tape measure. Why don't you try that handstand hold as well, just so we can see where we're at?"

"With splits?"

"No, just a normal handstand for now."

"Excellent, I've got to see this." Jared slams the oven door shut and runs to get a seat in the lounge.

"Right, I have a data sheet to write it all down." I go grab a pen from the kitchen drawer and stop to peer inside the oven as Jared is cooking something.

"And why exactly are you cooking six chicken breasts Jared?"

"I said I would help. I'm also going to cook some brown rice and vegetables so you have a few meals ready to go, that way you won't be tempted to eat rubbish."

"Ahh, bless. Thanks sweetie, that is actually helpful." I make my way into the lounge.

"Get your kit off," commands Meg. "We'll start with your ample bosoms."

"If you're going to start with ample, you might want to start with her butt."

"Jared!" We chastise in unison.

I pull away squealing as Megan wraps the tape measure around my bust.

"Wanda, stand still."

"It's bloody freezing."

"Don't be such a wimp." She pulls the tape together and makes a note of the result.

"Well, don't keep me in suspense. What does it say?"

"Forty-two inches exactly."

"It's this bra, it's slightly padded."

"Nice one Wand', can't wait to hear why your arse is so big."

"Jared, go away."

"Ignore him. Let's do your waist." Meg moves the now warm tape measure to my tummy. "Do you want me to measure your smallest part or the bigger bit below your belly button?"

"In other words, do you want her to measure you for low-rise jeans or the type of jeans Mum wears?" Jared laughs at his own joke.

I shoot him a look. "Just do both, that way I have an accurate benchmark."

"Right, well your waist is 33 inches and your bigger bit is 37 inches." Meg grins, trying desperately not to make a comment.

"OK, it's not great for a Personal Trainer but it's just a starting point."

"Absolutely, you'll be back to your pre-university weight in no time. And at least your bust is still bigger than your belly."

Meg and I have been best friends since we got thrown out of Mr. Hewitt's economics class at school. She is still at university studying geography or is geology? Well it's something to do with the environment but she has never had a problem with her weight. Although she is taller than me by 2 inches, we always used to weigh the same. Not now though; I have gained over a stone since starting my degree and now weigh in at 10 stone 1 pound. Oh well, it's just a place to start, I tell myself — again.

"Right, let's move this armchair and you can do your handstand against the wall," says Meg, grabbing the back of our cream leather armchair and heaving it to one side. I do a few stretches to prepare, take a deep breath and push myself onto my hands. Unfortunately, I only manage to get my legs half way.

Jared sniggers into his hand. "What was that? I've seen 5-year-olds do better than that."

"I was just warming up!"

My next attempt is way too enthusiastic and I slam into the wall with both feet and rebound onto the floor with a thud just as the doorbell rings. Megan runs to answer it as I punch Jared repeatedly for laughing.

"Hello, darling, what on earth is going on here?"

It's my mother. She often pops over since she and Dad divorced three years ago. Dad has recently moved back to Cyprus with his new girlfriend who Mum calls 'That Woman'.

"Hi, Mum," I call, looking up from the sofa. "Jared was being nasty."

"Why were you being nasty mister?"

I love the way she reverts back to talking to us as if we were six when she thinks we have been arguing. I pull a face at Jared who tries to defend himself.

"She started it."

"Behave the pair of you. Now what are you doing?"

"I told you about the competition Mum, well I'm just trying to do a handstand as I need to demonstrate balance for my routine."

"Oh yes, you did tell me. I think it will be good for you; you have put on a bit of chub since starting university darling."

"Yes, Mother I know and thank you so much for pointing it out."

"Unfortunately, you take after your father in that your weight goes straight to your cheeks. We used to call her chipmunk when she was little," she informs Megan whilst pinching my right cheek.

"How sweet you must have been, Wanda."

"Don't encourage her, Megan."

"Let's see this handstand then," Mum says, pushing her dyed-blonde hair from her eyes and perching a hand on one hip.

My final attempt was slightly short of the wall but not quite upright enough to be able to hold it.

"Oh for goodness sake, Wanda, it's just a handstand," Mum says. "Move over."

Jared, Meg and I all glance at each other. Good grief, my mother is about to do a handstand. At least she's wearing trousers. With that, my 46-year-old yoga-loving mother performs a perfect handstand, which she holds for at least three seconds. She then lands back onto her feet with the elegance of a ballerina. Oh great, even my mother is out-performing me.

"Way to go, Nina!" Meg shouts, whilst clapping and whistling through her fingers.

"Thank you, thank you." My mother bows to each corner of the room.

"Anyway, why are you here?" I ask feeling ever so slightly peeved.

"I've come to tell you all that I'm off to Tenerife with my yoga group. We are going to detox our bodies and our minds." This announcement is accompanied by her outstretching her arms and taking a deep cleansing breath.

"That's nice, Mum, when do you go?"

"Beginning of July, it's just for five days but I really need it."

"I can imagine; your life is so stressful," Jared says, curling his lip Elvis style.

"Don't mock darling. It's been very busy at the beauty counter recently; my company has brought out six new products this year already. By the way, I have brought you samples darling." She nods at me whilst rooting through her Mulberry bag.

"Do I really need anti-ageing stuff already?" I ask, pulling my cheeks to test their elasticity.

"It's never too early to start, Wanda darling; and Megan, you could use some dear. Roaming around beaches in all weather picking up fossils and things is terribly harsh for the complexion."

I suppress a giggle as I catch the look on Meg's face.

Saturday 30th June – Weight 9st 12Ib

It's been two weeks since I started training for the competition. So far I must have eaten ten whole chickens, ten turkeys, a sack of brown rice — which by the way takes ages to cook — a whole school of tuna and every vegetable under the sun. Jared has been helping as promised, but I need some flavour, not to mention a loan from the bank for all this poultry.

I'm going to check my weight this morning, even though I did have one glass of wine and a small slice of pizza this weekend, I feel as though I've lost something. I creep to the bathroom in my undies and stand over the scales. I have set them 'old school' to stones and pounds as losing weight in kilos takes longer at least it feels like it does. One whole pound lost feels infinitely better than half a kilo.

Whippee! I've lost three pounds. That may not sound amazing but I don't want to lose the muscle I have worked so hard for. I feel great. I am definitely on the right track. *Ooh* Meg has a snickers bar in the fridge — no, no, NO! I am totally focused. I look at the picture of Jennifer Aniston in a bikini which I have stuck on the front of the fridge for additional inspiration. I bet she doesn't reach for a celebratory Snickers bar every time she loses a couple of pounds.

Monday 2nd July

Watching Karen's routine has made me realise what I'm up against, so Meg and I spent a few hours yesterday at the leisure centre perfecting some of the simpler gymnastic moves. I can honestly say that I mastered a cartwheel, handstand balance and an Arab-spring — which is basically a cartwheel but twisting your body to land on two feet. I'm practising for the splits every day as I want to be able to show Jared I can do the same as Karen. If there's one thing that motivates me, it's proving someone wrong!

Back at work, I am about to go for a run around the gym field when I notice a tall blond guy running by the back fence. I'm not sure but I think it's Mike. I step outside and then retreat back in as he follows the fence back towards the gym. It is Mike, his solid thigh muscles contracting with every step. *Ooh lovely*, I mumble, peering around the door. Oh for God's sake Wanda, grow up he's just a guy. Oh poo, he's seen me!

"Hi, Wanda," Mike calls as he runs towards me.

"Hello. I wasn't sure if that was you."

"I'm just getting a workout in before lunch. How's your training going?"

"Good thanks, but I think I may have some competition."

It has just occurred to me that Karen wouldn't be able to not brag about being accepted in the same competition as me.

***

"Really, who's that?" asks Mike, pulling his foot to his sumptuous tight bottom to stretch his quads.

"I think Karen has been accepted too. Has she said anything to you?"

"No, why, is it meant to be a secret?"

"I'm not keeping it a secret but I think she might be."

"Can't see why, but I'll ask her if you like," Mike says stretching his other leg.

"Oh no, don't worry, I'll ask her myself."

"Listen, Wanda, can I see you a bit later, I want to ask you something?"

Not again. What does he want to ask me now? Something interesting I expect like what did I have for breakfast?

"No problem, I'll catch you later," I say smiling wearily as I jog away.

I enjoy a lovely tuna salad sandwich for lunch then run up the three flights of stairs to the gym — I've racked up about 150 calories so far today — as I am meeting my client, Vanessa. Reaching the last set of steps I remember that running after eating is not a good idea. I hold my tummy and breathe heavily as I hang onto the stair rail. I may be enjoying that sandwich again any second now.

After a minute I recover a little and push open the gym door. I can tell that Elliot and Zoe are on shift as I enter the gym, the music is so loud the floor is vibrating. I don't want to sound like my mother but are they deaf? The usual male —
— no, I don't mean penis, or do I? — W
this time, are grunting and shouting to

the free-weight section. To the right of the entrance is the cardio section, where the girls from the office across the road are grouped on the recumbent bikes. They gossip about their boyfriends' lack of commitment for thirty minutes and think this is aerobically effective. I straighten up and take a sip of water and look around for Vanessa just as she walks through the door.

"Vanessa you look great. I see that you have swapped the size twenty-two T-shirt for a more fitted top."

"Yes and thanks, Wanda, it's down to you. I just do whatever you tell me to. I can't wait for you to weigh me as all my clothes are loose." Vanessa spins around showing off her new figure. She has only been with me for two weeks but has stuck to her diet and exercise programme and it shows.

"There is nothing quite like revenge to keep one motivated," she says with a grin.

"OK, whilst you're feeling energetic and skippy, we'll take your workout outside to the games field for some interval training after your weigh-in."

"Great, let's do it."

Vanessa steps gingerly onto the scales whilst screwing up her eyes. Why is it we all think that the scales will provide a better result if we creep up on them?

"Oh my goodness, Vanessa, you have lost eight pounds!"

"Yes!" she exclaims, punching the air. "I knew that I had lost quite a bit but didn't want to check without you."

"You're doing great, but you need to realise that you won't and shouldn't lose that much in the next two weeks."

"I know that most of it is water but it has been a great boost. I have so much energy now."

I give Vanessa a goal of losing two pounds over the next week and we make our way to the games field.

"So how's your training for the competition going?" She asks as we begin our jog around the field.

"Good actually; my friend Megan has helped me choreograph a routine and it's really hard but I love a challenge."

"Why don't you show me after my work out? I'll tell you what I think."

"That's a good idea. I haven't performed in front of anyone yet, except Meg."

I put Vanessa through her paces for the next hour and we both return to one of the studios.

"I haven't got my music so don't expect too much," I warn her as I prepare myself.

"No problem, whenever you're ready."

"And we haven't finished choreographing it yet so this is just the first half."

"I'm sure it's going to be great."

I take a deep breath and begin my routine. It starts off quite slow and builds in intensity. My flexibility has really improved and I feel confident as I jump, stretch and spin my way around the studio. Until I get to the handstand; I can't hold it at the top and my right leg keeps on going, which turns my handstand into a crab. Motionless I try to control my breathing and figure out how I'm going to get up or down from this position. I'm not too fussy at this point.

"Excellent, Wanda, well done!" Vanessa is whooping and clapping from the corner. She thinks the walkover into a crab is part of the routine.

"I'm stuck. Could you help me up?" I croak.

I can feel the blood filling up my face and my eyes are bulging out. I must look like the closing sequence of *Total Recall*.

"Oh sorry, I didn't realise you were stuck. I thought you were pausing for effect." Vanessa laughs as she rushes to my aid.

"If I move my hands I'm going to drop onto my head."

"Here we go." Vanessa comes up behind me and supports my shoulders so I can stand.

"Thanks. That last move was meant to be a handstand but went a little too far."

"Never mind, you should keep it in, I was impressed."

"I'm not sure the judges will be, if I get stuck half way into my routine."

"Stick it at the end, they'll never know," she says with a giggle.

"They might guess when I have to engage the help of the stage hands before I can take a bow."

"Don't worry, Wanda, I'm sure you'll work it out. You've got time."

I do hope that Vanessa is right. I suddenly feel rather nervous.

Chapter Five

Saturday morning 7th July – weight 9st 10lb

No work for me today, so I'm going to have a 'superfood' smoothie and take off to a nearby country park to run for an hour. It will be a change from training in the gym and rehearsing my routine. I pull my wild hair into a bun, don my favourite shorts and fluorescent pink vest then head to the hallway to find my trainers.

"You're up early," Jared mutters, wandering into the bathroom.

"I'm going for a run. If I don't go now, I probably won't go at all; besides, it's 9.00 a.m. Jared, it's not that early. Meg has been at work for two hours."

"Oh yeah, anyway want me to come?" he asks with a look that says *please say no*.

"No, it's OK, I'm going for an hour, doubt if you would last."

"I meant on my bike."

"Don't worry bruv, I like running by myself, it gives me time to think."

"What about?"

"What I can eat when I get back! See you later."

***

As I enter the country park, I squint and hold my hand over my eyes salute style, wishing I'd worn sunglasses. The tables outside the Visitors Centre are already busy with dog walkers and the local running club who are stretching against the wooden benches. I secretly wish I'd already completed my run. To be honest, I've never been the best runner, even though I was in the relay team at school. Jared used to say I'm built for speed not endurance and he's absolutely right. Give me heavy weights to push or plyometrics – jumping – and I always excel but long distance running was never my favourite sport. Unfortunately, fitness instructors are always expected to be proficient runners, so I make it a priority to run as often as I can. Besides, it is great if you have something on your mind.

There is a pathway through the trees that gently slopes down towards a large pond. It is an easy jog so I tend to use it as my warm-up section. The air still has that cool morning feel under the shade of the trees and after ten minutes of gentle jogging, I stop and hold onto a large tree trunk to stretch my calves. I can see another runner approaching. Not wanting to look like a wimp, I forgo the rest of my stretches and start running again. We will probably exchange a 'runners' nod' as we pass each other, check our watches — not sure why really — and stride off with the satisfaction that comes from exercising whilst others are still in bed.

OK, here she comes, looks a bit like Karen Lester from a distance but luckily I know she's working today. She's getting nearer; still looks a lot like Karen. Oh poop! It is Karen. She comes to a stationary jog in front of me.

"Hello, Wanda, I didn't know you were a runner."

"Hi, I thought you were working today."

"I am, but not until later. Do you want to run together?"

My immediate thought is *No, you boring old fart*, but then I think that she may get chatty and give up whether or not she has been accepted for the Main Event competition.

"Why not, are you aiming for a particular distance?"

"I normally do eight miles, there's a lovely route around this park."

Eight miles! Jesus, I think that will take longer than an hour but I can't back out now.

"No problem, which way?"

We head back the way I came and open a gate to a field which is sitting on a steep hill. I love to challenge myself, so I step up a gear and stride out in front powering up the hill. I slow down and turn to see where Karen is. She is about 20ft behind me plodding along at a steady pace. At last, I have the upper hand. Steaming ahead, pumping my arms and breathing hard. It feels great. I'm eating up this hill and she can't beat me. Take that Karen Lester!

Reaching the gate at the top of the hill, I hold onto the post to catch my breath and use the bottom of my new vest to wipe the sweat from my eyes. Oh crap, I forgot to take off my mascara last night. I hate it when I do that.

I decide to be the better person and give Karen some encouragement, poor thing.

"Come on Karen, you can do it!" I shout, feeling ever so smug and up myself.

She reaches the gate looking as though she has just strolled up.

"Well done, Wanda," Karen says. "You took that hill really well."

I beat her and she *still* manages to congratulate me in a way that makes me feel inferior. She's not even breathing heavy. I hate her!

We continue on through a rough woodland patch fraught with muddy ditches and fallen trees. Karen navigates them with the agility of a panther, whilst my body appears to be aiming at every obstacle. My legs are starting to burn now and I may have to pull the old 'my shoelace is undone' trick to give myself a quick breather.

"How far have we run now?" I ask a while later, willing her to say seven miles.

"About four miles," she says, glancing at her watch.

You've got to be kidding! The distance passes much quicker when you're on a treadmill watching *The Jerry Springer Show*. I need to get some information out of her soon, as I may not survive much longer. I think I used up a lot of fuel reserves on that bloody hill.

"I hear you entered the Main Event competition a few years back," I manage whilst puffing and trying to avoid a tree root.

"Yes, two years ago."

"Mind if we get together some time so you can take me through what happens?"

"Sure, we'll set something up." Karen says, hopping over a puddle whilst I run through it.

She is being quite congenial, so I'm going to ask. "Did you not fancy entering this year?" I check her face for a reaction.

"Wanda, look out!"

As I turn my head to look forward I am just in time to see a low-hanging branch before swiping it with my face.

"Fuuck!"

"Oh my God, are you all right?" Karen cries, as she tackles the prickly branch which is now stuck in my hair.

"Yes, yes I think so."

I start patting my face with the back of my hand to evaluate the damage. There is blood, not loads, but together with the mud and scratches on my legs from earlier, it is enough for me to bow out.

"If you don't mind, Karen, I'm going to head back and get my face cleaned up."

"Yes of course you must. Do you want me to come with you?" she adds, looking suitably concerned.

"No, I'm fine. You finish your run. I'll see you at work Monday."

I turn back towards the park entrance and head home for some tea, green of course, and sympathy. I cannot believe that Karen looks more like she's been wafting through a field of poppies, than the assault course I have just experienced — Cow.

It isn't until I'm home and standing in front of an open refrigerator, that I realise Karen never answered my question. I went through all that torture for nothing. I grab a slice of ham and stuff it in my mouth, along with one of Jared's cheese triangles. They have always been my favourite even though I can never unwrap the damn things. As my anger subsides, the soreness on my face returns and I rush to look in the bathroom mirror. Oh my God, no wonder that woman and her little girl I saw on the way home crossed the road; I look like I've been sleeping with an angry kitten on my face! I open the cupboard and search for cotton wool and some soothing lotion. Meg usually keeps some for when she goes on her fossil finding jaunts. I find something pink and dab it over the cuts on my face and go back to staring in the fridge.

On the top shelf, is a plastic container with my name on it. For one brief second I get excited as I open it ... *huh*, what is that? I think it's cold tuna with brown rice and broccoli, yum. Reluctantly, I take my tuna and rice into the lounge and pick up this week's celebrity magazine. There is nothing like seeing a rich, privileged, celebrity and all their glorious cellulite caught on camera to make you feel better about your own life and lunch.

There is an interesting article on movie star Rachel Tallyman — the usual celeb, tall, slender, tanned and toned — and a day of her typical diet. Let's see: porridge made with water, peppermint tea, chicken salad for lunch and grilled fish with six asparagus for dinner. Usually I would be in awe of such a disciplined human being if it wasn't for the fact that only yesterday, whilst reading a different celebrity magazine; I saw a photo of her stuffing down a large hamburger and chips! I carry on checking out the rich and famous, imagining what I would do as their personal trainer. Obviously, my main job would be to get them to burn off the burgers they eat when they think no one is watching. Honestly, it's all fake, but I so want to be part of it; I can't help myself, I'm shallow. I want to live where the sun shines all the time so eating salad isn't a chore. I want to train on the beach and be on TV promoting my new ingenious way of keeping lean, which I haven't quite worked out yet. Just as I'm imagining myself working for the rich and famous, my phone rings.

"Hello"

"Hello, darling, how's your exercise thingy going?"

"Hi, Mum. It's going well I suppose. You all right?"

"Not really, darling, I was wondering if you would meet me for lunch today."

"I don't see why not. What's wrong?"

"I heard the most dreadful news today."

"Oh my God, what is it?"

"I'll tell you all about it at lunch. 1.00 p.m. at Antonios?"

"Yes that's fine, but can't you tell me now?"

"No, it's not the sort of thing one blabs about over the phone. See you at one."

I am left staring into my phone as my mother hangs up. She can be a bit of a drama queen but she did sound genuinely upset. I wonder what the dreadful news is.

***

I decide to take a bubble bath before getting ready to meet Mum. I can't get our conversation out of my mind. I wonder if Jared knows anything. I am about to submerge myself beneath a cloud of bubbles when I hear the familiar creak of the front door being opened.

"Jared, is that you?"

"Yeah, been having a coffee with Marcus in The Coffee Snob. Meg said she won't bring any pastries home as you can't eat them; so I went there instead."

"I'm in the bath; can you come in a minute?"

"Could, but don't want to," he shouts from the kitchen.

"Jared, get in here!"

The bathroom door opens and Jared pops his head around.

"What? Oh my God why is your face pink?"

"Oh yeah, I forgot about that. I had an argument with a prickly branch on my run today."

"I'm assuming the branch won," Jared says with a laugh.

"Have you spoken to Mum lately?"

"Not since Tuesday, why?"

"I got a call from her today; she said she wants to meet me for lunch; she's received some dreadful news."

"What news?"

"I don't bloody know that's why I was asking you."

"Why didn't you just ask her whilst you were on the phone?"

"I did, she wouldn't tell me. She sounded funny."

"Funny ha ha or funny weird?"

"Funny weird, I think she was genuinely upset about something."

"Well I'm sure you'll find out at lunch. Have fun." Jared grins and walks away.

"Jared?"

"Now what?"

"Want to come with me?"

"On yer bike, actually I can't as I'll be on my bike. Me and Marcus are doing a 20k this afternoon."

"Is that Marcus from the gym?"

"Yeah."

"*Oooh*, Jared and Marcus sitting in a tree, K.I.S.S.I.N.G."

"Grow up, Wanda," he says walking out of the bathroom.

I finish my bath and look in my wardrobe for something to wear. If I wear jeans, Mum will make some comment about me being scruffy, so I opt for my blue and white tea dress, denim jacket, pink socks and flat brown boots. I don't do elegant, and at least I'll be wearing a dress.

Antonios is in the town square, serving mostly Italian food and lunchtime Panini's. It is clean and bright with red and white gingham tablecloths and they give you tumblers for your wine, which they serve in carafes. I look around for my mother but she hasn't arrived yet so I ask for a table at the back of the restaurant, just in case there is going to be crying. I take off my jacket and check my phone. No messages.

"Could I get you something to drink?" asks the waitress.

"Yes please, I'll have a sparkling water." I may need alcohol later but I'm not going to waste the calories unless I need to. Just as the waitress walks off with my order, I see my mother navigating her way around the tight formation of tables.

"Hi, Mum." I go to hug her but she stops, holds me at arms length and stares at me in horror.

"Darling, what happened to your face?"

"Oh, it's nothing; I had an argument with a branch on my run this morning." At least it took her mind off what I'm wearing.

"Oh dear, perhaps we should have met at your flat."

"It's fine, Mum. I'll get the waitress."

She places her jacket over the back of her chair and leans to one side.

"What *are* you wearing?"

My hideous face was obviously not enough to deter her from disparaging my wardrobe.

"I thought I'd wear a dress for you."

"It's lovely, darling, but did you have to ruin it by wearing those hideous boots?"

Luckily I am saved by the waitress who takes Mum's order of a bottle of red wine and some olives. A *bottle* of wine; there's definitely going to be tears.

"So, what's the dreadful news?" I ask, leaning forward.

"It's your father," she says, dropping her eyes to the table.

"What. Is he OK? For God's sake woman, just spit it out!"

"He phoned to tell me that he's getting married again."

The waitress has impeccable timing and arrives to serve the wine. I must remember to tip her well.

"Oh, when?"

"I don't know. I really don't care. He said he wanted to tell me first. Like I'm even interested in what he and 'that woman' do," she says, taking a large gulp of wine.

As usual in these situations, I have no idea what to say, and before my brain has a chance to filter any stupid comments, I blurt out. "Perhaps she's pregnant."

"Pregnant, but he's nearly fifty-years-old!"

"I know, but Laura is only...." I begin before realising what was coming out of my mouth.

"Has he told you she's pregnant?" She spits across the olives.

OK, that was bad. I need to say something comforting. "No, he hasn't said anything. In fact, he told you about the wedding first so he must still care about you." I smile encouragingly. My mother just looks up from her glass with a stare that would have cracked mine if it were not a sturdy tumbler. Right, now I need wine. I wish Jared was here, he always knows the right thing to say.

"I swear, Wanda if it wasn't for the fact that I am so centred from practicing yoga, I wouldn't be able to cope sometimes."

"Yes, Mum it's great, otherwise you could easily be a drama queen."

She calms down as our lunch arrives and spends the next hour telling me how wonderful George is. This is her yoga instructor, who by all accounts is the Yoda and the Dali Lama all rolled into one. I'm just glad we are off the topic of Dad getting married and am encouraging her babblings about the wonders of yoga — I think she ignores the fact that I teach it — when my bag starts to vibrate.

"Wanda, you're not going to answer that are you? You know how rude I think it is when you do that."

"No," I sigh, "heaven forbid would I even glance at my phone whilst in your company."

"Good girl, it's just good manners, darling. Anyway, where's the toilet in here?"

As she leaves for the loo I sneak a peek at my phone. It's a message from Gary.

Chapter Six

Saturday 7th July

It's been three weeks since I met Gary at Povkas Bar. We've been texting back and forth ever since. He makes me laugh but I still can't remember exactly what he looks like. We haven't met up yet what with my shift work and his conferences across the country. I feel rather like Meg Ryan in *You've Got Mail.* But when he texted me at the café this afternoon, he asked to meet me this Friday.

I need to ask Meg how much she remembers about Gary before I say yes to a date. I made a mistake once when I agreed to go out with a guy I had drunkenly snogged at a party; he arrived at my door wearing tight white jeans and a Hawaiian shirt. I was not about to make the same mistake again.

As I walk through the door of our flat, Jared calls from the kitchen.

"I know what Mum's news was and I'm sorry you had to go through that on your own."

I walk into the kitchen where Jared is halfway through a piece of toast with the phone in his hand.

"Did Dad just ring?"

"Yeah, wanted to tell us he's getting married and he wants us to be at the wedding. How did Mum take the news?"

"Not well. Plus I think I made things worse," I reply with a grimace.

"How could you possibly have made things worse?"

"I may have inadvertently suggested that Laura could be pregnant."

"You said what? Oh my God, Wanda you actually did make it worse. Did Mum freak out?"

"She may have." I cringe and hang my head in shame.

"If she was pregnant, Dad would have told me on the phone, so I think it's safe to assume that she isn't."

"When's the wedding?" I sigh, grabbing a bottle of water from the fridge.

"End of August sometime."

"Bloody hell that's soon and it's the same time as my competition. Did he say exactly what date?"

"No, said he would get back to us when he was sure about the date."

Just as I contemplate calling my dad to tell him when my competition is, Meg comes home from work.

"Hi, Meg, how was work?"

"The same; Craig insists that his flirting all over me with his sweaty armpits is actually one of the bonuses of working for him."

"You know you love it, you dirty little chippy!" Jared nudges her against the fridge.

"Anyway, Meg, I need your advice, so sit down and I'll make you some tea."

"Great, what's the problem?"

Before I can open my mouth, Jared pokes his nose in.

"Dad's getting married and Wanda decided to plant the seed in Mum's head that Laura is pregnant."

"Oh my God, really, what happened?"

"That wasn't what I was going to ask you about, but yes, I stuck my Doc Martins straight in there as usual."

"Tell me more later. So, what *were* you going to ask me?"

"Do you remember Gary from Povkas?"

"Yeah, did he call you?"

"No, he texted again and wants to meet me this week, but I can't remember whether he was cool or not — any opinion?"

"I remember his voice was in tune more than yours," she says with a laugh.

"That's not helping."

"OK, he was nice looking, and he rescued me from singing with you. That's pretty cool, I'd give him a chance."

"What if Mike finds out?"

"You mean Mike from work?"

"Yes, I'm sure he's into me and I don't want to ruin my chances. What do ya think?"

"I think you're delusional. Has he been anything more than friendly?" she asks, squeezing her tea bag against the side of her mug.

"He did say he wanted to ask me something, the other day."

"Go on a date with Gary; you told me he was funny, besides you can always blow him out if Mike declares his undying love for you in the next two days."

"OK, I'll text him back."

"Why don't men call anymore, it's like we are all having virtual relationships?"

"Yeah but it's easier to blow someone off by text."

"That's true"

"Anyway, I'll wait 'til tomorrow to reply and let you know what he says."

Thursday 12th July - Manham Leisure Centre

Walking into the hall at the leisure centre always reminds me of school. I was the captain of the hockey team and a member of the netball and basketball teams but somehow gymnastics eluded me. Looking around the large hall there are wall bars covering two walls, a large matted area for floor work, a balance beam and a pummel horse. I puff out the air in my lungs as I contemplate the workout to come.

"Right, let's warm up," Meg says swinging her arms, "we are going to attempt a flick flack today. That will show Karen how brilliant you are."

"Or how easy it is to break your neck attempting the impossible."

"Don't worry babe we have this." Megan holds up a harness.

"What the fuck is that for?"

"Wanda, do you have to use such foul language? This will keep you from landing on your head."

"Then why not just get me a helmet?"

I resolve to do my best when I catch the look on her face and after a ten-minute warm up, we start off with some forward rolls.

"*Wheeee,* I can do these; shall we put them in the routine, Meg?"

"Well you could, but I'm just using them to stretch your spine. The more flexible it is, the less likely you are to injure yourself. Oh and plus, you're not five! Now grow up and let's take this seriously."

"Sorry Megan."

"Just do exactly as I say. You can start by stepping into this."

I step into the harness and Meg attaches it to a bungee, which is hanging from the ceiling.

"Right, bend your knees and jump up as high as you can," she says, placing her right hand on the small of my back. I jump high and bounce off to the left.

"*Whooa*, this thing has a mind of its own."

"I know you just need to get used to it and then get the confidence to flip your feet over your head."

I look directly at Meg who is still smiling. "Can you do a flick flack?"

"Don't be ridiculous. I haven't done gymnastics at this level since I was 14-years-old."

"Can I just say, Meg, that you are pretty bad at instilling confidence into your student."

"Sorry Wand'. Let's try again."

For the next thirty minutes I jump and fling my head back and wish I was seven again. Why is it kids have no fear? Is it because they are nearer to the ground so hitting it with their heads doesn't seem quite so daunting?

My final three attempts I manage to flip backwards but still can't land my hands on the floor before my feet land. The room starts to spin.

"Perhaps I *should* wear a helmet," I tell Meg, tired and dizzy from all the jumping.

"Well let's leave it there for now; you do look a bit peaky."

"I've got to get this if I have any chance of beating Karen."

"Are you more concerned with winning the competition or beating Karen?" asks Meg as she begins to put the mats away.

"Well if I don't win the competition but still beat Karen in points then at least I won't have to leave the gym. That cow will never let me forget it if she beats me."

"The other scenario is that she wins and sods off to LA to work. At least you would be free of her."

"Megan Beekin, do not even allow such a scenario to enter your brain! Can we give it one more try before we leave?"

"Are you kidding? You're too tired, let's try again tomorrow."

"*Pleeease,* just one more time, I know I can do it. I'm psyched and ready to give it my best shot."

Megan shakes her head as she replaces the mats for one last attempt.

"OK, Wanda, now remember everything I have taught you. You *can* do this."

I take a deep breath assume a squat position, swing my arms back and tuck in my knees as I spring up and over. My feet successfully follow my head; I place my hands on the floor and land like a professional. I did it! I actually did it. Megan and I jump up and down screaming.

"I can't believe it! You are the best gymnastic teacher ever. Let me do it again before I lose confidence."

"One last time, then we are going home."

My final back flip was not quite as successful. I manage to land on the side of my right foot and tumble onto the mat only to bounce back up again. I'm in pain and can't get control of the bungee.

"Wanda, are you OK?" Megan shrieks.

"No," I whimper, holding onto my ankle and trying not to cry.

"I told you, you were too tired to carry on didn't I?"

"Meg, I don't think the 'I told you so' speech is what I need right now. Help me up would you."

"Sorry mate," Meg says, heaving me up off the floor.

"*Ouch!* Oh poo, I think it may be broken. I can't stand on it."

Megan sighs and gives me that motherly look. "Better get you to accident and emergency. Come on, lean on me, we'll get you to the car."

***

Luckily my ankle is just badly sprained, but it still means at least a week hobbling about on crutches and limited training. I can't believe my luck, just as I was getting into the training and diet zone. I decide that this is just a blip and I can still keep to my diet and do some upper body training. 'Think outside the box' is what we were taught during our rehabilitation course, so that's what I'm going to do.

"Anyone want pizza?" Jared shouts from the kitchen as we enter the flat.

"Yes please, I need something nice."

"Are you sure; won't it ruin your hard work?"

"Just one slice and I'll pile some salad on the side."

I must admit I'm feeling a little sorry for myself, but previously I would have eaten the whole pizza.

Friday morning 13th July –Weight 9st9lb

I will need to phone work today and let them know I won't be in this week. I hope Karen isn't in; I could do without her fake sympathy. I scroll down to the number on my phone and hit 'Call'.

Annie answers. "Good morning, Phoenix gym, how can I help you?"

"Hi it's Wanda, I need to speak to Karen or Mike; preferably Mike."

"OK, Wanda, I think Mike is in Karen's office at the moment, I'll put you through."

There is a pause on the line followed by a click.

"Hi, Wanda it's Mike, everything all right?"

"Yes fine. You OK?" This is the first thing that comes into my head, which is ridiculous as the reason I am calling, is because I am not fine.

"Erm I'm good thanks. Did you call for any particular reason?"

"Yes, I'm sorry, Mike, I have badly sprained my ankle so I'm on crutches for a week. I thought I had better let you know I won't be in."

"Oh dear you poor thing, how did you manage that?"

I must admit I was hoping he was going to ask, how cool is it to say "I was practising a flick-flack and went over on it."

"You mean like a proper somersault?"

"Yes, I think I was tired as I'd been training for two hours." I decide not to mention that the first hour was performing forward rolls.

"Wow, that's really impressive."

Yes! I can feel his adoration growing.

"You and Karen are like gymnasts."

What?! "Oh, has she been doing flick-flacks then?" I ask, listening to the sound of my bubble bursting.

"Don't know if it was called that, but it involved some sort of tumbling. In fact I wanted to tell you something."

"What?" I sigh, not really caring what he has to say.

"Karen was bragging to me about some competition she has entered. I asked her what it was but I can't remember what she said. Sorry."

"You're joking, was it called The Main Event?" I ask, hoping against hope that he says no.

"Yes, that was it. Is that the one you're competing in?"

My life sucks!

"Yes, thanks for letting me know, Mike."

"She was quite discreet about it but technically she didn't swear me to secrecy."

"Well thanks again, I'll see you next week."

"OK, no flick-flacking 'til then, I need you here."

Mike Diamond needs me, how lovely. Karen is competing against me and tumbling like Nadia Comaneci — how shitty. I'm just about to hang up, when I suddenly blurt out a question I need answered.

"Mike! Sorry, before you go, I meant to ask you what it was you needed to ask me the other day." Please let it be '*I need to know if you have a boyfriend*.

"Oh yes, listen don't worry about it, I'll wait until you are back on your feet. See you next week."

What the fuck does that mean? Does he want a running partner or someone to slow dance with at the summer party? I say goodbye, put my phone on the kitchen table and open the fridge. I think refrigerators are the source of all knowledge. I have come to this conclusion as I find myself standing in front of ours during any crisis.

"Get your head out of there."

I didn't notice Meg behind me. She enters the kitchen bashing two supermarket bags against the doorframe. Noticing the pouty look on my face, she sets down the bags, grabs my shoulders and sits me down.

"What's happened?"

"I just spoke to Mike at work; Karen is definitely in the competition."

"Well, that's not really big news is it? We were sure she was anyway."

"I know but I didn't want it confirmed, especially now with me like this." I lift my foot into the air.

"You've still got time to be brilliant, besides, *you* can do a flick-flack," Meg says beaming.

"Apparently, so can she," I groan and relay the rest of my conversation with Mike.

Meg takes a breath and grabs my hands. "Look, the good news is that you still don't know what he wanted to ask you, and I know your competitive side will come through to beat Karen. Besides, Mike said he saw her tumbling, which could just have been a cartwheel," she says and hands me low fat toffee yoghurt.

I was rather looking forward to being taken out on a date, but I will have to let Gary know that I can't see him now. Making myself comfy on our large squishy sofa, I surround myself with celebrity magazines, put my foot up on a cushion and begin composing my text to Gary.

Hi Gary it's Wanda, I was looking fwd 2 meeting up this wk

but have sprained my ankle. Am on crutches. Really sorry.

Call u when up and around if ok.

I give out an audible sigh and drop my phone on the coffee table. Even the sight of famous actors with acne in my gossip mag cannot lift my mood.

"Here you go." Meg enters the lounge with two mugs of coffee and places one on the table next to me.

"Thanks." I smile weakly.

"What's up?"

"Oh nothing except; Mike is not interested in me, Gary probably thinks I'm blowing him off, Karen is going to whip my arse in the competition thereby ruining my dream of becoming a celebrity trainer. I can't work out and I haven't had any fun since this competition thing started because I can't eat or drink anything unless it has no fat, calories or dare I mention it —.taste!" I take a deep breath in, exhale and flop back onto my cushion. Meg is looking at me with her eyebrows raised, looking as though she is struggling to find something to say.

"Well," Meg begins, just as my phone vibrates its way along the coffee table.

"It's Gary," she says, looking at the screen before passing it to me.

I open the message which reads:

Hi Wanda, sorry 2 hear bout ur ankle. Don't worry

Just be ready by 7 tonit. Text me ur add I'll pick u up.

Wld fone but in meeting. Gary x

As I read out the message, Meg and I look at each other in shock.

"Wow, I was not expecting that."

"Oh my God Wand' that is so sweet."

"Where the hell are we going to go with me in this state?"

"You could still hobble to a table for dinner."

"I could, but I'm supposed to keep my foot up as much as possible."

"That's OK, you'll have the perfect excuse to finish the date early if he starts talking about his ex-girlfriends, his car or his mother."

"Good call. Actually, it's a great first date prop. I may have to use it on later dates if this one doesn't work out."

We clink coffee mugs and get to work on my outfit.

Chapter Seven

Friday 13th July

"Wanda, give it up babe; you're not going to get them on."

"But they're my favourite jeans," I cry, whilst lying on the floor trying to heave one leg of my skinny jeans over my swollen ankle.

Meg stands over me with a pair of her wide-legged trousers hanging over the hook of her arm. "Try these on. You can't really wear a dress so these will cover the strapping on your foot."

"OK." I sigh, resigned to not looking my most fabulous.

The trousers are a little tight around the tummy and rather long, but once teamed with my new white T-shirt, silver jewellery and faithful denim jacket, I look pretty good.

"What do you think?" I present myself, crutches and all, to Jared who is on the computer learning French.

"*Tres chic*," he says, looking me up and down. "Mind you don't trip over those trousers, they're a bit long aren't they?"

"Yes but they cover my shoe thingy I got from the hospital and I can't just wear one heeled shoe."

"Wanda, he's here!"

Meg has been looking out the window to catch a glimpse of Gary arriving.

"Oh my God, does he look cute Meg?"

"The good news is he hasn't got dandruff."

"What?"

"We're three floors up; I can only see the top of his head."

"Really helpful, thanks a bunch."

I grab my bag, sling it across my body and bash my way towards the front door. I should have practised on my crutches a bit more.

The doorbell rings and Jared knocks me as he rushes to get past.

"I'll get it."

I look around. Megan is poking her head out of my bedroom.

"Hi, Guys," Gary says smiling. He steps inside the flat.

I'm relieved, as although he isn't as gorgeous as Mike, he has a happy face with a crooked smile. Plus, he's taller than I remember.

"Hi, come in. I don't know if you remember my brother, Jared."

"Yeah, all right mate."

"And that head poking out from the bedroom is Megan."

"Oh yeah, I remember you from Povkas. You didn't want to sing."

"Yes, thanks for the rescue."

"No problem." Gary turns back to me. "Shall we go?"

"Yes, where are we going by the way?"

"Surprise," he says, opening the front door a little wider to let me out.

***

I must admit Gary has impressed me. Not deterred by my present handicap, he has brought me to a Moroccan restaurant where I am sitting on a floor cushion leaning against a wall, my injured foot propped up on a smaller gold cushion. We are eating with our fingers — my mother would never approve — and he hasn't once mentioned his ex-girlfriend or his car.

"So, do you like Moroccan food?" asks Gary whilst topping up my glass.

"I've never really had it before, but so far it's good."

"That's a relief; some people find this dish too spicy."

"Believe me, after eating nothing but plain chicken, brown rice and steamed veg for three weeks, my taste buds are having an orgasm." I enthusiastically stuff more harissa lamb in my mouth.

"*Oops*, did I say that out loud?"

Gary almost chokes on his couscous. "Yes, but I'm glad your taste buds are happy." We both look at each other and giggle. He really does have a lovely smile and his eyes are an unusual shade of grey; almost lilac really, but I suppose that could be the lighting.

Once back at the flat, Gary helps me out of the car and back upstairs.

"Here we are, now give me your keys and I'll open the door."

"Thanks, it's the big one." I nod my head towards the set of keys I've just pulled out of my bag.

Gary helps me through to the lounge and sets me up on the sofa with my foot elevated.

"I had a lovely time tonight. The Moroccan restaurant was a great idea."

"I'm glad you enjoyed it. Perhaps we could go out again?" he asks, tucking a pillow behind me.

"I'd like that."

"Well, you stay there and I'll see myself out. Hope your foot gets better soon."

Gary leans over and kisses me gently on the lips. In fact, apart from the fact that my foot is throbbing like a jackhammer, the whole evening has been a success.

Thursday 19th July

I am feeling rather sorry for myself this morning; I haven't heard much from Gary since Friday; Jared is on a flight to Cyprus and is stopping over to visit

Dad and Laura, Meg is at work and it's raining again. Not to mention, Karen is probably training like mad and flirting with Mike, whilst I'm stuck watching daytime TV and eating too many slices of jam on toast. I flick through the channels on the TV and wonder what to eat next. To be honest, my good intentions of keeping to my diet and finding other ways of training lasted all of two days.

I pick up my phone and idly scroll through the contact numbers. As it gets to D, I realise that I haven't even rung my dad to congratulate him. What a terrible daughter I am. I tap 'Call' and wait.

"Dad?"

"Hello, is that you, Wanda dear?"

"Yes, I meant to call earlier to congratulate you and Laura on the wedding but it's been a bit hectic here, so congratulations, I'm really happy for you both."

"Thank you. I did call your mother but I don't think she took it too well. She was rather hostile in fact."

My poor soft-spoken father is bewildered because he and my mother officially parted as 'friends'. He doesn't understand women very much, bless him.

"Oh, I'm sure she was just having a bad day, Dad. She seems fine now," I lie.

"That's good. Did you know your brother is coming to stay?"

"Of course I do, Dad, I live with him. Listen, have you set a date for the wedding yet, only I have a competition in August that I need to be ready for."

"What competition is that?"

"It's a fitness thing but it could be great for my career if I win, so I can't miss it."

"As far as I know, we are looking at the 24th I think."

"24th of what?"

"August."

"Dad that's the day before my competition; any chance you can change it?"

"All right dear, leave it with me. I'll have a word with Laura."

***

I spend the next couple of hours working out an intense training programme to take me up to the competition. I'm already a week behind and I won't be able to train at a hundred percent just yet. My diet is going to have to be perfect. I just need to get myself back in the zone.

As I'm working out my protein, carb and fat ratios, the doorbell rings and I hobble to open it.

"I'm coming," I shout towards the door. If it's one of those idiots again asking about our energy provider, I may stab them with my crutch.

"Hello, darling, I thought you may need some company."

It's my mum. She pushes her way in and air-kisses me on her way to the kitchen.

"Thanks, Mum, I am rather bored. What's in the bag?"

"I brought some lunch. Now you go and sit down whilst I make us a nice cup of tea."

She may drive me mad sometimes, but she is always around when we need her. She's around quite a lot when we don't too, but I'm glad she's here today.

"So how is everything?" Mum calls from the kitchen. "Have you spoken to your father yet?"

"Yes I rang to congratulate him." I leave out the fact that it was today.

"When's the wedding then?" she asks, noisily moving crockery in the cupboard.

"He said they had provisionally booked the 24th August but I told him about my competition so he is going to try and change it."

"This August!"

The noise stops.

"Yes. And no, Mum, Laura is *not* pregnant." I'm pretty confident that she isn't anyway.

"Well, seems a bit sudden to me. That woman is obviously pushing him into it."

I don't really know what to say to this so I change the subject.

"What's for lunch?"

Mum enters the lounge carrying a tray.

"Hummus with crudités, some olives, anchovies and salad. Kept it healthy as I thought you may have gone off your diet since you sprained your ankle."

"You're right actually. I've been eating from boredom as I can't train."

"Thought so, plus I can see your cheeks are a little chubby again. Tea?" She asks, pouring me a cup.

"Thanks a lot Mother."

"I'm only being honest darling. Look, I've got some pills in my bag, they help with weight loss."

"Mum! I've told you about those things before. They are dangerous, throw them away."

"Oh don't be such a drama queen darling, all my friends use them."

"Yes, but all of your friends are delusional. They think that they can hold onto their youth with pills, potions and having poison injected into their faces every three months. A healthy lifestyle doesn't get a mention. You should try taking them to yoga with you."

Mum turns to me with her '*ooh*, hark at you' look and laughs.

"Anyway, talking of yoga, I am off to Tenerife this weekend don't forget. I shall be glad to get away from this awful rain."

"Oh yeah I forgot. Wish I was going."

"George says that focus is the key to achieving all of life's goals. You just need to keep focused darling; you'll get there."

"Oh yes, and how is the all-knowing, all-seeing George?"

"Inspirational. I can hardly wait to be taught how to reach a deeper level of meditation," she says rolling her neck from one side to the other.

I've never met this bloke but he really gets on my nerves!

***

When I look at my mother, I wish I had her body shape: lean and athletic. Although she's never been overweight, I have heard her complain about getting fatter since she hit forty. Unfortunately for me, I take after my Greek father in the body department. Loosely translated, it means I'm predisposed to having a big arse and voluptuous bosoms.

"Well I must dash, darling. Don't get up. Can I get you anything before I go?"

"No thanks, Mum I'll be fine."

"OK, well take care and I'll see you when I get back." She kisses me on my 'chubby' cheeks and heads for the door; leaving me with another two hours of boredom before Meg gets home from work. I decide to do a workout.

Hobbling over to get my Dynaband — big rubber band — and hand weights, I hop around the coffee table and manage to push the other two armchairs against the wall. I crank up a workout mix album on my I-Pod and begin to feel the anticipation that comes before a great workout. It's a mix of dread and excitement. First, I stand still and squat for 20 repetitions, my foot is fine as long as I don't move it too much. Next, stationary squat with dumbbell punches, 17...18...19...20 and twist. Feeling good after my warm up, I hop over to the sofa and grab my Dynaband for some lat pull downs. I hold the band at full stretch above my head, and then lower my arms, making sure I squeeze my back muscles. My left arm starts to shake. I'll just do a couple more reps, 14...15. ..*ouch!* My elbow gives way and my head flinches to the right with pain as the band whips me in the eye.

I hold my hand up to my face and hop to the bathroom where I lean on the basin before inspecting the damage. It looks red and watery. I splash my face with cold water. Everything is going against me. I flop my big Greek bottom onto the toilet seat and start to cry.

Chapter Eight

"Hello, Wanda you here?" calls Meg as she enters the flat.

"Where the hell else would I be?"

"Sorry; hey you all right?" she asks, when she sees how red my eyes are.

"I'm fed up."

"Have you been crying?"

"No," I lie. "I was doing a workout and lost grip of my Dynaband. It whacked me in the eye."

"Oh, babe you poor thing, tell me all about it." Meg folds her arm around me in a bear hug.

I am just whinging about how horrid my life is, when my phone buzzes. Meg releases her hold. It's a text from Gary, which lifts my spirits a little.

hi Wanda, how's the foot?

be home fri eve. want to get tog

sat sometime? cld come 2 u if easier.

Gary x

"That must be from someone you like, you're smiling."

"It's Gary; he wants to come over Saturday."

"Say yes. Jared and I can make ourselves scarce."

I am about to text Gary back when my phone starts playing *'Build me up Buttercup'*, it's work calling.

"Hello."

"Wanda, it's Mike from work, how's your leg?"

My heart leaps at the sound of his voice.

"Oh, it's getting better thanks, but it's only ankle sprain. I should be back to work Monday."

"That's great; you're missed around here."

"Really?"

"Yeah, no one else knows as much about weight-training as you."

"Oh." Could have said he missed my beautiful face/laugh/legs, anything really. "Is that why you rang?"

"No not really. I wanted to ask if you are going to the Summer Ball on the 28th."

Yes! At last. I punch the air as Meg walks over looking quizzical.

"Yes, I should be going all being well with my ankle."

"That's great I'll..."

I can hear someone calling Mike in the background.

"Sorry, Wanda I've got to go, Pat is having a problem at the front desk."

"Oh, OK. I'll see you Monday." I'm beaming as I press 'End Call'.

"Well?" Meg asks grabbing my arm and shaking it.

"Mike wanted to know if I was going to the ball."

"*Yippee*, I told you something would happen."

"No you didn't. You said he had no interest in me whatsoever."

"Well he hadn't."

"He bloody has now." I beam in triumph.

Friday 20th July -9st 11Ib

Friday morning, I take the bandage off my ankle and decide to weigh myself. After two trips to the loo and stripped naked, I gently place one foot onto the scale then the other. I exhale the breath I have been holding and squint down to check the damage. Thank goodness, I have only put on 2Ib although it's still not acceptable. I drink another cup of strong black coffee, take another trip to the loo, run around the lounge in nothing but my thong trying to build up a sweat and step back on the scales. It's the same. As I calm down and look for my grey training bottoms amongst the pile of clothes in my bedroom, I realise that I'm doing exactly what everyone else does; trying to dump excess weight down the toilet. Honestly, I'm so embarrassed. I really ought to know better. I need focus, determination and a large supply of chicken breasts.

I decide to get out of the house and walk into town for supplies. The Coffee Snob is in town so I'll stop off there for a break and a quick chat with Meg. By the time I get there, I am limping slightly and my hands are white from clutching the carrier bags of chicken, vegetables and quick cook rice. It's good to see Meg's smiling face as I walk through the door.

"Hello, Wand' what are you doing here?" she asks, helping me to a table next to the window.

"I thought I'd get some exercise and supplies. I wish I'd driven now, my foot is throbbing."

"You poor thing, I'll get you a coffee and no muffin."

"Very funny. Thanks mate."

As I look up from examining my ankle, I notice a tall gorgeous guy in jeans and a white linen shirt opening the door to The Coffee Snob. It's Mike Diamond. Oh my God, what do I do? I try to decide whether to hide – I look a mess – or greet him with my best smile, when I notice he's holding the door open for a petite fair-haired rather pretty girl. She smiles at him and squeezes his arm as they share a joke on their way to the counter. I suddenly wish I was sitting in the large squishy chair in the corner, so I could slide under the table.

I discreetly change to the chair on the other side of the table so I'm facing away from the counter. With any luck they will sit outside.

"Why have you changed seats?" asks Meg as she brings over what looks like a large bucket of coffee.

"That's Mike, over there with that girl in the blue T-shirt," I whisper.

"Mike from the gym?"

"Yes."

"Wow, you were right, he is ruggedly handsome. Who's that girl he's with?"

"How the hell do I know?"

"She could be his sister," Meg offers as she takes a seat opposite me.

"Do they look alike?"

Meg squints a little to examine them both. "Not really, no."

"Great. Well don't let him see me, I look like crap."

"OK. Actually, they are taking their drinks to go, so you should be safe."

I stare into my bowl of coffee and wish I had stayed at home.

"Just my luck. Why did I have to see him today?"

"Well you can ask him who she is on Monday. You may as well know now."

"I suppose you're right. By the way, what size is this coffee, Bucket Grande?"

"I thought you may need a large one for the journey home. It's a cappuccino."

"You do realise that I could have had a normal size cappuccino and a muffin for the amount of calories in this thing."

"Oh, really? Sorry, Wand'."

I manage to finish most of my coffee, give my bags to Meg to bring home later and take a slow wander back home; my bubble having been burst yet again.

Saturday 21st July

I'm glad not to be at work today as my foot is sore and Gary is coming over with a take-away later. Jared is due home, and then he and Meg are off to meet some of our friends for dinner in town. I may attempt to put on my stilettos tonight with my skinny jeans and a flowery blouse that fits in all the right places. Mike Diamond doesn't know what he's missing.

Despite being fed up yesterday, I managed to cook lots of meals ready for the next few days. I even told Gary that I can't eat anything too fattening so he's going to ask for my Indian take-away to be cooked without ghee. Bless him, he really is lovely and I'm not just saying that because Mike has pissed me off.

Jared and Meg get ready for their evening out whilst I wander around the flat straightening cushions and wiping the tops down in the kitchen.

"Wanda, I don't think Gary is coming over to inspect the house," Jared comments, as I wipe around the sink for the third time.

"I know. I'm just a bit nervous that's all."

"Why? You've been out with him before."

"I know, but it's different when we go out; I know I can come home any time.

"You women make me laugh. I'm sure if you're not getting on, you can tell him to sod off. I've heard you do it before."

"He certainly was. Now, Wanda just be yourself and relax. Don't drink more than one glass of wine or you'll end up overeating. You only have five weeks left before your competition."

"I know Jared, but thanks for drumming it in to me anyway. Besides, I'm having chicken tikka – no sauce – with a little boiled rice and some spinach cooked without ghee."

"Good for you," he says, before shouting at Meg to hurry up.

Gary turns up at exactly eight o'clock with a big smile and a bag full of food. I have opened a bottle of wine and put it in the fridge. He looks good in a pair of beige cargo pants with a navy striped top and khaki jacket. He leans down to kiss my cheek.

"You look great, and taller than I remember."

"Oh yes, I'm wearing heels this time." I kick up my right foot to show him my stiletto.

"They look dangerous. Where shall I put this?"

I take the bag and offer him some wine.

We sit on the sofa with our food on the table and chat about everything and nothing really. He is so easy to talk to. I find out more about his job and the fact that he has two younger sisters. One of which really fancied Jared until Gary told her he was gay.

Another bubble burst. At least it wasn't mine this time.

When Jared and Meg walk through the door at 11.45p.m., Gary and I are playing on the Wii as Gary thought it would be a good way to stop me wanting anymore wine. He was right. Plus, I just beat the crap out of him in the tennis. Winning feels so great. I can't wait to beat Karen in five weeks time.

"Want to join us for a game?" Gary asks Meg and Jared.

"What are you playing?"

"Wanda has just beaten me at tennis so we could play bowling or something if you want."

"Right you two, move out the way and let the dog see the rabbit," says Jared, grabbing one of the controls.

Meg and I giggle as we know how competitive he gets.

I give Gary a gentle nudge. "Jared will try and put you off when it's your turn, so you need to ignore him."

"Got it," Gary says and nods at me with a steely look in his eyes.

The boys start playing whilst Meg and I go and make coffee.

"Wanda, Gary's great."

"Yes he is. He's really easy to talk to. We had a nice chat earlier."

"Well dish all. I'm a woman waiting for gossip."

"He did tell me something rather funny about his sister." I lean in for effect.

"What, *what?*" Meg leans closer nearly hitting my head with hers.

"His sister fancies Jared!" I laugh, knowing that Meg was expecting something really juicy.

"But he's gay."

"*She* didn't know that. Not until Gary gave her the bad news last week. She thought that because Gary was seeing me, she would get to meet Jared. Poor thing."

"*Ahh* that's sad. I wonder if he's aware of the torment he puts us girls through," Meg jokes.

We are still laughing when we walk through to the lounge with a tray of coffee and biscuits.

"Wanda I'm glad you're back, it's our turn and your brother has just got a strike."

"Did he cheat?"

"No I didn't it was pure skill." Jared protests.

We continued playing until 2.00 a.m., when Gary announces that he should go. As Jared and Meg pack up the game, I walk him to the door. We haven't officially kissed properly yet; not that I can remember anyway. The first time we met I couldn't even remember what he looked like and last time was so brief, it didn't really count.

"I had a really good time," Gary says, grabbing my hand in his.

"Me too; and thanks again for helping me stick to my diet."

"No problem. I'm impressed with what you're doing to achieve your career goals. You're pretty amazing actually." Gary pushes his fringe back and looks directly into my eyes.

Oh my God he's going to kiss me; I hope it doesn't suck. Thinking about it, I hope *he* doesn't suck either. I hate it when guys do that.

Gary gently puts one hand on my face as his lips move closer. I close my eyes and tilt my head further back, wishing I had put my shoes back on. He kisses me softly at first and as I respond his arms wrap around and pull me closer. His tongue starts doing a loop-the-loop around mine which I find amusing but not unpleasant. He pulls away and places his hands on my shoulders before asking;

"Do you want to come to my sister's BBQ with me next Saturday?"

"Oh, erm, I actually have a work thing next Saturday," I reply, trying to look disappointed.

"Oh, right, well it's not a problem we can go out another time."

"Absolutely, I'll look forward to it."

"Give you a call in the week then," Gary says as he opens the door to leave.

As I walk back into the lounge Meg is looking expectant again.

"Well, did he kiss you?"

"Yes he did. It was nice."

"Nice. Is that it?"

"What do you want? He kissed me and it was pleasant."

"Oh how exciting," Meg retorts in dreary monotone.

"Feel a bit guilty actually."

"Why, what did you do?"

"He invited me to his sister's BBQ next Saturday and I told him I have a work thing."

"Oh yes the party at the gym. Why don't you ask him to go with you?"

I tuck my hair behind my ear and look up rather sheepishly.

"Oh my God! You won't ask Gary in case the lovely Mike Diamond decides to pay you some attention. Really, Wanda you need to forget that guy, Gary is really nice."

"Yes he is nice."

I can't believe I'm so shallow.

Chapter Nine

Monday 23rd July

So I'm back in work after a week of overeating to the point of gaining back two of the six pounds I lost. I have been good over the weekend though; Jared came cycling with me for two hours yesterday and I've dutifully eaten my chicken brown rice and vegetables.

"Hi, Wanda how's the ankle?" Elliot asks as I enter the gym.

"Good thanks, how's things been here?"

"Same as ever; Karen has been wafting around spreading love and encouragement to her staff, head office has decided to give us all a raise and the men's showers have been problem free."

"That's nice," I say with a grin. I'm glad to be back at work.

Later that morning, I am taking one of my classes though a cool down in the studio when I notice Mike's face smiling at me through the window. I catch his eye and he waves before moving off.

"Well done everyone, you worked hard today. See you all next week," I shout through the chatter as my class pick up their mats and congratulate themselves on a good workout. I turn off the audio equipment and head out of the studio.

"Hi, Wanda," says Mike, "how's the ankle?"

"Good thanks, almost back to normal in fact."

"That's great. You look really well after your break," Mike calls out as he walks back into the office.

I look over at Annie on reception. "Do I look fat?"

"No. Why do you ask?"

"Normally when someone tells me I look well, it's because I've put on weight and my cheeks are chubby. Do my cheeks look chubby to you?" I start patting each side of my face.

Annie is looking at me as if I just asked her if she farted. "Wanda what are you talking about. Now let me have your class figures."

"Sorry, I had eighteen today."

I'm trying to discreetly look into the office to see if Karen is in when Mike walks out and beckons me over. My tummy does a mini-flip as I wander casually towards him.

"You beckoned?"

"I just wanted to ask you again if you're going to the party on Saturday."

"Yes of course I am. You going?" I ask as casually as I can manage.

"Yes, only I need to ask you a favour if possible."

"Ask away, your wish is my command."

"Great, it's just that I have a guest coming and I wondered if you would be your lovely self and befriend her for part of the evening?"

He looks at me anticipating my answer.

"Oh, of course I can. Just introduce us when you arrive and I'll look after her," I say smiling, whilst the word 'Bitch' is bouncing around my head.

"Thanks, Wanda I knew I could rely on you. I wouldn't normally ask, but the gym will still be open until 10.00 p.m., so I'll be on call until then."

"Glad I can help. Anyway must get back upstairs, see you later," I say through gritted teeth and make my way back to the gym.

I am slumped against the gym desk when I see Elliot out of the corner of my eye.

"Elliot, what are you doing?"

"Jumping," he says breathless and bouncing off to the left.

"OK, my next question would be why?"

"I'm bored. Try it, you look fed up."

"I am a bit but I don't think jumping around the room like Tigger-on-crack is going to make me feel any better."

Elliot stops suddenly as he collapses into a fit of laughter.

"Oh my God, that is *sooo* funny!" he says, when he finally calms down. "I am so going as Tigger to my next fancy dress party."

I lean my chin into my hands. "If I keep putting on weight the way I have the last week, I may join you as Winnie the Pooh."

Elliot laughs and turns to look at two large ladies walking into the gym. It's Mrs. Clamp and her daughter Fiona. They are flushed, sweaty and look like they have just finished a workout. They obviously took the stairs. I straighten up and put on my professional face. I'm taking them for a training session today and looking at them, I'm glad my first aid is up to date.

Thursday 26th July

I'm waiting for Vanessa to arrive for her training session and cannot help but look at the scales. I don't want to weigh myself yet but Jared has been cooking my meals this week and Meg has been working on my flexibility with me so I'm feeling pretty good. As I slip off my trainers, my phone buzzes in my bag — it's my mum.

"Hi, Mum how was Tenerife?"

"Fabulous actually, the resort was the perfect place to revive oneself."

"So did you manage to go within yourself and unfold your chi or whatever it was you were hoping to achieve?"

"To gain a deeper state of meditation and yes George helped us all achieve it."

"That's great Mum but I can't talk now as I have a client coming in."

"Oh sorry, darling. Listen would you meet me for lunch?"

"I suppose I could if you came into town. How about the Coffee Snob at 1.00 p.m.?"

"That's fine. I'll see you then."

As I put my phone away I can see Vanessa talking to Elliot. She looks really happy and even has a new hairstyle.

"Vanessa, you look great. I love your hair," I exclaim, walking towards her.

"Thanks," she says, flicking it with her fingers, "does it go with my new body?"

"It certainly does. Are you coming to the party Saturday?"

"Yes, I have my eye on someone so I've bought a new dress, which shows off my cleavage."

"*Ooh* hark at you, you wild thing. Who's the lucky guy?"

Vanessa points out a short stocky guy on the bench press machine. I casually wander closer to get a better look.

"Wanda! He'll see you," she hisses, backing up behind the wall.

"I'm just checking he's good enough for you."

"Do you know him? I think his name's Bradley."

"You're right his name is Bradley. I haven't spoken to him that much, but he seems nice. Better get on with your workout so you can knock him out on Saturday."

"Let's do it!"

The next hour, I take Vanessa through a gruelling circuit with very little rest. When she wants to give up I push her harder. By the time we are finished, she is soaked with sweat and not looking quite as attractive as when she arrived. The good news is Bradley looked impressed.

**

The Coffee Snob is busy as I peer through the door trying to see if my mother has arrived. She is queuing at the counter and I manage to get her attention.

"Sit down I'll get your coffee and sandwich." She mouths at me.

"Chicken salad for me please."

I set my sports bag down by an available table. The holiday definitely agreed with her, she looks fabulous in her cream jeans and turquoise top.

"You look great, Mum." I say standing to kiss her as she places the tray on the table.

"Thank you, darling I feel great, how's your diet going?"

"Not bad but I need to be really strict after gaining weight. Jared and Meg are being great by not eating crap food around me."

"Well, I still have those tablets if you change your mind."

"Mother! Most parents discourage their offspring from taking drugs."

"Don't be silly darling, they just make you tinkle it out that's all. Here, take these."

She hands me a packet of blue pills — she's so gullible they're probably Viagra — which I decline and excuse myself to use the ladies.

Returning from the loo, I notice my mother is tapping her false nails on the table. She only does this when she's nervous.

"What's wrong?" I ask, sitting back down.

"It's George." She looks at me and tilts her head.

"Your yoga instructor?"

"Yes. Wanda I need to tell you something."

I'm pretty sure I know what's coming. Mum hasn't had a date since her and Dad split up, but I think she has fallen for this George bloke. I feel quite sorry for her she looks so guilty about it.

"Go on. You can tell me anything, Mum."

"Thank you sweet; it's just that I think I'm in love with George." She looks at me smiling like a teenager.

"Mum that's great! I'm really pleased for you. And frankly, it's about time."

"Really, you mean you don't mind?"

"Of course I don't you idiot."

"I'm so relieved, darling. Can I bring her over to meet you and Jared at the weekend?"

"Yes do. We are out Saturday but... sorry, did you say *her?*"

I think I'm losing the grip on my mug but I can't put it down.

"Yes she's so great you're going to love her. I told her you teach yoga. You'll have lots to talk about. Actually, I said I would meet her today so do you mind if I scoot?"

I'm still dumbstruck as she drains her cup and gathers her bags to leave.

"Bye, darling, kiss, kiss. And thank you for making this so easy. See you at the weekend."

She doesn't seem to notice that I haven't moved. The enormity of what I just heard begins to sink in.

Oh my God, my mother is a freakin' lesbian! Is the gay gene in my family I wonder? Not that I have anything against them at all, how could I, half my family are gay, but I am curious as to whether I have any urges I'm suppressing. I look down at the other half of my sandwich and push it to one side. I need to speak to Jared.

Chapter Ten

Saturday 28th July - The Summer Ball

Weight -9st 8lb

Jared has Kings of Leon blaring from his iPod station which I can't help but dance around to. I love getting ready for a night out. Meg joins me for a short boogie around my bed whilst trying not to spill her wine. I grab her glass and take a deep sniff.

"A cheeky little Sauvignon Blanc if I'm not mistaken?"

"It is. Do you want a sip?" Meg waves her glass under my nose as she sways and bobs her head to the music.

"No, I'll wait."

"Good girl. I was just testing you anyway."

Meg dances back to her room and I sit on the floor in front of my mirror with my make-up bag. I apply my new 'Bold Brown' eye shadow and highlighter with great precision. My mum has worked on the beauty counter in a large department store for years and taught me the best way to accentuate my brown eyes. As it's a party, I dig around for my gold face glitter, which my mother hates because she's too old to wear it. The final touch is my 'Barely There' lip plumper. It feels like you have burnt your lips in the sun, then eaten raw chillies. I never reapply if things start to heat up with a guy though as it is rather painful when it comes in contact with his boy bits! I learned this the hard way — long story.

Now for the *piece de resistance*, as Jared would say. Carefully slipping my dress off its hanger, I step into it and ease it over my thighs. I yank a little harder as it reaches my bottom. There! It's over the worst. I adjust my boobs, thread my arms through and call Meg to zip me up.

"Wanda you look fabulous," she says as I turn to face the door.

"Thanks Meg but I don't have it zipped up yet."

"Turn around then."

I cross my fingers as she pulls the dress with one hand and jerks the zip upward with the other. I can feel her struggling.

"Oh my God, it's too tight isn't it?"

"No, no it's fine. Just breathe in for a second."

"I am bloody breathing in!"

"Oh. Well keep it up, it's nearly there."

I take one large breath in as Meg pulls the zip to the top.

"There, no problem," Meg says, sounding relieved as she pats my bottom, "now get your shoes on."

I examine myself in the mirror. From the front, I look rather beautiful if I say so myself, my arms are more sculptured and my legs are leaner. Unfortunately, the side view leaves a little more to be desired. I stick my chest out and pull my tummy in. There, that looks fabulous. Not sure I can keep this up all night though; I look like I have a pole stuck up my arse! So, I have a choice of looking 'lumpy' or like I have a pole up my poo-pipe — great.

I look for my shoes and remember they are in a box at the back of my wardrobe. Meg may need to unzip this dress so I can bend down to reach them. I decide on the lady-like curtsy approach, lower myself and grab a hanger to hoick the box forward.

My heels are stunning with the dress and even make me stand taller which helps pull my tummy in. I am feeling rather good as I present myself to Jared. "*Ta dah!* What do you think?"

"Looks great. We should take a picture for Mum." Jared says as he spins to show me his outfit.

"Well?" He stops and waits for my verdict. I don't know why, as he knows he always dresses impeccably.

"Fabulous as usual darling! Let's take a photo for Mum."

We call Meg in to take a picture for us. She looks really pretty in a floaty pink and white dress with beige wedges. Meg doesn't do stilettos.

After taking several photographs on our phones and sending a couple off to Mum, I make a last quick trip to the loo. As I'm washing my hands, I catch the reflection of a slightly 'lumpy' tummy in an otherwise perfect outfit. I stare into the mirror looking for an angel or devil on my shoulder as I remember the little blue pills.

Chapter Eleven

The party was being held in the restaurant area just to the left of the gym entrance. As we arrived, Colin Steen the DJ was still setting up his unit at the far end and was busy sorting through boxes of vinyl. The evening sun still shone brightly through the full-length windows of the cafe, even though it was nearly eight o'clock. Meg, Jared and I walked up to the bar where Annie and Zoe were engrossed in conversation.

"Hi, guys. You both look great!"

"Hi, Wanda, you look fabulous — and very tall," Annie says as she looks me up and down.

"Thanks. Not sure how long I'm going to last in these shoes though. By the way this is my friend Meg, and you both know Jared."

"Yes, hi Jared and nice to meet you Meg."

As everyone introduces each other, I try and grab the attention of the woman behind the bar. I'm so ready for a glass of wine now.

"Blimey, I didn't realise that was you from behind," Elliot says, nudging next to me at the bar.

I'm not sure what that means, so I ask. "Is that a good or bad thing?"

"Don't be so needy, you know you look amazing."

"You're so sweet. Thanks Elliot."

I must admit, at this rate I'll completely forget to hold in my tummy as I obviously look like a supermodel. Jennifer Aniston, eat your heart out. I may have to take you off the fridge door and replace you with a picture of myself.

I order our drinks and hand Meg a glass of wine and Jared his bottle of beer.

"I wonder what Karen 'Crapface' Lester will be wearing," Meg says, glancing around the room.

"A brown paper bag over her head hopefully."

We chink glasses.

"Anyway, it looks quite busy, and the Deejay is good."

Colin had put on *Chasing the Sun* by The Wanted, which is Meg's favourite.

"Let's hope he doesn't ruin it by moving on to 'The Wedding Selection' later on." I look at Meg who makes a face. "Oh God, let's hope not."

"Anyway, what time is Mike Diamond meant to be getting here?" Meg asks.

"He's already here. I told you he's working until nine or ten. Not sure what time his girlfriend is coming though. With a bit of luck she won't make it."

"Well, Karen just made it." Meg nods towards the door. Karen walks in with Kerry, one of the aerobics instructors. She is wearing a tight-fitting grey Herve Leger knock-off with black T-bar heels.

"I didn't realise she was so tall," says Meg. "I've only seen her sitting behind her desk."

"I see she picked a colour to match her personality," I mutter before turning back to Jared.

I'm enjoying my second glass of wine — I'm going to have two waters in a row next — when Karen approaches.

"Hello, Wanda."

"Hi, Karen." I manage a smile although I cannot seem to pries my teeth apart. "You look lovely."

"Thank you. Luckily I've lost half a stone so I got into this dress easier than I thought — and you look nice," she remarks without even looking at me.

I notice Meg stifling a laugh as Karen walks away. I grin at her whilst making stabbing movements towards Karen's back.

"I can't believe she was so overtly rude."

"I know I have to put up with that every day at work. Honestly, she can be such a ..." Meg is making a weird face and jerking her head to one side.

"What is wrong with you?" I ask, just as I notice Karen hovering behind me.

"I forgot to ask if you've seen Mike. I know he's working, but his girlfriend might be coming tonight."

"Yes we know," I snap. "Mike asked me to look after her for him. He said he wanted to make sure she had fun."

"Oh, that's good. Wouldn't want her to be stuck on her own."

"Well don't worry yourself; we'll make sure she has a good time." I can feel myself snarling as Karen walks off again.

"I really hate that girl," I say, just as I notice a red-haired girl laughing and dancing with Bradley who trains in the gym. It's Vanessa; she looks amazing and confident in her new blue dress. I walk over to say hello.

"Vanessa, you look fantastic!"

"Thanks, so do you, that dress is gorgeous. Did you see who I came with?"

"Oh, you came with Bradley?"

"Yes, he asked me a couple of days ago. He's really sweet and the best thing is, I saw my ex-husband yesterday and the look on his face was worth every bead of sweat that dripped off mine. I he's broken up with that girl he was with."

"Does he want you back?" I lean in so Bradley doesn't hear.

"Don't know, don't care. I'm happier than I've been in ages. I'm so grateful to you Wanda."

"No worries girl, it's my job."

We agree to chat later and I make my way back to Meg and Jared, just as Mike walks in with the girl from The Coffee Snob. Oh my God, he looks positively perfect in his black jeans, blue and black striped shirt and wavy hair sitting just right on his perfect head.

"I take it from the look on your face, that Mike has just walked in." Meg nudges as she turns towards the door.

"Yes he has and he looks perfect." I watch them make their way towards us. The girl is dressed in skinny jeans and a black lace top with sky-high stilettos. She's a bit young for him but she looks amazing.

I put on my best smile when I greet them. Mike looks at me and mouths the word WOW. A this point, I'm torn between being chuffed to bits and appalled because he's with his girlfriend. I take a gulp of wine.

"Wanda you look stunning." Mike kisses me on the cheek. "This is Lauren." He places his hand on the small of her back as he presents her to me.

"Nice to meet you, Lauren; this is Meg and that bloke there is my brother, Jared, and that's Elliot."

I look at Mike and introduce him to Meg.

"Lovely to meet you, Meg," Mike says holding out his hand. "Would you all like a drink? I have to pop back upstairs for a while but I shouldn't be long. Most members are here so I'll close up early."

"White wine please," Lauren says, grinning at Mike. He narrows his eyes at her then smiles gently.

"Erm, the same for me please." I show him my wine glass. Megan shoots me a look.

"Same for you, Meg?" he asks, pushing his way to the bar.

"Thanks." Meg raises her eyebrows at me, which I ignore. I'll have water next time.

"So how did you and Mike meet?" I ask Lauren, in an attempt to make conversation.

She looks at me like I'm mad. "*Err...* well my mum is his sister."

"Sorry?"

"I'm Mike's niece."

Meg and I look at each other in shock. I want to run around the gym shouting *yippee!*

"Oh, he didn't say who you were," I say smiling, a big smile.

"You didn't think I was his girlfriend did you?"

"Well, someone did say something." I try to think of how to put it.

"*Eww*, gross! I'm only sixteen," Lauren says screwing up her nose, "I live in Lincoln. I'm just staying with Uncle Mike for a week during the school holidays as my friend lives here."

This night is getting better by the minute.

***

The party heats up as Colin plays a stream of dance hits and a couple of the younger male members – again, not penises – start break dancing. Everyone makes a circle around them and claps their encouragement. This leads to them attempting somersaults from a standing position, which doesn't end well. Actually, 'penises' may be appropriate in this instance, or is it peni when describing more than one?

I'm on my fourth glass of wine, which is making me feel a bit funny. I did order water but I think I left it at the bar. Mike has been really attentive and I'm sure he patted me on the bum earlier. I can't be absolutely sure, as this dress is so tight my butt is numb. Lauren is sucking face with a young guy who is much shorter than she is but to be fair he isn't wearing six-inch heels. I caught them earlier and promised not to tell Mike.

Jared is proving very popular with girls and guys alike. He was talking to Elliot for ages earlier so I thought I'd ask the question that's been bugging me for months.

"So Jared, is Elliot gay?" I poke him with my elbow, hush, hush wink, wink style.

"No, course he's not. He is stylish for a straight bloke so I can see where your vibes were coming from."

"Did you use your gaydar?"

"Yes and he didn't even give off a peep."

"Thanks babe. I knew you would be able to use your superpower to find the truth." I gesture with open arms, flicking the last of my wine over Karen who luckily is facing the other way and doesn't seem to notice.

"Wanda!" Meg rushes over from dancing with Kerry and Zoe.

"How much have you had to drink?"

"I don't know but they are only small ones. I'll get water next time."

"Do you feel drunk? Only I've had more than you and I feel fine."

"I do feel a bit spacey actually. Perhaps it's because I haven't been eating much."

"You look like you're on drugs. Has anyone given you anything?"

"Not unless you count my mother," I reply, pursing my lips as Meg looks rather stern.

"What do you mean your mother? Wanda what have you taken?"

"Well I did take a couple of those blue pills of hers. I just needed a jolt to lose another couple of pounds."

"I thought you told her you didn't want them. Oh really Wanda, you really ought to practise what you preach more often."

"She must have slipped them into my bag when I went to the loo at the Coffee Snob the other day. I thought a couple would just make me wee a lot so I'd lose some excess fluid. This dress is really tight Meg." I look at her doe-eyed and drop my bottom lip. Of course I have just realised that peeing for England would make me dehydrated, thus effected by alcohol much quicker. I really didn't think it through.

"Stay there, I'll get you some water, which you *will* drink!"

Meg wanders off to the bar and I lean on the table; my feet are throbbing.

"You all right?" Mike says handing me a shot glass.

"Yes fine. What's in this?"

"Not sure, I think it's Sambuca. Big Pete who runs the restaurant has bought one for each the staff."

I look at the small clear liquid as my stomach turns. I am just about to say I'd better not, when Mike smiles showing his lovely dimples.

"Down in one!" he says, clinking my glass.

Oh well, can't make much difference. I clink him back and down the shot in one. I then quickly hide the glass whilst coughing and spluttering as I can see Meg coming over with my water. Mike excuses himself as he needs to lock up the gym but not without booking a dance with me for later.

"Looks like it's going well with Mike," Meg says with a grin.

"I can't stop looking at him. If he kisses me I think I'll faint."

"What about Gary?"

"Who? Oh, Gary, I'm not sure. I really like him, but Mike makes my tummy do cartwheels."

"You sure it's not that shot I just saw you neck down?" she asks, raising her eyebrows.

"I couldn't say no, he clinked my glass."

"Oh, if he clinked your glass then you *had* to drink it." Meg shakes her head at me and hands me a bottle of water.

"Drink that. All of it!"

Colin the DJ continues to keep everyone dancing and I have two dances with Mike. Unfortunately, neither one a slow dance but maybe later. Karen dances like my dad, side step and an arm swing. Very demure and very unlike the Karen that is able to bend and bounce around the aerobic studio.

Jared and Marcus have been leading everyone in various dances for the last hour and I caught Elliot kissing a *girl* called Sam!

Mike wanders off intermittently to look for Lauren and I agree to search the gym with him when he can't find her. It could lead to a romantic moment of our own. Fingers crossed.

"Let's see if they're in the sauna; it's the perfect place to hide."

I grab Mike's arm and drag him towards the stairs. Unfortunately, his face changes as we reach the spa area.

"Why the hell is it steamy down here?"

His jaw tightens. We turn the corner, and hear giggling and there, covered in a cloud of bubbles, is Zoe, Lauren and four other members half-naked and bobbing about in the Jacuzzi. I can't help laughing but Mike is definitely not amused.

"Who is responsible for this?" Mike bellows waving his arms in the air. He sounds like my old maths teacher. I cover my mouth so he can't see me laughing. Actually, I would really like to join them. It looks fun.

"Mikey baby, come on in," Zoe calls through the billowing bubbles. She has obviously taken her shampoo in with her.

"Get out. All of you — now!"

"Uncle Mike," Lauren says, popping her head up and raising her bottle of beer. "Don't be angry; come and join us, but take that stick out of your arse first. It'll rot in here!"

OK, that's it. I can't hold it in any longer. I nearly fall off my heels laughing and have to stumble back around the corner; Mike looks as though he's about to explode. Luckily, he seems to have forgotten that I'm here.

I take refuge in the sauna and sit on one of the benches, bending over to hold my stomach as I think of Lauren and the stick comment. I take a deep breath to try and calm down and have to wipe the tears from my eyes. As I lean back, the sauna begins to sway from side to side. I hold my head but my face feels cold and I think I'm going to be...*Errwah!*

I don't feel very well. I lean over the sauna bucket I have just thrown up in, and try some of that short exhaling they make women do when they're in labour. This just makes my head spin more and then I see black.

Chapter Twelve

I wake up, blink and try to establish where I am. I can see the Christmas photo of me, Jared and Meg on the shelf above the television and this is definitely our ugly brown carpet. Rubbing both eyes, I look over at the armchair. There, curled up like a kitten, is Lauren, one shoe on the floor and the other hanging off her foot. I cannot figure out what she is doing in our flat and my brain hurts too much to try.

"Hello sleepy head, how you feeling?" Mike smiles as he enters the lounge.

Now I'm really confused. I feel like I'm at his place, but what would he be doing with our ugly brown carpet? I manage a smile and sit up.

"I'm fine I think. How come you're here, where are Meg and Jared?"

"In the kitchen making coffee. You have great coffee here; I may have to come back. Would you like one?"

"No thanks, I'll stick with water." I reach for the glass of water that someone has left for me on the coffee table. "Is Lauren OK?"

"Yeah, bit wrecked but she'll be fine. I'll drink this and get her home."

"How come you brought me home, not Jared?" I ask, curious as to what had occurred.

"None of you were in a state to drive so I brought you all home. Thanks for not throwing up in my car, by the way."

I cringe and cover my face with my hands.

"It was that bloody Sambuca that tipped me over the edge, it's your fault," I say jokingly.

"Yeah right," Mike says, walking over to Lauren. "Anyway I'd better get this one home."

"Wanda you're alive!" Jared comes in from the kitchen.

"Yes, very funny. Where's Meg?"

"Getting changed into her pyjamas. Think you should do the same Wand', I can see right up that dress."

"Jared!"

Mike laughs as he encourages Lauren to her feet.

I push myself off the sofa and do a quick head check. No spinning, a little banging but not too bad.

"I'll see you out Mike. It was lovely to meet you Lauren, although I think you were a bad influence on me."

Lauren laughs as she gives me a hug. "I thought you were the bad influence on me."

As we reach the front door, Lauren calls goodbye to Meg and Jared and makes her way down the stairs, stilettos in hand. Mike hangs back.

"See you guys and thanks for the coffee," he calls to Meg and Jared. "And thank you for the dance. Sorry we didn't manage a slow one." Mike says, lightly touching my fingers with his.

"Thanks for the rescue." I look up at his perfect face which looks like it's getting nearer.

He leans down and kisses me firmly on the lips and squeezes my hand.

"I'll give you a call," he says with a wink, "If you don't mind of course."

All I can do is nod and smile back at him with a closed mouth. I have just been kissed by the most perfect looking man I have ever seen in my life, after throwing up and not cleaning my teeth! Oh the shame.

I close the front door and rush to the bathroom to assess how bad I look. My beautifully applied smoky eye is now more Gothic and my hair looks like Mum's Kate Bush album cover. I cannot wait to get out of this dress. After weeing buckets and throwing up, I'm a bit disappointed that I don't look slimmer than I did at the start of the evening.

"All right babe, how you feeling?" asks Meg as she walks out of her room in her pyjamas.

"OK I think. You?"

"Just knackered. Did Mike say anything at the door?"

I make a face and Meg jumps on the sofa to get herself comfy. She knows I am about to dish.

"Well?" She tucks her feet under herself and grabs her coffee mug.

"He kissed me."

"*Eww* that's gross, you've been throwing up!" Meg clasps a hand over her mouth.

"I know!" I laugh, doing the same.

"Have you cleaned your teeth?"

"No. I'm so embarrassed. What on earth did he have to kiss me for? He could've waited until we were on a date or something."

"Did he use tongue?"

"No, thank God."

"What's going on?" Jared shouts from his bedroom.

"Mike kissed Wanda and she hasn't brushed her teeth after being sick!"

"Wanda that's disgusting!"

"I didn't know he was going to kiss me. I could just see his head was getting bigger and then he was too close for me to pull away."

"What did he say before he left?" Meg asks.

"He said 'I'll give you a call'."

"He might change his mind when he finds a bit of sweetcorn stuck in his teeth." Jared says as he wanders into the lounge.

Meg spews her coffee over the sofa and practically falls off it laughing.

"Jared! That's gross."

"Well the good news is..." Meg says, trying to compose herself. "He's definitely seen you at your worse and he still kissed you."

"Yes he did, and you're right Meg, I can't possibly do anything to put him off now. Anyway, I'm off to bed. I'll see you all in the morning."

Sunday 29th July

Today, my mother and her 'girlfriend' are coming over for tea. I can't say that I'm looking forward to it but I want my mum to be happy and who am I to judge. When I told Jared after my lunch with Mum, he just sat there with his mouth open for ages. Actually, he seemed to take it worse than me.

"What time are Mum and George coming over Wanda?"

"I said about five. Thought that would give us time to get over our hangovers and pop to the shops to get some tea stuff."

"What's 'tea stuff': is it like bread and jam and lashings of ginger beer? *Phenah phenah!*" Jared pokes the end of his nose up in an attempt to look posh.

"I don't know you're the one who's good at that sort of thing. Just get a quiche, cheese board and some cakes."

"What are you going to eat?"

"I'll have a tuna sandwich and sliver of cake, oh and lashings of green tea."

"Do you want me to go out?" asks Meg, who is cleaning the kitchen sink.

"No. Why would I want you to go out?"

"Well it might be awkward and it's a family thing."

"Don't be ridiculous, besides this is your flat too and you are family."

"Can I go out?" asks Jared.

"No! Now get dressed and come shopping with me."

***

Jared and I stroll to the local supermarket and wander around the aisles picking up various bits and pieces.

"What about these?" Jared holds up a packet of sausage rolls.

"Don't get those, I love sausage rolls."

"So what you're saying is, if you can't eat it, we can't get it."

"Precisely, now get a quiche I hate quiche."

"Thanks, so kind of you, Wanda." Jared bows. "Hey what if she's a vegetarian? Has Mum said anything?"

"Oh yeah, good thinking. Mum didn't mention it but all those yoga types seem to be vegetarians so we had better get the spinach and goats cheese."

I pick up two of my least favourite cakes to put in the basket. I would get ones that I don't like but there aren't any.

We arrive back at the flat and Meg is still busy hovering and fluffing pillows.

"Meg baby, any coffee on the go?" Jared asks.

"Not yet, but I'll make some," Meg replies, unplugging the Hoover. "By the way Wanda, you forgot your phone and you have a message."

"Was it Mum?"

"No, it was Gary."

"Oh bugger! I forgot, he said he was going to come over today. Shit, what shall I tell him?"

"I know," says Jared, "tell him your mum just came out as a lesbian and she's bringing her lover to meet her kids. Oh and your boss, whom you snogged last night, may be calling later. That's if you want to get rid of him. If not then tell him you're ill and you'll call him tomorrow."

I find my phone and check the message. It reads:

Hi Wanda. Hope you had a great night.

Be round about 6 as won't get home til 5 x

I dial Gary's number but am transferred to voice-mail.

"Hi, Gary it's Wanda. Can you call me when you get this? Hope you had fun at your sisters'. Speak to you later."

Oh well, that's all I can do for now.

By five o'clock, we have not only cleaned the flat but Jared has also made ham and cucumber sandwiches with tomato focaccia and egg mayonnaise on brown bread. We have spinach and mushroom quiche, some potato salad and two different cakes. Meg has even washed the good crockery.

"Guys, they're here!" Jared calls from the bedroom.

"Can you see what she looks like?"

"Nah, but I think she's wearing a hat."

"Who, Mum or George?"

"George. Quick put the kettle on she'll be here in a minute."

The doorbell rings and I do a quick check that everyone is ready before opening it.

"Hi Mum," I greet her with a kiss on the cheek. "And this must be George." I look at the scrawny, tanned woman standing next to my mother in the doorway.

"Yes, hello, you must be Wanda. It's good to meet you." George lunges toward me and grabs my hand. I get the impression she is a little nervous. That makes five of us!

Mum and George make their way to the kitchen where the rest of the introductions take place.

"We didn't know if you were vegetarian or not George, so we made sure we had options," Jared says, showing her his plates of sandwiches. I decide not to mention that I saw him using the same knife to cut the ham and the egg sandwiches. She'll never know.

"I am vegetarian actually, that's really considerate of you all."

Meg sorts the cups for tea and ushers everyone into the lounge. George sits next to Mum on the sofa; her hair is wild and unkempt, it makes her head look too large for her tiny body. And she wasn't wearing a hat. That was her hair!

"I was telling George that you teach yoga, darling," Mum states as she inspects the inside of an egg sandwich.

"Oh yes, but I've not taken that many classes yet."

"What form of yoga do you teach Wanda?" George asks.

"Ashtanga mostly," I reply whilst handing out the plates. "Help yourselves to sandwiches."

I head to the kitchen and Jared follows, leaving Meg to keep them entertained.

***

"What do you think?" asks Jared, grinning like someone who just did something naughty.

"They look really weird together," I whisper. "And what is that on her head?"

"Now you know why I thought it was a hat!"

"She doesn't even wear make-up. Mum can't put the rubbish out without full war paint. I just don't see it!"

"Oh God, I hope they don't intend to start holding hands and stuff in front of us," Jared says screwing up his nose.

"You should be the tolerant one here." I can hear my name being called.

I make my way back into the lounge. "Did you call, Mum?"

"Yes, Megan was just telling us how well you're doing with your training for that competition you're entering."

"Yes, and you'll be pleased to hear that I can hold my handstand and do the splits. I'm not even eating any of this." I gesture towards the food on the table. "I'm having tuna and salad, but I will have a tiny slice of cake."

"That's good Wanda darling. I can see you have lost some weight."

My mother then informs George about how my cheeks get 'chubby' when I put on weight.

"So George, do you teach yoga full time?" asks Meg as she tucks into some potato salad.

"Yeah, pretty much. I actually own the studio, but I'm an artist too, so I sculpt in my spare time."

The leather thong necklace she is wearing with some sort of symbol on it is flipping up and down as she speaks which is rather distracting. I can see that Meg is trying to ignore it.

"Wow, that's cool," Jared says, nodding his head. "What, like out of clay or do you use something else?"

"All different; sometimes I'll sculpt from something I find on a dump site. Those places are great to rummage around," George enthuses, leaning forward.

This revelation is obviously news to my mother who is unaware of the look of disgust she now has on her face.

"This one sculpture I made from bits of old bicycles and a mattress, gained the attention of a local art dealer. Nothing came of it but I was proud of that piece." George smiles and continues to bob her head as though recalling a special memory.

Mum's face is now a contorted grimace, which she trying to pass off as a smile. Her idea of art is the cushions she made on an interior design course last year.

George is very friendly and starts to loosen up after a while. She touches Mum's hand a few times when recalling some of their experiences in Tenerife, it's probably me but I'm sure I caught Mum flinching slightly.

"Who wants coffee and cake?" Meg jumps up during a lull in conversation. She takes everyone's order and makes her way to the kitchen. Jared is playing Mum and George his new CD and we all try to talk above the noise. I am just relaying a funny incident that happened in the gym last week when I stop mid sentence. There, standing by the lounge door is Meg with Gary. Oh poop!

"Gary, hi I rang you earlier but you didn't call me back." I rise from my chair with what I realise is a fake smile. I can see Meg grinning like a scary puppet behind him.

"I did call but it went to voicemail, so I came over as arranged. I hope that's all right?" Gary smiles looking from me to Mum.

"Yes of course it's fine. Erm let me introduce you. Mum, George, this is Gary."

Mum looks at me with a 'and why don't I know about him?' look on her face.

"Lovely to meet you Gary."

"Hello." George nods.

"Let's go in the kitchen and get you a coffee." I drag Gary out of the lounge.

"Sorry, Wanda, I didn't know your mum was coming over. Do you want me to go?"

"No stay, it's fine." Meg is still sporting the scary puppet face as I look to her for support. "I do need to tell you something though," I add, trying to think of how to put it.

"Don't tell me, you met someone else last night." Gary says as his shoulders drop. Meg's mouth is now a wide gurn. I would laugh if I wasn't suddenly suffering from pangs of guilt.

"No, of course not, it's about my mum and George."

Gary is looking intense and raises his eyebrows. "What about them?"

"My mother decided to reveal that she's a lesbian. George is her 'girlfriend'," I tell him, using air quotes on the word girlfriend.

"No way! Seriously, I'm so sorry Wand'. You sure you don't want me to go?"

"No, just act normal and we'll all get through it."

The next hour passes quite pleasantly with a game of bowling on the WII and Gary helping George with a problem she has with her computer. I only have tuna salad and one minuscule piece of cake and two coffees. I am just walking to the kitchen with the empty mugs threaded through my fingers, when I hear a knocking from somewhere. I stop to listen. It's someone knocking on the front door. Most people ring the bell. I place my bouquet of mugs on the kitchen table and go to the front door peephole to see who it is. All I can see is a large spray of flowers. Ooh lovely, someone sent me flowers. I quickly open the door, wondering if they're from Gary or Mike.

"Hi, Wanda thought I would drop by and see how you were after last night," Mike says smiling as he hands me the flowers.

Chapter Thirteen

I quickly check the hallway before dragging Mike into the kitchen. The sensible thing would have been for me to go onto the landing but I panicked.

Mike looks shocked as I swing him around, banging him into the fridge door.

"Hey, Wanda what's going on?"

"Nothing sorry," I reply, breathing heavily, "lovely to see you but I need you to go."

"Oh sorry, I know I should have rung first but..."

"No, it's not you, Mike, it's just that..." I am about to explain the mother situation when I see Meg sporting her scary puppet face again and creeping along the hallway. Mike turns to look at her and I make my own 'what the fuck do I do now?' face behind him.

"Hello, Mike," Meg says grinning. "What lovely flowers."

"I was just telling Mike about the situation," I whisper.

Meg's eyes widened with shock. "You were?"

"Yes, about Mum and George being here." I nod vigorously.

"Oh, I see, yes of course it's a delicate situation."

"It doesn't sound like it," Mike says, cocking his ear towards the lounge as Jared and George scream with laughter at something.

"That's just Jared overcompensating. Anyway, I'll call you when they've gone home."

"OK."

Half my mind is panicking that Gary will see him leave whilst the other half is wishing I had some emergency mints by the front door. Still, if he does decide to kiss me, tuna is still a step up from vomit.

I place one foot into the hallway when I see Gary out of the corner of my eye.

"Meg!" I shout. But there's no need, as she's body-checking him back to the lounge with cries of "No, no it's all fine, go back and enjoy yourself."

"Who was that?" Mike asks.

"Who?"

"That guy who Meg just tackled in the hall."

"Oh erm, that's her brother, Gary." Oh God another lie. This is not going to end well.

"Why is he here? Does your mum know him?"

"Yes he's like a second son to her, a straight one!" I try a laugh, but it comes out as more of a snort.

"Oh I see. I'm sorry, Wanda I'll go and let you" he begins just as his phone rings.

Mike smiles apologetically whilst checking the front of his phone. "Sorry," he mouths.

I can't help but glance at the caller ID that says 'Chloe calling.'

Now, I'm no angel in this scenario, but honestly — WHO THE HELL IS CHLOE?

Mike clears his throat and cancels the call. He looks a little sheepish.

"Anyway, call me later if you can," he says, tucking his phone into his jeans pocket.

I'm feeling a bit miffed but I need to get him out of the house, so I rally.

"Thanks Mike for being so understanding. I'll call you when they leave." I check the hall again before escorting him to the front door and pushing him through it as casually as I can.

"No problem and good luck," Mike says with a smile. His dimples almost make me forget everything else that's going on. He leans down as I hear a shuffle by the lounge door and see Gary looking at me. I pull back in reflex calling "Thanks so much, speak soon, bye!" Poor Mike falls forward, smacking his head on the door as I slam it shut. Gary is practically pounced on by Meg who was in the middle of her turn at bowling.

"Meg! What are you doing?"

"Oh, sorry Gary," she apologises, realising Mike has been safely expelled from the flat.

"I thought Meg was a calm, sane person," Gary says, shaking his head. "She's a nutter!"

"I don't know what's gotten into her today." I tut, and wipe the sweat from my face. "Anyway, thanks for being so great with Mum and George."

"No problem, they're good fun. Who was that at the door?"

"What door?" I ask, walking back to the kitchen.

"The front door," Gary says, in a slow deliberate manner.

"Oh, him, he's my neighbour; he brought some flowers." I present the flowers, which I had slipped into the sink. I grab the card before he has a chance to see it and open the kitchen draw.

"What for? I haven't missed your birthday or anything have I?"

I'm not really listening, as I want to read the card before popping into the draw. It reads: I'LL BE YOUR HERO ANY TIME. LOVE MIKE X

I'm smiling at the content of the card when I realise Gary has asked me a question.

"No, my birthday's in February. These are because I did him a favour last week. Anyway let's get back to the game shall we?" I turn towards him giving him my loveliest smile.

***

We manage to get through the rest of the visit without incident and Mum and George leave about 8.00 p.m. Luckily, Gary is ready to leave about 9.00 p.m., as he has some work to do before the morning. He really has been great today. I let out an unexpected yawn whilst walking him to the door.

Gary puts his arms around me and kisses me on the cheek. "Bit of an exciting day eh?"

"You could say that." I smile wearily, looking up at him.

"Fancy that new adventure movie at the cinema this week?"

"Yes, that would be great. I'm working Tuesday evening so it will have to be Wednesday."

"Great, I'll look forward to it." Gary leans in and kisses me ever so gently on the lips. I can't help but respond as he pulls me tighter. His soft kisses increasing in passion. I stand on tiptoes to meet his lips again, aware that his hands are slowly roaming over my butt. I hear Meg walking up the hall and we break away, both breathing heavily.

Gary calms himself before asking "Would you like to come to The Lighthouse next weekend if you're not busy." He looks at me expectantly.

Oh no, what do I say? The Lighthouse is an old manor house about an hour away. The grounds are stunning. At this moment, I really want to say yes, but I'm still not sure what's happening between me and Mike. I feel very shallow, but manage to blurt out. "Yes I'd love to!" I can always cancel it if something happens before then.

"Great," says Gary, "only my company have been given special rates for next weekend as we have done some work for them recently and it would be nice to spend a bit more time together."

"I'll look forward to it. Bye, speak to you tomorrow."

"Wanda Mikos, you made me look like a flaming lunatic today!" Meg is in the hall with her hands on her hips.

"I'm so sorry Meg. Was kinda funny though wasn't it?"

Meg shakes her head and laughs. "I'm going to clean the kitchen. Come and tell me what happened."

"Wait for me if you're gossiping!" Jared runs to the kitchen and plonks himself into a chair.

I relay the unfortunate events of Mike's attempted kiss and the subsequent head butting of the door.

"Oh my God, Wanda, first you leave him with vomit breath, now you've given him concussion. I can't believe he still wants to see you." says Jared, holding his hands up in disbelief.

"Actually he may not, I think I should ring to apologise. Plus, I need to find out who Chloe is."

Jared and Megan both turn to look at me. "Chloe?"

"Oh yes, I didn't tell you about the phone call."

Megan pulls off her rubber gloves and takes a seat next to Jared as I tell them about Mike's phone call from someone called Chloe.

"Do you think that's who Karen was talking about, Wand'?" Meg asks, remembering the conversation we had with her at the party.

"No idea, but I think I'll give him a call anyway to apologise for being a lunatic today."

"Will you ask him about Chloe?"

"I want to. Gary has invited me away next weekend and it would be helpful to know if Mike has a girlfriend so I won't feel so guilty."

"Oh, Wanda, what a tangled web you weave." Meg says, shaking her head and replacing her rubber gloves. "So are you going to go away with Gary?"

"I said yes, but I'm not sure."

"Because of Mike?"

"Yes, I'm feeling guilty enough about seeing them both but if I agree to go away with Gary, he's going to expect lots of kissing and whatnot."

"Whatnot? You mean sex?"

"Yes, it'll change everything. I don't know if I'm ready yet."

"Why didn't you say 'No' then?"

"I couldn't help it, it just came out."

"Wanda, really, you do need to engage your brain before you speak."

"I know, I know."

"Well, you're just going to have to have 'whatnot' with Gary and worry about Mike and his girlfriend another time. Are you going to call Mike?"

"Yeah, better do it now."

I am quite nervous as I press the 'Call' button under Mike's name in my phone. He answers straight away.

"Hello, Wanda, how did things go?"

"Not too painful I guess. They just left." Another small lie. "I just wanted to apologise for acting like a loony. Is your head alright?"

"I'll survive. Why did you slam the door? Was it something I said?"

"No. Please don't think that. It was just...." Why did I not prepare for this call? I should have known he was going to be curious about why I shut his head in the door. Think, girl think!

"I saw my mum coming and was embarrassed," I blurt out. Actually, that's not bad.

"Oh I see. Didn't realise I embarrass you."

"Of course you don't, you know what I mean. Anyway, the other thing I called to say was thank you so much for the flowers and I loved the card too. It should be me sending you flowers after you rescued me."

"Glad you liked them and you're forgiven for the concussion. Listen do you want to train together tomorrow lunchtime. You said you like to be pushed."

"Don't see why not. I'm doing chest, biceps and hamstrings tomorrow that suit you?"

"No problem. Can I stand behind you when you do bent-over bar lifts?"

"Don't be cheeky! And that's not the correct name for the exercise you're thinking of."

Mike laughs. "Whatever it is, can I still stand behind you?"

I rub my arms as my hairs stand up on end. I cannot believe that this man can give me goose bumps over the phone. We decide on meeting at 1.00 p.m. the next day.

"Wanda, before you go. Perhaps we can arrange to meet for dinner when we train tomorrow."

At last, a proper date. "That would be great, I..."

"Only there's something I want to talk to you about."

Well, that's it. We all know what that means. Mike has a girlfriend.

Monday 30th July

Training with Mike would be a lot easier if he didn't turn up looking so sexy. He just walked into the gym wearing a pair of white tennis shorts and a Fred Perry top with the collar turned up slightly. Not usual gym wear as such, but he's more a running, cycling and tennis kind of guy. Plus, he smells masculine and spicy. I don't mean his body is emitting last night's vindaloo; it must be a body spray or something. If it's one of those that make women fall over with lust, it's totally working. I, on the other hand, have managed to get back into my favourite pink training bottoms and have teamed them with a brand new white vest. I have even put my hair in plaits as Meg thinks it makes me look cute.

"Right Miss, where shall we start?" Mike asks, obviously expecting me to lead the session.

"Well I need to improve my upper body strength for some of the moves in my routine, so can we start on the bench press?"

"No problem," he says, walking over to the bench and unloading the two 20-kilo plates that have been left on the bar. "How much shall I load on?"

"Let's warm up with the bar first."

I must admit I feel a bit nervous but I'm determined to impress him as I push out twenty repetitions.

"Excellent," Mike says, placing the bar back on the stand. "I'll just put some weight on for my warm up."

"Are you trying to impress me, Michael Diamond?"

"Not with this weight." He grins and loads the bar with a 5-kilo plate on each side.

I stand behind him to help replace the bar as he finishes his set.

"Leave the fives on, I'll use them on my next set."

He's looking suitably impressed as we change places. I lie onto the bench and stretch my head back to release my neck and realise, to my embarrassment that I can see right up Mike's shorts. I'm either looking at his pubic hair or hopefully a pair of black briefs. My face is burning as I take a breath, close my eyes and start pushing the bar.

"Not bad for a girl," Mike mocks, as I finish fifteen reps. "Do you always bench press with your eyes closed?"

Oh no, what do I say?

"I didn't realise I was; must have been concentrating."

We are starting to flirt more as we go on to training biceps, when Karen arrives in the gym.

"Hi you two, who's training who?" Karen asks jokingly.

I assume she's being nice as Mike is here. He looks up from the weight rack.

"Hi, Karen, I think Wanda is kicking my arse." He looks over at me and winks.

Well us 'Main Event' girls are pretty strong and fit you know," Karen says walking over to me and bumping shoulders in a girlie *we're best mates* way.

Stunned, I look up at her but she is smiling at Mike. Oh my God! I can't believe she has finally admitted that she's entering the competition.

"I didn't know you were entering," I say, as casually as I can.

"You know I am," Karen replies, looking at me with a puzzled expression. "I told you weeks ago when we went for a run in the country park."

"Sorry, I must not have heard. I was busy being struck in the face with a branch."

"Oh yes, I'd forgotten about that. It seems to have cleared up nicely," she says, moving her eyes around the contours of my face.

"So, Karen, how's your routine going for the competition?"

"Great actually, I have a much better chance this year I think."

"Why's that?"

"I've taken what I learned two years ago and improved in every area. How's your routine going?"

"Fantastic, thanks for asking. I've never been good at gymnastics, but I've had a coach teaching me for the last month or so." I know that Meg is not exactly a coach but I couldn't help myself.

"I think I'll come and watch you both in the competition," Mike says, picking a couple of 9-kilo dumbbells off the rack. "In fact, we could organise a trip for the whole gym."

Karen and I form a synchronised look of horror on our faces.

"Anyway I have a meeting to get to," Karen says as her face returns to normal. She spins on one heel and heads for the door, then stops, spins back around and announces. "Oh yes sorry, I actually came to tell you something, Mike."

"Chloe called," she says smiling. A genuine smile this time.

Chapter Fourteen

Mike looks paralyzed in an awkward position as Karen wafts out of the gym door. My heart begins thumping loudly. Eventually, Mike stands and makes an apologetic face at me.

"Wanda, I'm so sorry, I meant to tell you about Chloe. That's why I wanted to meet you for lunch or dinner or something." He walks towards me and sighs as he waits for my reaction.

"Who the hell is she?"

"She's my girlfriend — was my girlfriend. We broke up when I moved here to take this job."

"OK," I say slowly. "So why does she keep calling you?"

"Because she wants us to get back together," Mike says pursing his lips into a smile of sorts. He takes a seat on the bench behind him.

"Right, so is that what you want?"

"No I, well I'm just taking her calls because she sounds so desperate. I did love her once; I can't just tell her to piss off."

I take a seat next to him and lean my elbows onto my knees whilst I think.

"No, you're right, you can't. That would be a shitty thing to do. I just wish you had told me about her. I mean I know we haven't been out on a date or anything but…"

"I have tried to tell you a couple of times but then you were off with your ankle and…"

"Oh, is that why you kept telling me you wanted to ask me something?"

"I wanted to ask you about Lauren but also to see if you'd be cool about the whole Chloe thing." He looks at me pleadingly.

"It's fine. I understand; maybe you should sort things out with her before we go any further."

I can't lie, at this point I am thinking a short break between us means I'm still connected to Mike but I can say yes to a mini break with Gary.

"Maybe you're right," Mike says, nodding his head and looking at his feet.

What? He is meant to say No; please Wanda my love for you is growing like a spring flower in bloom! I know what I just said about the break but he didn't have to agree so quickly.

Mike and I finally agree to give ourselves two weeks before going out on a date and head to the changing rooms.

"See you later," Mike says as we part ways.

"Hey, Mike."

"Yeah?"

"Shall we still keep flirting on the menu?" I ask.

"Absolutely!"

***

I've been mulling over the situation with Mike during my shower and have convinced myself that saying 'yes' to Gary's proposal would not be totally out of order.

"Hey, Wanda," Zoe calls over as I step out of the shower cubicle, "what were you and the Mikester talking about so intensely earlier?"

"Nothing interesting," I say, wondering how much to tell her.

"You looked so cute training together. By the way, what happened on Saturday night after the party? Mike freaked out a bit when he found us in the Jacuzzi; is he still mad?"

"No, don't think so. Actually he drove us all home. I was smashed and woke up in my flat. Mike was still there to make sure I was all right."

"Oh my God, that's so sweet." Zoe says, making herself comfortable on the bench whilst I get changed into my work clothes.

"Then he kissed me at the door," I whisper, checking there is nobody around.

"No way, *ahh* that's so romantic."

I decided to leave out the bit about throwing up in the sauna.

"Yes, he even popped round Sunday to see how I was and brought me flowers."

"He must really be into you, Wand'."

"I'm not sure actually, as he still technically has a girlfriend, Chloe," I say looking sideways at her.

"What a wanker!"

Her reaction makes me laugh and I swear her to secrecy with a promise that I will keep her updated.

Attempting my usual run up the stairs two-at-a-time for maximum calorie usage, I notice Elliot and Karen outside the gym door on the floor above me. I slow down to listen to their conversation. Karen is shaking her head and waving her hands in anger. Elliot looks like he is trying not to laugh.

"Just get it done please Elliot. Honestly, some people are animals!" Karen stomps off still shaking her head.

"Hey Elliot," I call before he enters the gym, "what was Hitler having a hissy-fit about?"

"You are never going to believe this. A few of the members were complaining about a foul smell in the spa; when Karen went to investigate, she found that someone had thrown up in the sauna bucket. *Ehwww!*"

"Oh no Elliot, that was me," I exclaim, as both hands cover my eyes, tying to conceal my shame.

"No way! You are a sick animal Wanda Mikos." Elliot gives me a shove as we make our way into the gym.

"Don't you dare tell anyone," I warn him.

"No worries, I think it's hysterical, except for the fact that I've got to clean it up." He turns slowly to look at me.

"I'll do it. Just don't tell anyone."

"Deal."

"I'm meant to be seeing Mrs. Clamp and her daughter at half past so can you tell them I won't be long when they show up?"

"Will do Chicki."

The thought of clearing up sick from two nights ago is filling me with dread. It wouldn't have been so bad if we had been open yesterday, but there was work being done on the changing rooms so the gym was closed for the day. I think that must have been the reason for the party; get all the members too hung over to want to train on the Sunday will result in fewer complaints.

I spend the last hour of my shift training the Clamps and trying to smile through their constant whinging. I did perk up when I checked their weight loss progress, as they had both lost another three pounds each.

I arrive home and am about to tell Meg about my decision to go away with Gary when she interjects to inform me that Karen from work has called.

"What here, on our house phone?"

"Yes, she just left a message but I didn't listen to it."

"Why didn't she speak to me at work or ring my mobile?"

"I don't know."

"I wonder what she wants to tell me. Probably going to let know that Mike is in fact married with two children."

Meg shrugs her shoulders and switches the coffee maker on.

"I suppose I had better get it over with. Why didn't she just see me at work? I've seen her loads of times today."

"For goodness sake why don't you listen to the message and find out, instead of second guessing the whole thing. Anyway, she might be calling to tell you something nice," Meg says, with a look of doubt on her face.

"Yeah cos that's gonna happen!" I fling my arms into the air and make my way to the lounge. I want to hear this message for myself.

***

As Meg enters the lounge, carrying two mugs of coffee, I slowly lift my head. Eyes wide and my bottom jaw nearly in my cleavage.

"Good grief, Wanda what's wrong?" Meg quickly places the mugs on the table and rushes towards me.

I am still trying to get my head around the news I've just received and can't quite speak. Meg starts shaking my arm. "Wanda! For goodness sake, tell me what's wrong." Meg is now looking as pale as me. I stand up straight and manage to close my mouth.

"Listen to this." I press 'Play' on the answer machine. Karen's normally haughty voice sounds quite cheerful as she starts her message. *'Hi, Wanda, sorry, I meant to catch you at work, I got a call from The Main Event organisers to inform us that the Channel 10 film crew will be filming our section of the documentary from next week. Anyway, I won't be in for the next ten days so they are going to start with you. They will call you or the gym on Friday to confirm. Good luck, bye.'*

As this point, I realise that my eyes are still owl-like as my face is aching.

"That's great. I thought it was something terrible by the look on your face. Anyway, how is it you didn't know about the filming? Surely they would have given you details in the information they sent you," Meg says, picking up her coffee and taking a sip.

I am still standing owl-faced and motionless.

"Oh, Wanda, you did read the rest of the information they gave you?"

"I kept meaning to get around to it, but I forgot."

Meg gives out an audible sigh and shakes her head at me. The annoying thing is, I may have stuck to my diet and training even more if I knew I was going to be on television.

"I thought you signed some papers and sent them back."

"I did."

"It may have been an idea to read it first Wanda; that document probably included your consent for taking part in the filming."

"I'll get the papers." I sigh and go in search of my application package, which I find in the side pocket of my training bag and take them into the lounge. Meg and I sit close on the sofa and scour the papers. Sure enough there it is in black and white.

All participants will be required to take part in a full-length documentary, which will be aired on Channel 10 next spring. The camera crew will follow each competitor for a short period, to get an insight of the training and discipline involved in entering The Main Event competition. Please complete the consent form below and return to the address given.

Meg and I just look at each other and burst out laughing.

"Well, you said you wanted to be famous," Meg giggles, shrugging her shoulders.

I drain my coffee and leap off the sofa. "We need to go to the leisure centre and practise my moves. Do you think it will be available?"

"Yes, they don't have classes until Wednesday. I'll call and let them know we're coming. Grab your music."

Meg and I set off for the leisure centre with a renewed sense of determination. I am going to turn this unexpected news into a positive and work even harder than before.

Chapter Fifteen

Tuesday 31st July

I'm beginning to dread pressing the message button on our house phone; no good ever comes of it. And this time was no exception. My dad's girlfriend Laura called to say she had managed to change the wedding to the 17th and wanted to ask if I would be her bridesmaid. My first thought is, the 17th of what? Surely she can't mean August; that's the week before the competition!

I am sitting with my head in my hands, when Jared enters the room.

"What's up?"

I slowly pull my hands away from my face and look up at him. "That was Laura; she is pleased to tell us she managed to change the date of the wedding," I announce sarcastically.

"Well that's good isn't it?"

"It's now on the 17th."

"Of what?"

"Exactly, I think she means the 17th of August." I sigh and flop back onto the sofa.

"Hang on, that's the week after next," Jared says, calculating the days in his head.

"No shit Sherlock! How the hell can I go to Cyprus one week before the competition?"

My mind is whirring more than when I overdid my flick-flack last night. I need to call Dad. I grab the phone and try to calm myself with some yoga breathing. Punching in the number I rehearse what my first words will be.

"Hello."

It's Laura, Oh crap; I would rather speak to my dad.

"Hi, Laura, it's Wanda; I got your message about the wedding."

"Excellent, how do you feel about being a bridesmaid? Don't worry, you can pick out your own dress and if you want to buy one there, we'll give you the money when you come over. Oh and your dad was meant to ask Jared to be his best man, do you think he will? We weren't going to have either but I insisted. I can't wait for you to see the little chapel in the mountains. It really is the perfect place for a wedding and — ."

"Laura, can I just ask something?"

"Yes of course, sorry sweet, I get carried away."

"You said the 17th; my question is the 17th of what?" At this point, I'm begging her in my mind to say September.

"August silly, I know it's sooner but the only other time we could have the chapel would have been next summer. Your dad said any other time than the weekend of the 25th should be fine."

There is a stretch of silence as I try desperately to think of some way of saying I can't come to the wedding, without bursting her bubble.

"That's great! And of course I would love to be your bridesmaid."

Jared is in his bedroom getting his stuff ready for work when I poke my head around the door.

"Well, what date was it?" he asks, stuffing a T-shirt into a bag.

"The wedding is definitely on the 17th of August you're best man and I'm going to be bridesmaid."

"I get to be best man, cool." Jared lifts his uniform off the back of the door and tucks it into his suit bag. He turns and sits on his bed.

"So what did you tell Dad?"

"Laura answered the phone." I join him on the bed. "She was so excited and they can't get the chapel again until next summer."

"So you told her it was fine and you can't wait to be her bridesmaid." Jared nudges me and smiles.

"You know I did. What else could I say?"

"Listen, your routine for the competition is great, your diet is going well so what's the worst that could happen?"

We look straight into each others eyes and laugh. What indeed.

I'm getting my things ready for work when Megan walks through the door.

"Hi guys," she manages through a yawn.

"Hi Meg, I'm just off and so is Jared. How was work?"

Meg places her bag down in the hallway and tilts her head to one side. "Good actually, but what's up with you?"

Jared walks out of his bedroom carrying his overnight bag. "Don't ask!"

"Why what's wrong?"

"I'll let madam tell you, I'm off to work. *Au revoir mes amis.*"

"Yeah see you later, Jay. Wanda, come and tell me the latest drama."

I grab my sports bag and meet Meg in the hallway.

"Dad's wedding is the week before the competition — and I'm going to be bridesmaid." I look desperately at Meg who purses her lips together. I think she is trying not to smile. "Meg, it's not funny! I can't have anything disrupting my training before the competition."

"Wanda babe, don't be such a drama queen. It's not ideal, but if there's one thing I know about you, is that you thrive on a challenge." She looks at me hopefully.

"Well," I say slowly, "I do love a challenge and it will mean I can have a bit of colour for the competition."

"That's a girl, now get yourself off to work and we'll discuss strategy later."

I smile and give Meg a big hug. "Thanks mate, see you later."

"Oh by the way," I call as I turn the doorknob. "I need you to come shopping with me. I have to get a dress."

"No problem."

"Oh and one last thing," I shout just as the front door behind me is closing.

"What?"

"Can you tell my mum I'm going to be bridesmaid?" I quickly slam the door and run down the stairs before she can say no.

Tuesday Evening 31st July

I arrive at the gym and the car park is rammed. There are people milling about in reception and Mike is talking to a group at one end of the desk.

"It's busy tonight," I remark as I walk over to Annie, who is trying to take a photo of a new member on the computer camera.

"I know. It's always busier after people have been paid; plus Karen has given out some free passes."

As I check the class schedule and make my way to the gym, I notice Vanessa walking up the stairs in front of me. She has finished her six-week course with me and looks amazing.

"Vanessa!" I run to catch her up.

"Wanda hi, how's the routine going?"

"Great thanks; you look amazing by the way. How is your training going?"

"Not bad, but it's not the same as working out with you. I know you taught me how to train efficiently but I think I've been personal trainerised."

I look at her and laugh. "Personal trainerised?"

"Yes, you know what I mean. I didn't have to think when I was with you. Now I have to think for myself."

"Well you know that I'm still here to help you."

"I know and I do appreciate it, but if I can, I'm going to start seeing you again just once a week if that's OK?"

"Of course it is. Come and see me later. Oh and I also need the gossip on you and Bradley." I wink pushing the door to the gym. Vanessa looks embarrassed and whispers, "It's all good."

I am excited by the prospect of continuing to train Vanessa. She is definitely more fun to work with than Mrs. Clamp and her daughter. They have been in three times and done nothing but whine through the whole session.

My next consultation is a woman and her husband who are local doctors. This is quite intimidating as I know I'll be taking their blood pressure and resting heart rate, which is something they do every day. However, after spending the next 45 minutes with them, I find out that they seem to know diddlysquat about nutrition and exercise. My confidence increases by the minute. So much so, that by the time they leave, having booked sessions with me, I am feeling less intimidated and rather more 'up-my-own-bottom'.

The rest of my shift is taken up helping Elliot with a couple of big guys who cannot figure out why their legs are still skinny after eight weeks of training, and a class in the studio. By 9.45 p.m., the gym has emptied out and I suddenly remember that I wanted to ask Elliot about Karen. I find him bent over an Olympic bar trying to pull off the clips.

"Need any help?"

"These bloody clips are so hard to get off. Grab the other end could you."

Elliot and I squeeze and slide the clips off the bar, followed by the 20-kilo weights.

"So where's Karen then?" I ask casually.

"Dunno, think she's on holiday or something. I don't care as long as she's not here."

I decide to go in search of information. First stop Mike. She would have told him about her plans.

I am in mid bounce down the stairs, when I look up and *Oomph*, I bump straight into Mike who appears to be running up the stairs two at a time.

"Sorry!" We both call out in unison. Mike goes off to the left, just as I do the same. *Oomph*, we collide again and can't help but look at each other and laugh. Mike places his hands on my elbows and guides me gently to the left of him. I don't take my eyes off his. He smiles; his eyes crease and almost disappear but for a sliver of bright blue. He turns to face me and pulls me closer. My tummy performs a flick-flack as his full lips reach mine and...

"Wanda! Have you seen — oh sorry you guys," Elliot pulls an *'oops'* face as he leans over the stairwell.

I jump back trying to make out that we were not about to kiss. Although it's quite obvious Elliot saw us.

"Have I seen what Elliot?" I shout up the stairs.

There is no reply. I look up at Mike and tut.

"You go and check what he wants," he says, kissing me on the cheek. "I'm going to go back down and lock up the office."

As I make my way back up the stairs and enter the gym, I'm greeted by Elliot who is facing away from me with his arms wrapped around himself rubbing up and down his back. He is also attempting a snogging motion with his head.

"Ha, ha very mature," I say, throwing my pen at him.

"I didn't know you two were doing the dirty!" he gasps, turning to throw my pen back at me.

"We're not really. We agreed to not get involved for now. It's complicated."

"Looked pretty involved from where I was standing. Come on Wand' what's the skinny?"

"What's the skinny?"

"Yes. The gossip, the 911, the Word."

"Can I tell you tomorrow? I really want to get home, I'm knackered." I look at him pleadingly.

"OK, but I need details."

I shake my head and laugh as I start to clean up the gym reception and realise that I still haven't asked Mike about Karen.

I pick up my sports bag and check my phone, there's a text from Gary to let me know he had to book the horror movie as there were no tickets for the film I wanted to see, and he has booked the hotel for Saturday night. I admit to feeling a pang of guilt as I think about the 'almost kiss' that just took place.

I head out of the gym and make my way down to reception. Annie is announcing the gym closing over the Tannoy, and Elliot is checking the toilets for stragglers. As I pass Karen's office, I can see Mike putting away some papers.

"Night Mike," I say smiling as I'm not really sure what to say after the 'kissing' incident.

He looks up and indicates for me to come in.

"Sorry about earlier," he says, sitting on the edge of Karen's desk. "I know I said I'd leave you alone for now but you looked really cute and I couldn't help myself." He smiles that sexy smile and I my knees buckle so that I have to lean on the desk too.

"It wasn't just you," I say, looking directly at him. "Perhaps we should..."

I am interrupted by Mike leaning towards me and kissing me gently on the lips. He pulls away and sits up straight. "Sorry, you were saying?"

My heart is banging against my ribcage. I'm sure we are about to engage in a full-on snog at last, when Annie appears at the door to wish us both a pleasant evening.

Mike shakes his head and laughs. "We just can't catch a break."

"Maybe it's the universe telling us something," I offer as I pick up my bag.

"Maybe — anyway, will I see you tomorrow?"

"Yes if you're on late shift again." I turn to walk out of the door. Before Mike can say 'goodnight' I remember something. "Oh, I meant to ask you if you know where Karen has gone." I put on my cheekiest smile.

"Technically, it isn't a secret I suppose. She's gone to the Brecon Beacons in Wales."

"Oh my God, that cow!"

Mike seems somewhat taken aback by my reaction.

"Is that bad?"

"She has gone to a famous fitness training camp. I can't remember the name of it but they train athletes and stuff."

I drop my bag and start pacing back and forth looking at the carpet.

"What's wrong with her going to this training camp then?"

"It's cheating!" I exclaim, throwing my hands in the air but secretly wishing I had thought of it first.

Eventually, I stop pacing and look up at Mike who hasn't moved.

"You all right?" he asks.

"Yeah, sorry didn't mean to freak you out."

"It's fine, I knew you were nuts." He says moving towards me and placing his hands on my shoulders. "You're not really bothered by this are you? I didn't think you were that insecure."

"I'm not!" I protest, a little offended by this remark.

"You can take on anyone; I have no doubt about that."

"Yes you're right, I'm just a bit freaked out by the whole TV thing and on top of that, I have got to go to my dad's wedding in Cyprus the week before the competition."

"Oh yeah," Mike says, "Karen did tell me about the TV cameras coming to film you both. Should be entertaining."

I look sternly at him out of the corner of my eyes. He just laughs.

"Right, I'm going home, see you tomorrow." I say, walking into reception.

"One more thing, Wanda," Mike calls after me.

"Yes?"

"Fancy dinner with me Saturday night?"

Chapter Sixteen

Wednesday 1st August

I am sitting at the kitchen table sniffing my French roast and thinking about last night with Mike. I didn't know what to say when he asked me to dinner, so I told him that I had to dye my mum's hair! I have no idea where that came from. Lying is not a good way to start a relationship, but I need time to sort my head out. Meg's mum would say *'Lying is like a rabid dog; at some point it's going to chase you down and bite you on the arse!'* For my sake I hope she's wrong.

I did agree to meet Mike on Sunday night but I may need to cancel depending on what happens with Gary on Saturday. Hey look at me, Wanda Mikos, keeping her options open!

I'm just considering my predicament, when my phone nearly vibrates its way off the table. It's Mum.

"Hi, Mum, how are you?"

"Not too bad darling. I wondered if you wanted to come over for lunch. I'm off work today and wanted to catch up."

"Don't see why not. I'll get to you about 12.00 p.m.?"

"Lovely, see you then."

***

As I pull up to my mother's house, I can see she has been hard at work in the garden. There is a small patch of grass to the right of the drive, which is bordered by a host of flowers in full bloom. There are two bay trees framing the red front door and at least four hanging baskets on the front of the house. I knock twice and Mum opens the door looking flustered.

"Hi, Mum, you look frazzled, you all right?"

"I've just poured some eggs into the pan, I'm making a Spanish omelette," she says, rushing back to the kitchen.

As I close the door, I make my way to the kitchen where wafts of cheese are emanating.

"Smells lovely, what's in it?"

"Peas, sweetcorn, mushroom and feta cheese."

"Sounds great."

"I thought you would want something high protein and low fat, so we have a small green salad with avocado and a fruit salad for dessert."

"Mum, you're a star." I give her a squeeze and kiss her on the cheek.

"Can you get the knives and forks out; I've laid the table in the lounge."

"Will do."

I walk through to the lounge, which is a contradiction in styles. The walls and sofas are cream; there is a large cream and brown rug sitting on dark wooden floorboards and the dining table has a glass top. All very modern, until you look at the oak sideboard behind one of the sofas and the cushions, which Mum made in her interior design class. They would look more at home in a country cottage. It represents her perfectly — slightly confused.

"Here we are now go and grab the salad could you?" Mum walks in with the whole frying pan and places it onto a mat.

As we sit and portion up the omelette, my nose prickles as I get a hit of her special salad dressing. It's really potent and includes a whole clove of garlic and English mustard.

"This tastes fab Mum; how come you and Jared are so good at cooking and I'm crap?"

"You're not crap darling, you just don't have the patience to learn, you never have."

She's absolutely right. I remember when we were growing up, Jared standing on a chair next to Mum whenever she was cooking. I did sit on the draining board when our nana was baking cakes, but I think that was to make sure I got to lick the bowl first.

"So how is George?" I ask casually.

"Oh she's fine I suppose."

"It doesn't sound as though it's going too well. What's up?"

"I'm not really sure we are made for each other."

"Why's that?" I ask, knowing exactly why they are not right for each other.

"She's a bit too much of a hippy for me. I tried to get her to shave her armpits recently and she really took offence."

I can't help but choke on my rocket leaves as I try not to laugh.

"Well, that's not much to ask is it?" I say supportively.

"I didn't think so. Besides, in this weather, she was getting a bit whiffy." Mum screws up her face and raises her arm to demonstrate.

"*Eww*, nice."

"I got one of those new air fresheners that look like an ornament. It puffs out a lovely smell whenever someone walks past."

"Did it work?"

"Oh no, she gave me lecture on how it wasn't natural *et cetera* and brought some incense sticks which made the house smell like a dead hippy's boudoir. Seriously, it smelt worse than her armpits!"

I picture my perfectly groomed mother wafting away the stench of her girlfriend's armpit pong. "So what's the situation between you at the moment?"

"Well, I haven't seen her since Friday and that's fine by me. Her yoga classes are amazing though, so I want to remain friends."

"At least you're putting yourself out there again. It's about time." I smile and touch her hand.

"Then you will be really impressed when I tell you that I'm off to a speed dating evening with Sandra and Jayne tomorrow night." She looks at me expectantly. "What do you think?"

"Mum, the last date you brought home was a woman. You going speed dating is hardly going to shock me."

"Do you think I'm too old though?"

"Don't be daft. Go, have fun. As long as you tell me all the gossip on Sunday."

I can't help thinking how great it feels talking with Mum like we are friends as well as mother and daughter. It hasn't always been the case.

"Can I call you Saturday, or are you working?" She asks.

"No, I'm not working; I'm going away with Gary on Saturday." I can feel my face burning as I put more black pepper on my food.

My mother looks up eyebrows raised. "*Oooh*, I didn't realise that this was a real relationship," she teases.

I cringe and rub my forehead with my hand. I wouldn't normally tell her anything about my relationships but I feel like I can tell her anything today.

So I tell Mum the whole bit about Mike and Gary, the near snogging incident yesterday and the quandary I'm facing regarding this weekend with Gary. Mum listens without saying a word until I have finished.

"What do you think I should do?" I ask, hoping my mother will be the wise woman she ought to be at her age and give me a solution.

"Jeeez Wanda, what do you get yourself into?" she replies, eyes all-agog.

"That's not helpful Mum, what should I do?"

"I don't bloody know do I? I've never been in that situation. Your father was my one and only, so I'm afraid I have no experience with trying to juggle two men at once."

This is a revelation. The only man my mum has ever slept with is my dad! I suddenly see her in a whole new light.

"You really didn't have any other boyfriends before Dad?"

"Well I did, but I was only young and it never went pass the kissing stage. Don't forget, I met your father when I was sixteen." She smiles at the memory and I suddenly realise why she was so lost after they divorced.

I was going to tell Mum about Laura asking me to be her bridesmaid, but I can't.

Thursday 2nd August

It's my day off today and Meg is coming shopping with me to get a dress for the wedding. I still feel awful that I didn't tell Mum, but I just couldn't bring myself to. I make myself some porridge out of a packet and some peppermint tea. Meg is getting an early start on a project for uni and is sitting on the lounge floor surrounded by books.

"Morning Meg, you look busy," I say, plonking myself on the sofa with my tea and porridge.

"I thought I'd get an early start as we're shopping for your dress today — and we all know how long that's going to take," Meg says through gritted teeth.

"There's no real rush. It's not like I'll wear it again." I make a face and pick up my new celebrity magazine. The front cover is a collection of pictures featured within the magazine. There are two female celebrities in bikinis; one showing her usual svelte figure, the other a before and after shot of how the celebrity has let herself go. Plus, a woman who weighs two hundred pounds and is paid to sit on men's faces. I look over at Meg who is deep in thought.

"What's your paper about, Meg?"

"The changing shape of our coastlines. What are you reading?"

"The changing shape of celebrity waistlines."

"That's an intellectual read, Wand'."

"It's research, plus, there is a helpful article about calories."

"Wanda, I can't imagine there is one thing that you don't know about calories."

"Well this is about how many calories you can use up during sex."

"You mean 'whatnot'?"

"*Ha ha*, but seriously, it says here that if Gary and I keep it up for an hour, we would use 288 calories. Plus, if I add in some moaning and sighing that would burn up an extra 18-30 calories. I could have a large glass of wine and not ruin my diet. *Yippee!'*

"I assume they're talking about the military position; what happens if you keep changing positions. Surely that could use up even more?"

"Let's see. Oh yes, here it is. Also try a position where you squat on top of him and then bounce up and down. This is a great workout for your thighs and butt, and it can burn up to 207 calories in 30 minutes." I look at Meg who is grinning and nodding her head.

"I've got it," she says, "why don't you take that watch thing you have that reads your heart rate and how many calories you've used. I'm sure Gary won't be put off by you treating your first time lovemaking as a fitness training session."

"Do you think he would mind wearing a heart rate monitor?"

Meg laughs as she looks up from her books. Then, she looks directly at me and pouts. "I've just realised how much I am going to miss you if you win the competition — which of course you will," she adds.

I make a pouty face back at her. "It will only be for three months initially; besides I may not win. I might embarrass myself so much when the film crew get here, they ban me from competing!"

"Don't be daft. What's the gym like you'd be working at?"

"Haven't I shown you the website?"

"No, let's have a look," Meg says, pushing her books to one side and picking up her laptop.

We go onto the Move Makers website which is a blast of colour and flashing adverts. The gym is the first picture at the top of the page. The building is two stories high with windows from floor to ceiling. Inside, the gym floor is about 1000ft square and there is a running track on the floor above.

"Good grief, those people look really ripped." Meg gasps as she checks out the members on the gym equipment.

"I'll look just as good by the time I get there," I say confidently. "Do you think they used models for the website?"

Meg is looking rather scared for me as we check out the famous actors they have worked with. We scroll down to a group picture of the Personal Training staff, all of whom are tall, tanned and ripped to shreds. I suddenly feel a bit sick.

"Come on," says Meg, seeing the colour slide from my face, "let's get ready and go shopping."

"OK, but can we just do my weight and measurements first. I need to know where I'm at before the big dinner and 'whatnot' with Gary."

"Fine, I'll get the tape measure. By the way, I've never heard sex called 'whatnot' before. Is that what all the cool kids are calling it?" Meg laughs as she gathers up her books and makes her way to the kitchen drawer.

I close my eyes and step onto the scale saying a silent prayer. As I look down, a smile spreads across my face and I punch the air. Three pounds lost! I'm now 9st 9Ib. Still more than I wanted to be at this stage but it's going in the right direction.

"Well?" Meg leans into the bathroom.

"I've lost another three pounds."

"Well done babe! Shall we do your measurements as well?"

"Please."

Meg rushes back with the tape measure and we get started. I have lost two inches off my waist, *hoorah*! And one and a half inches off my boobies, boo!

***

We have been trawling the shops of Briford shopping centre for four hours; so far, I have tried on seven dresses, and although I can now get into a size smaller, it hasn't made them look any better. They were all either too floaty, tarty, or too much like my mother's to be considered as suitable for the wedding.

We decide to pop into The Coffee Snob for a quick breather and a much needed caffeine hit.

"Meg, what is that shop opposite?" I ask, noticing a shop across the road I hadn't seen before.

"Oh yes I forgot about that. It's just opened. I haven't had a chance to look yet but one of the girls here said their stuff is great."

"Oh my God, could you not have told me this four hours ago? I nearly ended up with a dress from the granny section in Marks and Spencer!"

"Don't be so dramatic. Anyway, Marks don't have a granny section — it's all granny." Meg laughs at her own joke and punches me on the arm. Luckily she's weedy.

We finish our coffee and make our way over the road to Riches, the new boutique. There is a faint fruity smell as we walk through the door. It isn't massive, but it has been well set out and the decor is modern. Straight away I can see three things I want to try on. Admittedly, none of them are dresses but I remain hopeful.

"This is lovely," says Meg, holding up a cornflower blue dress with tiny white flowers in the material. It has short sleeves and a crossover neckline, which has a white lacy bit across the cleavage. It looks just like one I saw on Alexa Chung in a magazine. I have to try it on.

"*Ta dah!*" I open the curtain in a dramatic reveal. "Well, what do you think?"

"Wand' it's gorgeous. You have to buy it. And I'm not just saying that so we can go home," she confirms, looking sincere.

"This is great, I finally have a dress at last," I say, walking back to the changing room.

Meg looks at me with a big smile of relief. "Thank goodness."

"Now all I need are shoes."

Meg's smile drops.

"Your face is a picture!" I laugh. "Don't panic pet, I have a pair that will be perfect with it."

"Thank God! Let's go home I'm starving."

***

I'm off to see some horror movie with Gary tonight, I hate scary movies but I'm looking forward to seeing him. Plus, it will give me a chance to check how I feel about him before committing myself to Saturday.

Not wanting to succumb to the many calorie-laden snacks available in the cinema, I'm going to have a jacket potato with tuna before I go, and chop some carrot sticks to take with me.

The doorbell rings as I'm lacing up my boots, so I tie a bow as quick as I can and run to answer the door. Gary is standing there looking cool and sexy. His hair is casually flopped over one eye and his cheeky grin looks like he has mischief in mind. I do love that about him.

"Hi, you look nice." Gary bends down to kiss me and gently strokes my arm. He looks into my eyes and smiles. "Sorry I had to change the film choice. Do you like horror? I didn't have time to call and check with you before I booked it."

"No problem, I love horror," I lie again.

I'm wearing my dark skinny jeans, a long-sleeved white top and my flat boots. It means I feel really short next to him but I can't wear heels all the time.

"Hello, Gary," Meg says as she makes her way to the kitchen. "What are you going to see tonight?"

"*Demons Down Below*," Gary replies.

Meg looks at me as I make a face behind Gary's back. She knows I hate horror films but she plays along.

"Wanda will love that, won't you Wand'?"

"Yes. Shall we go Gary?" I tug at his arm before she can say anything else.

We are standing in the queue at the cinema and I look up at Gary who is holding my hand.

"Do you want some popcorn or sweets?" he asks.

"No thanks. I've brought some carrot sticks. I can't afford to go off my diet."

"*Mmmm* carrot sticks, you'll make me jealous."

"I've got the television guys coming Monday so I need to look as lean as possible. The camera adds ten pounds you know."

"Does that mean you're only going to be eating chicken, rice and carrot sticks when we go away Saturday night? I was hoping to order a bottle of champagne."

Gary puts his arms around me and pulls me close.

"Don't worry," I say, looking up at him seductively, "I've figured something out."

"Oh yes, and what's that?"

"Tell you later." I nudge him to let him know the woman behind the counter is waiting to take his order.

The film is about half an hour in and I am still waiting for something scary to happen. I'm a bit bored to be honest. I slowly lean down to get my carrots out of my bag. The sandwich bag I put them in rustles loudly, I stop still and look around. Everyone, including Gary, is watching the film. I gently place my carrots on my lap and slowly pries open the bag. The character on screen is creeping down the stairs to investigate a loud noise in the kitchen. The cinema is silent. I watch with my mouth open as the actor turns the corner at the bottom of the staircase. She sees a shadow moving. I absentmindedly bite into my carrot....*cruunch!* Everyone within earshot jumps out of their skin, and turns to look at me just as the girl on screen is attacked by a demon. I slide down into my seat and look at Gary who is laughing and shaking his head.

The film gets progressively scarier. I have put my carrots back in my bag and snuggle a little closer to Gary. The girl in the film is now standing in her hallway getting ready to go out and the dark shadow figure is standing behind her. My heart is thumping and I realise I'm squeezing Gary's arm. The tension in the cinema rises just as we hear……*La Ta Da DaDaDa Dah Dah Ta Da Da.* Some woman behind us has left her mobile on and it's playing the Can-Can. I collapse with laughter as does everyone around me. The woman quickly scrambles about in her bag and is apologising profusely as she pulls out her phone and switches it off. This makes me feel better about the carrot incident but I decide to check my phone is off and reach into my bag. My phone lights up with a message. It's from Mike.

How about dinner Sunday night?

I catch Gary glancing across and snap my phone shut.

"Mum, wants me to have dinner Sunday," I whisper as I put it on 'silent' and place it back in my bag.

Chapter Seventeen

Friday 3rd August

I'm in work early as I need to practise my routine as much as I can. God only knows what Karen is doing at her fabulous Brecon Training Camp. Still, I love a challenge, and I just realised how much I keep saying that phrase. At least I can go through my moves knowing she won't be watching.

My music begins slow and steady as I stretch up from a crouching position like a flower unfurling. That's the idea anyway. The beat of the music increases and my moves match its throbbing rhythm. My spin is perfect, as are my balance and strength poses. The smile on my face is permanent as I kick and jump higher than ever before. I end with the flick-flack — I figured at least if I balls it up; it will be at the end — which I perform with the ease of a national champion. As I finish, I catch my reflection in the mirror. I am definitely ready — bring it on!

Ten minutes into a PT session with Mrs Mary Clamp and daughter Fiona and as usual they have whined through the warm-up and I'm losing the will to live. However, as a professional, I smile and give them all the encouragement I can muster. What I would actually like to do is pin the both of them to the weights bench with a 60 kilo bar!

"So, Mary, how does that feel?" I have just increased the gradient on the treadmill to three percent.

"It's too steep. I'll have to hold on with both hands," she replies, shaking her head.

"You don't need to, I'm pretty sure you walk along streets that are steeper than this. Keep pumping your arms, you'll be fine." I turn to Fiona on the other treadmill before she can protest.

"Right Fiona, let's try a jog for 30 seconds then walk for 30 seconds."

"I can't, I'll fall off," she says, staring forward as though she's scared to move her head.

"For goodness sake, we go over this every week; besides, you haven't fallen off yet have you?"

"No," Fiona replies sulkily.

"Well, if you want to lose 60 pounds, you are going to have to get that butt moving more. Come on let's go!"

Fiona's face is panic stricken as I increase the speed. She starts to move her feet a little faster; I increase the speed again.

"OK Fiona, you're doing great; just 30 seconds and we'll take the speed to an easy walk. You can do it."

"Don't make it any faster," she pleads.

"I won't, just keep going."

As Fiona's arms begin to pump, her boobs start swinging to and fro and her cheeks turn purple.

"Can I finish now?" Mary shouts behind me.

I turn briefly to tell her she has five more minutes, when I hear an almighty thud. This is followed by another thud as I turn back to see Fiona hanging onto each side rail. Her tongue is hanging out and her feet are dragging behind her. She is attempting to right herself without success.

"Oh my God," I gasp, hitting the emergency stop button, "Fiona are you all right?"

I help her to her feet and guide her over to the mats where she can sit down. She doesn't say anything, but I think that's because she can't.

"Can I get off now?"

It's Mary shouting from her treadmill. She doesn't seem to be at all worried about her daughter. She just wants an excuse to do as little as possible — lazy cow.

"Yes I'm coming." I sigh, making sure Fiona is OK before I leave her.

I manage to get through another mind-numbing session with the Clamps and just as I am giving them their updated diet plans, I hear Mike's voice over the Tannoy.

Could Wanda Mikos please come to the general office? You have a phone call from Channel 10.

I'm sure I can hear a smile in his voice as he says it. Git!

"Why is channel 10 calling you? Are you going to be on television?" asks Mrs Clamp excitedly.

"Erm yes," I reply, rather embarrassed.

"Mum, our trainer is going to be famous, how exciting."

"I'd better go and take the call," I say backing into the rowing machine. "I'll see you ladies next week. Bye!"

As I run down the stairs to reception, I am stopped by several members trying to find out why Channel 10 is calling me. I manage to brush them off and reach the office flushed and nervous. Mike is standing there smiling and holding the phone. I narrow my eyes at him and grab the receiver.

"Hello, this is Wanda Mikos." I say whilst trying to calm my breathing.

"Hi there, Wanda, this is Sergio from Channel 10; I hope this is not a bad time to call."

"No, not at all, I have just finished training two clients actually."

"Great. Now as you know, we need to get some footage of you and Miss Lester preparing for the competition."

"Miss Lester is away at the moment," I interject, hoping that this will cause some aggravation.

"Yes we know. We will be travelling to the Brecon Training Camp later in the week to catch up with her."

I knew it! They're even going to travel up there to film her. I could spit. "How lovely," I manage, through gritted teeth.

"Yes, but we would like to shoot some scenes with you, starting on Monday if that's agreeable?"

"Right, what do you need me to do?"

"Nothing special, just some footage of you training in the gym and rehearsing your routine. Plus, we would like to come to your home and see what sort of things you prepare nutrition-wise."

"Oh, erm yeah that's fine, no problem. See you Monday."

I replace the handset and look at Mike.

"You look terrified," he says, trying not to laugh.

"I am. It's going to be horrible. I'm bound to make a fool of myself."

"You'll be great, as always," Mike says, stepping forward and kissing me on my head.

I look up at him; God, he's shaggable.

"Anyway." he looks sternly at me. "I am still waiting for a reply to my text about dinner Sunday night." He starts tapping his toe and crosses his arms.

Oh bugger, what do I say?

"Lovely. What time shall I be ready?"

**

I am looking forward to Jared coming home today. I have really missed him this week; not only because I had to make my own food, but he would have been much more patient shopping for a dress than Megan. And he always has great advice so he is coming home just in time.

"Jared is that you?" I call out as I hear the front door.

"No babe it's me. I just saw Gary's friend at work and he's asked me out for a drink tonight. Get the kettle on, we need tea and gossip."

I get off the sofa and rush to meet Meg in the hall.

"Did he know you worked there?" I ask, helping her with her bags.

"Yes, I told him that night at Povkas. He said he wanted to ask me ages ago but he was seeing someone and had to wait to break it off."

"Took him long enough."

"I know, but he said she has been away and it was her birthday so he decided to wait."

I put the kettle on and grab a sneaky slice of ham out of the fridge. Meg catches me as I am closing the fridge door and slaps me on the head.

"Your diet Wanda!"

"*Ouch.*"

I'm taken aback by this sudden display of forcefulness. Jared is rubbing off on her.

"So, you haven't told me if you're going out with what's-his-face yet."

"I said I'd meet him at Povkas at 8.00 p.m. At least I can walk home if he turns out to be an idiot."

"Good plan." I nod, passing her a mug of tea. "I got a call from Channel 10, which Mike announced to the whole gym over the Tannoy."

"Oh yes, I forgot they were calling you today. What did they say?"

I relay my conversation with Sergio and the fact that I was right about Karen.

"I think you just need to forget about Karen and concentrate on your own training," Meg says, sipping her tea and walking into the lounge.

"I know, you're right, Mike said the same sort of thing. Then he kissed me here." I smile, pointing at my forehead.

"Not again? How confused are you now?"

"Well I'm hoping you and Jared will have some great advice on whether or not I should go tomorrow."

"I have no idea what you should do," Meg says. "Maybe you'll have better luck with Jared."

Luckily, Jared arrives home ten minutes later. He has only been gone for a few days but I can't help thinking how much I would miss him if I lived in LA.

"*Bon soir,* girlies, how's tricks?" Jared calls as he bashes his way towards his bedroom loaded up with bags.

"Hi, Jared," we call back, "how was France?"

"*Magnifique.* In fact, get me a drink I need to hear all your gossip, after you've heard mine!" he exclaims, jumping out into the hallway.

"Well I think we need to open a bottle of wine for all the gossip flying around tonight," Meg says, pushing herself out of the armchair.

"Not for me. My head feels like I'm balancing a 10 kilo plate on it."

"Oh dear, tell me your gossip first," Jared says, sitting on the floor and leaning against the sofa.

I relay my tales of woe and end with the question, "So what should I do?"

"About what?"

"Jared, were you not listening?"

"Of course I was, Wand' but I don't see any dilemmas in the tales you just told."

"Why are you talking like that? Did you have elocution and literary lessons whilst you were away?"

"Sort of. Tell you later. Anyway, what's your problem girl?"

"Listen carefully, I need these questions answered. 1. Should I go away with Gary tomorrow? 2. Should I have dinner with Mike on Sunday? 3. Should I kill myself now and avoid the embarrassment of showing myself up on national television?"

Jared drops his head as though he is thinking hard.

"1. Absolutely, 2. Abso-bloody-lutely, and 3. Nobody's going to watch that crap anyway."

I stare at him, eyes wide and mouth open. Jared just grins.

"Anything else you need me to sort out or can I tell you about Francoi?"

"Wait for me," Meg calls from the kitchen.

As Meg sorts the drinks and Jared waffles on about the guy he met, I grab my phone from my bag. I have two messages. The first is a text message from Gary to say he will pick me up tomorrow at noon. The other is a missed call from Mum. I press the left message button and listen.

'Hello darling I'm at my speed dating night. Can't believe I've not done this before. So far two lovely chaps have written my number on their sheets, so I thought I would ask you how much fun is it dating two men at once.'

I hear her laughing as she puts the phone down. Cheeky moo.

Chapter Eighteen

Saturday 4th August – Weight 9st 8lb

I've decided it's too late to get out of the overnight thing with Gary, so I've taken Jared's advice and I intend to have fun. I've even packed the dress I wore for the gym party to wear at dinner tonight. There is still a tiny puke stain on the hem but I'm sure he won't notice. To be honest, now that I've made up my mind, I'm really looking forward to it. I have decided to look a little more lady-like than normal, so put on a full-length multi-coloured skirt; white vest, a long necklace and a pair of blue wedges. The skirt is Meg's but the length is good and I feel sophisticated.

Gary arrives to pick me up looking smart in his dark jeans, white T-shirt and a grey V-neck jumper, which matches his eyes.

"Ready?" he asks, leaning down to kiss me.

"Yep. I think I have everything."

I walk back to the lounge to say goodbye to Jared. "See you tomorrow Jay."

"Bye guys, have fun. Don't do anything I wouldn't do with a cricket bat!"

Gary frowns. "What is he talking about?"

"I rarely know," I reply, shaking my head. "Shall we go?"

***

An hour later, we pull in to a long tree-lined drive leading to the most beautiful white manor house, surrounded by perfectly manicured gardens. The sun is shining and I can't wait to get out of the car. My bum is numb and I need to stretch.

"Not too shabby eh?" Gary smiles as he grabs the bags from the boot.

"It's fabulous. I can't wait to see inside."

We are greeted at reception by a very smart man in his thirties, whose head sits too large on his narrow shoulders. He asks Gary for his name.

"Mr Lydell and Miss Mikos; we have two double rooms booked for tonight."

I look across at Gary as he is given the register to sign. *Two* rooms? So he is not expecting 'whatnot' at all. Once again I am conflicted between how considerate and unassuming he's being and *why doesn't he grow a pair!*

"I will show you up to your rooms Sir," the smart man says as he walks around the desk and picks up my bag. "Follow me."

The stairway is grand, and there are gold-framed oil paintings leading all the way up to the top floor where our rooms are situated.

My room is large and imposing, with a chandelier hanging in the centre. The bed is enormous and the wallpaper is dark brown and gold. The furniture in the room is the same colour brown as the wallpaper, and the bathroom is modern, with a selection of toiletries next to the sink

The man with the big bonce shows Gary to his room, which is next door and once he has gone, Gary comes back to my room.

"Hope I did the right thing booking two rooms?"

"Erm, yes it's fine."

"I didn't want to assume anything; I just wanted to spend some time with you."

He pulls me towards his chest and raises my chin to kiss me on the lips.

"But of course if you can't bear to sleep alone in this scary old mansion, I will of course give up my room and come and stay here with you."

"Oh shut up and bring your bag in here. I can always send you next door later if you get on my nerves."

"Gary smiles and pulls his hair from his eyes before kissing me again. Right, are you ready for something to eat?"

"Starving. Can we get food downstairs?"

"I've already ordered lunch with tea and champagne."

"That's so sweet; I can't believe you did that." I stand on tiptoes and kiss him full on the lips. I cannot believe how thoughtful he is. My last boyfriend's idea of lunch was driving to the nearest burger bar.

***

So here we are sitting in the garden, eating a variety of sandwiches and drinking champagne. The view is breathtaking and the air is cool and fresh. It reminds me of one of the paintings in the hall.

By the time the server arrives with the tea and cakes, I am feeling rather 'squiffy'. The last time I drank alcohol was probably at the gym party. I know I've overdone the champers, because I'm starting to discuss deep and meaningful subjects with Gary who is doing his best to appear interested. I decide to have some tea. The cakes look amazing but I have already had too much today so I'll give them a miss. Well maybe just that meringue, there is no fat in those — except for that bit of cream in the middle.

We spend the rest of the afternoon walking hand in hand around the grounds, playing chess in the library and walking down to the local village, which seems to be in the throes of some annual festival. It's all terribly civilised and gives me a chance to sober up. Gary is perfect boyfriend material and I have convinced myself that I'm not doing anything wrong.

We get back to the hotel, just in time to change for dinner. Neither of us noticed how late it was and Gary has booked dinner for 7.00 p.m. We enter my room just as his phone rings. He looks at me with an apologetic smile.

"You take your call, I'll have my shower," I tell him, grabbing my toiletries and kissing his cheek.

"Thanks, I won't be long."

As I step into the shower cubicle, I close my eyes and breathe. It's been a wonderful day, but to be honest, I feel incredibly tired and would love to sleep for an hour or three. The competition training and diet has been taking its toll recently. It makes me question whether or not I would be able to keep up with those other trainers in LA. They were all so...so...perfect. Letting out a sigh, I console myself by thinking perhaps my body will get used to it; or better still, those PTs had all dieted especially for the website photograph.

I finish my shower and step out of the cubicle. As I reach for a towel, I catch my reflection in the mirror; my arms look toned, my abdominals are on show and even my legs look longer because they are so lean. I check myself out from every angle and decide that I am absolutely ready for Los Angeles and can't believe I ever doubted myself. I can still hear Gary chatting on the phone using his business tone of voice so I assume it's someone from work. I am quite happy he's taking so long, as it gives me more time to make myself gorgeous.

When I finally exit the bathroom, I am fully buffed, make-up on and wrapped in a complementary towelling robe which is at least ten sizes too big.

"*Wow*, look at you," Gary says adding a whistle. He is lying on the bed watching Top Gear, "love your dress."

"Lovely isn't it?" I grin, hoisting it up so I can walk. "Don't they ever have normal size people staying here?"

"Well I think you look gorgeous in it," Gary says, rolling off the side of the bed.

"I do think you'd look better out of it though." he winks as he walks towards me.

"Well I think you are going to have to wait. I'm sorry but I have only left you fifteen minutes to have a shower and get changed."

"No worries, I'll be ready."

Gary comes out of the bathroom ten minutes later with just a towel around his waist. I have never seen his torso before and it's rock solid! He has the V-shape of a swimmer and his abdominals, although not tight like Mike's, are flat and covered in a smattering of hair.

"You look amazing!" he gasps, seeing me in my dress and heels.

I feel amazing as the potbelly I had the last time I wore this dress, is nowhere to be seen.

"Thanks." I smile, twirling so he can get the full view.

The Green Room restaurant at the hotel looks out over the gardens. It is totally green – surprisingly – with round tables covered in white and green tablecloths. The candles and flowers in the centre of each table are also green. The ceiling is high, which gives the room a feeling of grandeur, and there's a young man playing music on a white grand piano in the corner. I'm feeling rather sophisticated as we are guided to our table, which is by the window.

"Would you like an aperitif?" asks the waiter, who has just handed us our menus.

Gary turns to me. "Shall I order champagne or would you rather an aperitif?"

I'm not actually sure what an aperitif is. Thought it was those little snacks you get before your starters.

"Champagne will be lovely," I reply, in my poshest accent.

"We'll have a bottle of Tattinger please."

"Yes sir, I'll leave you to look through the menu."

I choose the fish and vegetables for main course which should be low calorie so I allow Gary to pour me another glass of champagne. Unfortunately, when it arrives, the fish is covered in a rich sauce and sitting on a pile of buttery potatoes. Might as well have had the steak with chips.

"Well that's the last of the champagne," Gary says, as we finish our main course. "Shall I order another bottle?"

"Better not, I already feel a bit whoozy."

"OK. What about a glass of wine?"

"Great, dry white for me." I figure a glass is better than drinking half a bottle and this is my cheat meal for the week.

Once our main course has been cleared for a while, the waiter arrives with the dessert menu. I don't blink an eye before deciding on a chocolate fudge brownie with cream and ice cream. This is the reason why you shouldn't drink; it tends to lessens one's resolve – but apparently allows one to talk like Prince Charles.

"One chocolate brownie, and one cheesecake please," Gary informs the waiter.

"Certainly sir, would you like to try a dessert wine with that?"

Gary looks at me for confirmation and orders two glasses of dessert wine. I have no idea what the difference is between normal and dessert wine so I may as well try it. Perhaps they blob a bit of cream on top.

My brownie arrives and it looks amazing. I haven't had anything like this for so long; I may hoover it up in two seconds flat. I'm feeling really squiffy now and have taken to touching Gary at every opportunity. My head may not thank me in the morning but I'm having a great night.

"How's your dessert?" Gary asks.

"It's fabulous." I gush, shovelling the last spoonful in my mouth. "Oh sorry, did you want some?"

"No thanks, want to taste mine?" he asks in a 'come hither' tone.

"No, I shouldn't; besides, I need to use the loo." I realise that was not exactly the response he was hoping for, but I really do need the loo.

I am sitting on the toilet in the rather fancy bathroom, which smells of peaches. My head is spinning and I let out a spontaneous giggle. I definitely won't be ordering an Irish coffee. I exit the cubicle and wash my hands with the Molton Brown hand wash provided, before returning to the restaurant. As I turn the corner, I bump into Gary who is making his way to the men's toilet.

"I've ordered you a coffee," he says, touching my face and winking at me.

"Not Irish?"

"No, just normal. Did you want Irish?"

"No, normal is fine thank you."

"Right, see you in a minute."

The guy on the piano has just started playing my favourite Barbara Streisand song as I enter the restaurant.

I sit for a second and smile at my current situation. Great bod, great food and a great guy with a great bod — bliss.

"I didn't get decaf I hope that's all right?" Gary says as he arrives back at the table.

"It's fine," I reply, picking up my coffee cup and taking a large swig.

"I would hate to keep you awake all night," he says, giving me his sexiest smile.

***

Once back in our room, I practically fall off my shoes and land on the bed. I think someone has attached a small dumbbell to each of my eyelids as I'm having trouble keeping them open. Gary places his wallet on the dresser, turns to me and smiles.

"You look like you're about to fall asleep."

"No I'm not," I slur slowly, "I feel great."

Gary laughs and disappears into the bathroom.

Sunday 5th August

I open my eyes, yawn and blink several times. Where the hell am I? Oh I remember now, the hotel with Gary. Oh my God! I slowly turn my head to see Gary sleeping soundly next to me. What happened last night? Think Wanda think! I remember a bit of kissing going on but the images fade after that. Did we do the 'dirty' 'because if we didn't, that means I still have about 2,000 calories to work off. Plus it couldn't have been that great if I don't remember. Oh no, I think he's waking up. What do I say? Should I be embarrassed? Was I a tiger in the sack or did I pass out on him?

Gary makes a slapping noise with his lips and rolls towards me. I am going to make a dash for the bathroom to check my morning face and clean my teeth. As slowly as I can, I roll to the side of the bed and slide out of the covers. I am still wearing my underwear, well almost; my right boob is popping out of my plunge bra. I quietly grab my robe off the chair and creep to the bathroom. Looking in the mirror, I realise I didn't take my make-up off last night; my eyes resemble Alice Cooper and my hair is aping an early Michael Jackson afro. I hope Gary doesn't wake up soon as repairs may take a while.

"Morning Miss Mikos." Gary says as I exit the bathroom.

"Morning. Hope you slept well, you know if you wanted to. I mean sorry for being a bit out of it last night. Didn't do anything embarrassing did I?"

"Well you were fine until you started sliding around on top of the piano singing Barbra Streisand and the waiters had to coax you down."

"Oh my God, I did not do that!" I sit on the bed with my head in my hands.

"You didn't."

"What?"

"I was joking. You were rat-arsed though," he says with a laugh.

I jump on the bed and bash him with my pillow. He grabs the pillow off me and pulls me down on top of him. His sexy lips are cold but soft. We kiss gently at first, increasing in passion and I can feel him hard against me. My head spins as he rolls on top of me whilst simultaneously pulling at the tie on my robe. His body feels heavy. I look up at the ceiling, which is spinning, and my face just got cold. Oh crap, I'm going to throw up. Gaining a sudden freakish strength, I throw Gary off me and onto the floor, scramble off the bed and trample over him to get to the toilet. I spend the next ten minutes leaning over the toilet bowl wishing I was anywhere else but here.

I feel awful, I'm so embarrassed. He will never want to see me again. I'm going to jump out of the window and kill myself and….on the other hand, how many calories must I have thrown up? Not as pleasant as sex but hey, there's always a silver lining, it's just that sometimes you really have to look for it.

"Wanda, you OK?" Gary is gently tapping on the door of the bathroom.

"Think so. I'm so sorry. I really shouldn't have had champagne. It's just that I haven't had a drink for so long and this diet and training is making me insane and I'm sorry you had to put up with me and…"

"Wanda, shut up you idiot. I knew you hadn't been drinking so it's partially my fault."

He sounds sincere, but let's face it, I've left him with a 'stiffy' *and* I've stolen the bathroom.

Chapter Nineteen

Sunday 5th August

Gary has been so understanding but I continue to apologise all the way home and assure him that the next hotel visit is on me. He suggests I may want to leave it until after my competition.

We arrive home at lunchtime and Gary decides to drop me off as he has work to do before tomorrow. I'm not sure if that's true, but I can't really blame him if it isn't. As I open the door of my flat, I can hear Megan and Jared in the lounge, so I go to join them. They are drinking coffee and watching '*Twilight*' on DVD.

"Hi, guys."

"Hey Wanda, how did last night go?" Meg asks.

"Pretty good I reckon," says Jared, "you look like shit!"

I huff a little before dropping my bag and flopping into the chair.

"Well, it was lovely, the hotel was beautiful and we had lunch and champagne and then we…"

"You had champagne?" Meg exclaims.

"I know that's where it all went a bit tits up."

"Oh my God, you got smashed and passed out didn't you?" Jared says.

"Wand' you didn't."

"Oh, I'm afraid I did."

"He must have been gutted, poor bloke," Jared says still laughing.

"How much did you drink? You said you were going to stick to one glass." Meg has her disappointed face on.

"I know, I know, I didn't drink that much but I have been eating so clean lately that the effect of the alcohol was magnified. I did have lots to eat and used it as my cheat meal. But I still passed out on the bed in our room." I cover my face with my hands and shake my head. "I may have ruined things with Gary."

"No shit Sherlock," Jared calls as he makes his way to the kitchen.

"Honestly Meg, he was so sweet about it. Unfortunately, I haven't even told you the worst bit yet."

With that, I hear footsteps in the hallway. It's Jared.

"I was just coming back to ask if you want a coffee but I just overheard about 'the worst bit' so you'll have to wait. Right, dish."

He sits next to Meg and they both lean forward in anticipation. I tell the sad tale about nearly having sex before having to throw him off the bed and trampling him to death so I could puke. Meg gasps and places her hand over her mouth as Jared nearly falls over laughing.

"So, if Gary is so fantastic, does that mean that Mike is out of the running?" Meg asks raising her eyebrows.

"Oh I don't know. Why can't I have them both?"

"I've got an idea! Why don't we do a 'pros' and 'cons' list, like we used to at school?"

"That's so childish Megan. Oh all right, let's get some paper."

We grab a pad and pen, sit next to each other on the sofa and start comparing. Jared goes off to make us coffee.

MIKE — PROS: Gorgeous, fit as f**k, same interests. CONS: Ex-girlfriend, bit of a temper, money prospects not great.

GARY — PROS: Cute, loadsa money, laid back. CONS: Not as hot as Mike!

Just when I think we've finished, Megan leans over and pulls the pad towards her to make an addition.

WILLY SIZE: To be established — Wanda didn't actually see Gary's as it was under cover (not like a willy spy, just under the blankets).

"Megan!"

"What? Willy size is very important; trust me. When I went out with that bloke Bobby, he came out of the bathroom on our first night together and I thought he'd left it in the bathroom it was so small!"

"You are so mean. My list was very sensible until you added that."

"Anyway, let's analyse the results." She pulls the pad nearer. "Well, that confirms it," she says, nodding her head and tapping the list with her pen.

"What?" I ask, not quite seeing where she is going with this.

"You'll have to go out with Mike tonight in the name of 'willy research'. Then you can make up your mind."

"Oh my God Megan Beekin you are incorrigible!"

"What's happened?" asks Jared, bringing in a tray of coffee mugs.

I start to tell him about Meg's outrageous suggestion when there's a rumble in my bag. Meg takes over the story as I check my phone. I have a text from Mike.

Really sorry but won't get home til late.

Been visiting family. Will have to cancel tonight. speak tom. Mike x

Jared and Meg are still laughing at my misfortunes when I snap my phone shut and declare, "The willy-check is off anyway; Mike just cancelled."

"Oh no, did he say why?"

"He said he's visiting family and won't get home until late. This means, he is visiting his ex-girlfriend and she doesn't want him to leave." I can't decide if I'm angry or relieved.

***

I need to work on a new training programme for Vanessa, so I make some coffee and settle at the kitchen table. Half way through my note taking, I am interrupted by a call.

"Hi, Mum, how are you?"

"Good, that speed dating night was great fun. You and Meg should try it. I don't know if they do a special event for gay people but if they do, Jared could give it a go too."

"Well it sounds as though you had a good time."

I cannot believe my mother is so enthusiastic. It's as though she just discovered a calorie-free chocolate bar.

"So did you meet anyone nice?" I ask.

"Didn't you get my text Friday night? I met two men; both want to take me out, Jayne met a nice fella too."

"Sounds great. When is your first date then?"

"Tonight, Tony is taking me out for dinner. Dennis is meeting me for a coffee on Wednesday."

"*Ooh* hark at you, wild woman," I tease.

"I know I feel like I'm eighteen again. Anyway, how was your romantic weekend away?"

"It was good, the hotel was amazing and you would have loved the gardens Mum, they were stunning."

"Sounds fabulous but did you bonk him?"

"Mother!"

"Oh don't Mother me, what's the 'skinny' as a girl at work would say?"

I can't help laughing at her renewed enthusiasm for life. I tell her nothing happened but she doesn't believe me.

I change the subject quickly to the story of Sergio and Teagan from Channel 10, which she devours with the same enthusiasm. We agree to try and hook up for lunch this week and I go back to working on Vanessa's programme. I inform Jared that I think our mum is going through a mid-life crisis.

Monday 6th August

My shift starts at 6.30 a.m. today, but I arrive unusually early as the television crew are coming this morning. I didn't get much sleep last night; I'm petrified actually. I even wish Karen was here so I wouldn't be alone in my petrification — not sure if that's a word but it should be.

I am wearing my most flattering training bottoms, but can't do much about my top as its uniform. My new push-up bra is making sure 'the girls' are nice and perky, and my hair is pulled into a French plait. I'm inspecting myself in the gym mirrors when I see Elliot standing behind me. At least I think it's Elliot. He has had his hair cut into a short and may I say rather sensible style. He is also wearing his favourite training bottoms. Slowly, I turn to face him.

"Look at you. What's with the new doo?"

"Oh just fancied a change," Elliot replies, casually stroking his fringe.

"So it has nothing to do with the fact that Channel 10 will be filming here this week?"

"I didn't even remember that it was this week. Had the hair appointment booked for ages."

I smile at the 'new look' Elliot and notice Zoe out of the corner of my eye. My first thought is who the hell is responsible for that fake orange tan? She looks like an Oompa Loompa. And her hair, which is usually in a big bunch on top of her head, is quaffed to within an inch of its life. She could pass for an extra on *The Only Way Is Essex*. I burst out laughing, but stop myself when I see her face.

"You look lovely today Zoe," I call out with as much enthusiasm as I can muster.

"Oh shut up! I look like I've been Tangoed. That stupid new girl who does the spay tan was trying a new colour. I've had four showers this morning."

"Don't worry you can hide from the cameras until you can get Collette in beauty to give you an all over body scrub. That girl can sort out any beauty disaster."

"That's a good idea. Thanks Wand'."

I try to spend the first couple of hours keeping busy, so I don't have to think about the TV people coming today. Luckily, Vanessa has a session booked this morning so that should take my mind of it. I decide to do a quick weight check before she turns up. I allow two pounds for my clothes as I step onto the scale, 9stone 6Ib, not bad. I would still like to reduce my body fat more but it's all going in the right direction.

Vanessa arrives at 9.00 a.m. and she looks fabulous.

"Hi, Wanda, how are you?" Vanessa hugs me and means it.

"I'm fine, you look incredible."

"I know," she grins, "I've never had so much energy in my life. I just wish I had come to see you sooner."

"*Ahh* that's nice. Now let's get to the nitty gritty, are you still seeing Bradley?"

"Absolutely, he's so different from my ex, and in a really good way." She giggles as she places her locker key around her wrist.

I get her on the rowing machine to warm up and we finish with some interval training. I then start her on a new programme where she has to do each exercise to reasonable failure. This means she will be able to challenge herself when training without me.

Vanessa stretches her back and takes a sip of water. "How is the training going for your competition?"

"Good I think. Had a bit of a hiccough at the weekend but not too bad."

"Well you look amazing. I can see you have lost more weight but your muscles look even bigger."

"Thanks sweetie, it hasn't been easy and I'm so sick of chicken and rice but it'll be worth it if I win this competition."

"So, what's happening with you and Mike? I haven't really seen you to chat since the party; I remember he was all over you though. Have you been seeing him?"

I was just thinking of a reply to her question as Mike walks into the gym. I look over at him and Vanessa follows my eyes to see who I'm looking at.

"Speak of the devil," she whispers.

Mike walks towards us and smiles at Vanessa. "Hi guys, sorry to interrupt but Wanda, Channel 10 just rang to say they are running late so won't be arriving until lunchtime."

"Oh, that's good, the later the better really."

Mike puts his body discreetly between Vanessa and me. "Sorry about last night. Speak to you later," he whispers in my ear.

I feel my face turning red as I look back at Vanessa who is grinning.

"And what happened last night that he's so sorry about?" she asks as Mike walks away."

"Nothing really, shall we finish?"

I decide to work on my routine in the studio and after warming up, I switch my music on full blast. As the rhythm increases, I give one hundred percent effort to every move. My arms flow elegantly and my strength moves hold steady. The smile on my face is a permanent fixture and I try not to let it look too much like a cheesy grin. As the music moves to a crescendo, I'm about to perform my flick-flack, when I notice movement outside the open door. It puts me off but I manage to concentrate and pull it off with elegance, except for a slight wobble at the end. I grab my towel and turn off my music. The people at the door are still there, so I walk over to see who it is.

"Hi, Wanda?" A swarthy looking man asks. He is carrying a camera so I realise he must be Sergio from Channel 10.

"Yes, you must be Sergio."

The girl with him is skinny with bright red hair. She's wearing skin-tight black jeans and boots with a stripy red and black top. She shakes my hand vigorously.

"Hi Wanda, I'm Teagan, lovely to meet you."

"Hello, I'm sorry I wasn't at reception when you arrived."

"No problem, we got stuck at the studio this morning so ran a bit late. I hope you don't mind that we took the liberty of filming your routine just now."

"Oh erm yeah it's fine."

"It was amazing by the way," Teagan says enthusiastically.

"Really?"

"It was great," Sergio confirms, "do you want to see it played back?"

"No, not really, I don't even like catching myself in the mirror."

"You should really," Teagan says, nodding her head, "it can help you get a better perspective of what the audience is seeing."

"Do the other contestants watch it back?"

"Yeah, most of them get someone to video their routine every couple of weeks, so they can adjust it as necessary."

"Oh." I suddenly feel like I am totally out of my league entering this competition.

"All right, let's go into the cafe and I'll have a look."

We order coffees and take a seat in the corner. Sergio rewinds the film and presses play. The video starts almost half way through my routine. I'm really impressed that I can now smile through the whole thing. The routine as a whole is so much more polished than when I first started, but — yes there is a but, I look like an elegant rhino.

When I look in my mirror at home, my body looks lean and tight; I know that the camera tends to add pounds, but how many cameras were on me for goodness sake?!

"You look disappointed," Sergio says, tilting his head.

"No, not really. The routine looks good it's just that I look enormous."

"Don't be ridiculous, you look great," he assures me.

"Am I bigger than the other contestants?" I ask, still looking at a still of myself on the camera.

Sergio and Teagan look at each other shaking their heads.

"You guys are all the same. You're obsessed with the other contestants, but unfortunately, we aren't allowed to talk to you about them."

"So, I'm the fattest then."

"We didn't say that, and you're not fat, Wanda."

"Have you seen Karen yet?"

"No, not until Wednesday."

"Wait until you see her, you might change your mind."

"Is she skinny?"

"Tall, skinny, blonde and runs through rough terrain like a woodland nymph."

"Do we hate her?" Teagan grins at me.

"Not at all, she's perfectly lovely — more coffee anyone?"

Chapter Twenty

I'm feeling a bit deflated after my meeting with Sergio and Teagan. They are both really sweet but it appears all the other contestants know exactly how to prepare for this competition. Perhaps I should have waited until next year to enter. I have arranged to meet them tomorrow at the leisure centre as Meg is taking me for a session in the morning.

As I walk through the front door of the flat, I'm greeted by the warm aroma of roast pork. I realise that I haven't eaten since seeing myself on camera earlier. I'm starving, but I don't think one of Jared's fabulous roasts is going to improve my situation.

"I'm doing a roast. You want some?" Jared calls out.

"No thank you," I reply, following the smell into the kitchen.

Jared turns around and smiles at me. "What's up? You look like a dieter on the edge."

"I am." I sigh. "I met the TV crew today."

"Oh yeah, I forgot about that. How did it go?"

"Fine, they were really nice. They took some film of my routine and I look like a hippo." I pull out a chair and sit myself down.

Jared screws his face up like he doesn't understand what I mean.

"I'm still too fat!" I exclaim, getting up and opening the fridge door, whilst trying to ignore the perfect Miss Aniston staring at me. "I'm going to detox until Friday. No meat, dairy, alcohol, sugar or wheat."

"Don't be stupid Wanda; you know you have a rockin' body. Have some lean meat and veggies with a spoon of gravy. It'll make you feel better."

"Are you doing Yorkshire pudding?"

"Not for you young lady, I'll make you some tea. By the way, Meg is home; she's in the shower I think. When we have dinner, you can tell us how it feels to be a TV star."

"Very funny." I sneer still staring into the fridge.

Jared sighs loudly and shuts the fridge door. "Go and sit down, I'll bring you some tea."

I leave Jared and the mouth-watering smell of roast and go to my bedroom. In the corner next to my wardrobe, is a large pile of old fitness and celebrity magazines. I know that one of them has an article for a weekend detox. I flip through them one at a time and just as I find it, Meg appears at my bedroom door.

"Hi, Wand', what are you doing?"

"I was looking for this." I hold up the article about detoxing. "It involves drinking 2 litres of some vile tasting – I'm assuming here – liquid every few hours. I think Beyoncé used something like it to slim down for a movie."

"Surely you don't want to do a detox. You're hardly eating anything as it is."

"You didn't see me on camera. I just need to lose a bit before they come back on Friday."

"How are you going to have the energy to rehearse at the leisure centre tomorrow if you haven't eaten anything?"

"Oh, I forgot to tell you, the TV crew are going to join us tomorrow. Do you think the manager will mind?"

"Oh my God, they're not going to put me on television are they?"

"Why, are you wanted by the police?" I laugh.

Meg makes a face at me and goes to help Jared in the kitchen.

We are just about to sit down to dinner, when I hear a bleep in my sports bag. It's a text from Gary. I read it aloud to Meg and Jared.

Out wiv clients. Will call tom to see how TV thing went.

If they want to interview yr boyfriend,

I promise not to blab about wkend :)

I text him back:

Very funny! Speak tom.x

"So, he definitely thinks you're a couple now then?" Meg says with raised eyebrows.

"Yes, it seems so."

"What's going to happen with Mike when they ask to interview your boyfriend?"

"Nothing, it's not as though they're going to ask me in front of Mike is it?"

"But he will watch the finished programme won't he?"

"That's a long way off, so I'll worry about it then."

Tuesday 7th August

Meg and I arrive at the leisure centre by 10.00 a.m. and inform the manager that we will be joined by Channel 10. This news goes down extremely well and we are given every courtesy. We only have an hour and a half before they need the hall back so we get started with a warm-up straight away.

Sergio and Teagan poke their heads around the door about five minutes later. I look up, smile and nod for them to come in.

"*Yoo-hoo!*" Sergio waves. "Getting started already?"

I stop my warm-up and walk over to greet them.

"Hi, guys, good to see you. This is my friend Megan; she's my gymnastic coach." I indicate towards Meg who walks over to say hello.

"Hello, it's nice to meet you," Meg says with a smile, "we're just going through the warm-up."

"No problem," Teagan says, lugging some of the equipment to the other side of the hall. "You just carry on and pretend we're not here. We need to do sound checks *et cetera*; it's kind of our warm-up," she says.

As we make our way back to the mats, Meg catches my eye. "I can't believe you told them I was your gymnastic coach," she whispers.

"Well you are aren't you?"

"They're going to think I'm some sort of professional. How embarrassing is it going to be when they start asking questions about my experience?"

"Don't worry, we'll avoid the question. Besides, I had to say something. All the other contestants seem to be getting some form of professional coaching."

"Wanda, I don't think being assistant coach to a bunch of five-year-olds, classes me as a professional."

"*Sshh*, Sergio's coming."

"Wanda my lovely, we are going to follow you with the camera. Try to ignore it. Teagan may want to stop you occasionally to ask a question."

"Oh, OK."

I finish my warm-up and stretching, and then try to forget about the camera as Meg switches on the music. I usually perform the whole routine once over, then we work on the gymnastic moves, which are my weakest area.

My routine is going well until the bit where I spin on one leg then go straight into a straddle jump. My right foot sticks to the mat on the spin and my body continues on, twisting my knee and forcing me to stagger off course. I really hope they didn't record that bit. I continue on, but I think my smile is turning into a grimace. My knee is throbbing and I really want to stop. I can see Meg looking worried as I come to a balance which means standing on my right leg. The hold lasts for two seconds before I can't stand it and drop to the floor. Meg rushes over and Sergio follows with the camera.

"Are you all right Wand'?" Meg asks, grabbing my leg.

"Yeah, I just twisted it. I'll start again."

"No you won't. You've probably injured yourself because your concentration lapsed due to lack of food."

"No it wasn't, my foot just stuck that's all."

"What did she mean by lack of food?" Teagan asks as Meg wanders off to get an ice pack.

"Oh nothing; she's like my mother, always making sure I'm eating enough."

Teagan helps me up and I can see Sergio still following with his camera.

"So what have you eaten today?"

I notice she has switched on her microphone.

"Porridge and skimmed milk, plus I was going to have a protein shake after training." I lie.

Teagan looks at me suspiciously. I like her, but let's face it she's a journalist and they feed off stories of woe. I can see the headline now GIRLS STARVE THEMSELVES FOR COMPETITION.

Megan arrives with an ice pack and sits me on one of the sofas in the juice bar. I order a protein shake just for show. Sergio and Teagan join us after a short chat with Trevor Meesler, the centre manager who was obviously desperate to be on television. They look as though they are placating him with a short interview. He walks away looking suitably satisfied.

"How's your knee my lovely?" Sergio asks, placing his camera on the opposite sofa.

"Fine thanks. I'll be back to training tomorrow. Sorry to waste your time today."

"Don't be silly. The viewers love an injury. It's what keeps them interested."

"Perhaps we could ask Meg a couple of questions?" Sergio says looking at Megan.

"Oh erm sure." Meg smiles but looks terrified.

Sergio picks up his camera and Teagan grabs her mic and points it towards Megan.

"So, Megan, how often do you train Wanda?"

"Just once or twice a week."

"Do you train Karen from the gym as well?"

"No friggin' way! Oh I mean no, just Wanda."

"I take it you don't get on with Karen Lester then?"

"I don't really know her that much. I'm sure she's a lovely girl."

Teagan glances over at me before asking, "How do you think Wanda and Karen get on? It must be quite tense for them working together."

I narrow my eyes at Meg who quickly looks away.

"I erm...don't really know." Meg grabs her glass of water off the table and gulps it down in one.

Teagan turns her attention back to me. "Do you ever train together or help each other with the academic section of the competition?"

"No way! I mean we are competing with each other at the end of the day."

Teagan smiles as she looks to Sergio to wrap it up. I think she has just been given a conflict story for her gossip loving viewers.

***

Luckily, Teagan and Sergio have to leave for the Brecon Beacons to film an interview with Karen, who they now think is my archenemy. I decide to rest my knee and increase my cardio tomorrow to make up for not training enough today.

I don't drink my protein shake at the leisure centre but make up my detox drink when we get home. It's just until Friday I keep telling myself. As I walk towards my bedroom, after downing my drink, I check my phone. There are two missed calls; one from my mum and one from Gary. I flop myself onto my unmade bed and tap the contact number for 'Mum'.

"Hi, Mum, it's me."

"Oh hello Wanda darling. I tried to call you earlier."

"I know that's why I'm calling you. How did your date with thingy go Sunday night?"

"His name is Tony and he is a perfect gentleman. He took me to that new restaurant on the edge of town; the seafood one. The food was amazing and Tony was really good company."

"Are you going out with him again?"

"Yes, he's taking me to the pictures on Friday."

"Well, I'm glad it went well. Aren't you seeing some other bloke this week?"

"I'm just having coffee with Dennis tomorrow. I think we are meeting at the Coffee Snob so you can spy on us if you want," she says jokingly.

"I might just do that, just to check him out. In fact, I'm going to bring Jared too."

"Don't you dare? He'll do something to embarrass me. You know how cheeky he is."

"All right Mum, I'll call you for 'the skinny' on Thursday."

It's good to hear my mum going out on dates — with men.

My next call is to Gary. I haven't seen him since Sunday; I think I might actually miss him.

"Hi Gary, sorry I missed your call earlier but I have been training with Meg."

"No worries, it's been hectic here this week. How did the interview with the TV crew go?"

"They were really nice actually. They came to the leisure centre today but I twisted my knee so it got cut short."

"You really are accident prone, Wanda. You all right or have we got to go back to Moroccan restaurants so you can keep your leg up?"

"Ha ha, very funny. I'm fine; I just need to rest it for a couple of hours."

"Bet the TV squad filmed you falling on your arse. That's the sort of thing those people love."

"Yes they did and then they interviewed Megan who let slip that Karen and me are mortal enemies."

"Oh shit, did they ask you?"

"Not yet but they will. I mean they're nice people but at the end of the day they want juicy stuff that will keep their viewers watching."

"Well don't worry about it. I'm sure you'll be fine."

"Will I see you this week?" I ask, suddenly sound very needy. I hope Gary doesn't notice.

"Yeah, I thought we could get together Thursday; perhaps go to the pictures."

I am really grateful that he didn't ask me out for dinner. At least I don't have to eat at the cinema.

"Excellent, I'll look forward to it. Bye."

Chapter Twenty-One

Wednesday 8th August

I am awoken by the most annoying beeping sound from my alarm clock. This is one of Jared's jokes. He switches it from 'radio' to 'beep' as he knows it drives me insane. Although, it does ensure I get up without pressing the 'snooze' button. I look at the time, it's 5.00 a.m., and I'm so hungry my tummy is already rumbling. I may have to abandon the detox after today.

The reason I'm up at this ridiculous hour, is to go for a run before work. I need to catch up after cutting my training short yesterday. I pull on the training bottoms that I flung over my wicker chair last night, grab a T-shirt from the drawer and fumble about for my trainers. I'm going to prepare my detox drink and take it with me as I don't think I'll make it up the road without something to give me some energy. I creep into the kitchen and fill my water bottle with a mixture of maple syrup, lemon juice and cayenne pepper. I hate porridge, but I would wade through a room full of sweaty jockstraps to be able to have a bowl now.

The morning air is warm and damp and the only sound I hear is the birds chirping their morning greeting. I love this time of day before the world wakes up. Arriving at the park, I notice that the small woodland path to the visitor's centre is still in darkness due to the thick foliage. I am just about to take a sprint through it, when I am startled by someone behind me; a tall skinny man in a vest and shorts runs past me. He mumbles 'morning' as I turn and notice another three runners behind him. There are two more in the distance. They must be part of a running club. Whoever they are, I'm grateful for their presence. Feeling much safer, I follow them into the woods.

I stay within sight of the other runners for the remainder of my run and arrive home by 6.15 a.m. My head feels like it is still jogging. I don't want to take headache tablets as I haven't eaten, so I grab a bottle of water out of the fridge and drink the whole lot. I'm not looking forward to work, but at least nothing I do will be caught on camera today.

Luckily, I have a busy day set up, which means I will have less time to think about food. I have my two doctors coming in this morning for their first session. I can't wait to see how fit they are, plus I have a yoga class and a new circuit class. I have made up enough sugary crap drink to get me through. I hope.

I actually feel pretty good after my session with Mr and Mrs Sahoti. They are really impressed with my knowledge and are open to my nutritional advice. We arrange another appointment and I give them a programme to follow.

It is just before lunch and I am about to teach my beginners' yoga in the studio. My usual ladies are all here and I greet each one as they come up to grab a mat.

"Hi, Christine, how's the kids?" Christine is already slim and fit but uses yoga to de-stress.

"Still driving me mad. You look amazing by the way."

"Oh thanks. Not long before the competition now."

"You'll do great, Wanda. Just make sure you kick Karen's butt; I hate that cow. She encouraged me to join the gym on a Friday and reduced the prices the very next day. When I called her on it, she basically said 'tough shit'. I would have left but this is so convenient for me."

"I just hope I can beat her, even if I don't win. She has been at a special training camp for the past week."

"Well don't worry, that just means she needed more help than you do."

I laugh and hand her a mat. "I hope you're right."

The class is going well but I'm feeling a bit sick from lack of food. My eagle pose is wobbly and I am dreading down facing dog in case I throw up on my feet. The music is rather soothing though and I manage the poses even better than usual. I am much more flexible than I was two months ago when I started teaching this class.

We are going through the cool down and instead of feeling calm, my heart rate is increasing. There are a dozen butterflies flapping around my insides.

The same feeling as I used to get when I sat an exam at uni. My breathing is shallow but I convince myself that I'm fine and carry on.

"OK, from a standing position, you are going to drop your head and roll down towards your feet, one vertebra at a time." I get them to grab their calves or ankles and hold, just as a dark veil begins to form over my eyes. I am aware that I am swaying but I don't know why.

When I open my eyes, I'm lying on my mat with all my ladies standing over me and Mike holding my hand.

"Wanda, you blipped out for a couple of seconds. Drink this." Mike helps me up and hands me my water bottle.

I look around at all the concerned faces and smile.

"Sorry guys. I haven't had time to eat. I didn't mean to scare you."

"We're just glad you're all right." Christine smiles and ushers the others out of the studio.

I am left looking up at Mike who is smiling his most gorgeous smile at me. Those dimples make the butterflies in my tummy start up again.

"Let's get you into the office."

I am about to try standing when he lifts me into his arms. I feel like I'm in the last scene of '*An Officer and a Gentleman*' as he carries me through reception to Karen's office. I'm sure I can hear someone humming the theme tune. I know it's every girl's romantic dream, but I feel a bit of a tit.

"You don't have to carry me. I can walk you know."

"Are you embarrassed?" he says, swinging me around for everyone to see.

"Yes I am, please put me down."

"Would you be even more embarrassed if I kissed you?"

I look up at him eyes wide. He doesn't kiss me but gently places me onto Karen's office sofa.

"So, what happened? I'm assuming you are not plastered like the last time I had to take you home."

"No I am not you cheeky bastard!"

"Well?"

"It's nothing. I just haven't had time to eat properly."

"What have you eaten today?"

"Porridge and some energy drink." Another lie, but I did dream of eating porridge.

"I think I'd better take you home."

"There's no need for you to do that. I'll be fine."

"You're no good to me ill. Go and get your bag from the gym and I'll take you home. Let Elliot know if you have any classes or consultations.

"OK, I'm going."

"Meet me down here I just need to see Marcus before we go."

***

I enter the gym and Zoe and Elliot run up and fling their arms around me nearly knocking me off my feet.

"Oh my God Wanda we heard you dropped dead during your yoga class. Are you all right?"

They are well meaning, but their loud cries have started to attract attention on the gym floor. I can see some of the members coming over to check I'm not dead. I squirm at the thought of being asked questions so I smile brightly, declare that I'm fine and rush to grab my sports bag.

Mike is waiting with his car keys when I arrive back at the office. I smile briefly and walk as fast as I can toward the exit.

"Hope you feel better." Annie calls out from behind reception.

Without turning around, I shout "Thanks." and follow Mike out to his car.

"So, how you feeling now?" Mike asks as we drive out of the car park.

"I'm fine, really. I didn't need to leave work. I just didn't get time to eat much that's all."

"Well, better safe than sorry."

We drive in silence for a minute or two.

"So, how was your visit home?" I ask. "We haven't had a chance to chat since."

"Just the usual, you know what families are like."

I really want to know if he saw his ex-girlfriend but can't figure out a casual way of asking. So I settle for, "Did you see your ex-girlfriend while you were there?" Subtlety has never been my strong point. Mike looks across at me then turns his head back to the road.

"Yes, I didn't have much choice I'm afraid."

"She's not going to do anything stupid is she?"

"Normally, I would have said no, but she has been acting really strange. She even has it in her head that we were getting engaged, which is why she was so pissed when we broke up."

"Did you ask her to marry you?"

Again, Mike looks at me. "You are direct aren't you?"

"Just asking," I say casually, trying to keep the mood light.

"No I didn't."

"Are you sure?"

"I think I would know if I proposed to someone!"

"Perhaps you implied it at some point. You may have said something like 'when we get married' or something along those lines."

Mike sighs as he turns the car into my road.

"Oh look, we're here. Come on, I'll walk you up."

He parks the car in Jared's parking space, gets out and walks around to my door.

"Nicely avoided," I say as he opens the car door for me.

As we enter the flat, I am assuming it is empty as Meg and Jared are at work. I call out anyway just to check. No answer. I turn to Mike who has just brought my bag in for me.

"Just dump it there." I indicate the messy space behind the door. "Can I make you a coffee?"

"You should sit down. Here, let me make you some tea. I don't think you should have coffee at the moment."

Mike takes my hand in his and leads me to the lounge.

"You sit and I'll bring you tea."

"Mike."

"Yeah?"

"I'm sorry you keep having to rescue me." I throw him my sexiest pouty look.

He leans over me and whispers, "I can't think of anyone I would rather rescue." He then kisses me full on the lips, winks and walks off to make the tea.

I instantly feel tingling in my girlie parts.

Getting myself together, I switch on the television and start to relax when Mike brings in two mugs and a couple of biscuits on a plate.

"Here, drink this and eat these."

"Biscuits?"

"Yes you need the sugar."

"It's not the fact they're biscuits, I'm just wondering where you got them from."

"I had to search a bit. They were at the back of the cupboard where the cooking pots were."

"Oh, Jared knew I would never find them there, cheeky sod."

Mike sits down next to me and I grab one of the biscuits. He looks into my eyes, his are intense and my girlie bits are bubbling again. I stuff the last of the biscuit into my mouth.

"You are incredibly beautiful Wanda Mikos. Do you know that?"

"Of course I do," I say lightly. "I get to look at this face every day."

"You have no idea how to take a complement have you?" he smiles and strokes my – now not so chubby – cheek.

"I can take a complement as good as anyone."

He holds his stare and doesn't speak. I am just about to break the awkward silence when he leans in and kisses me hard on the lips. As I respond, he pulls me into his chest. His fingers find the bottom of my workout top and he slides his hand under, just enough for me to feel a little nervous but he isn't grabby. His other hand is on the back of my head as his kisses increase in intensity. I can hear both our breaths quicken as we move around so that he is on top of me on the sofa. His body feels hard and...*ooh* it's not the only thing!

His hand that was on my back is moving its way south. I can't help but ponder on my knicker selection this morning. Plain black thong I think. This is a relief as I nearly wore the grey one, which used to be white. Mike moves his tongue away from my mouth and down to my neck, kissing softly but with urgency. I am beginning to feel light headed again. I'm not getting enough oxygen. Mike continues to kiss my neck until he can't go any further as my yoga top is too tight. He reaches under it and begins to lift it over my head. Oh my God I am about to have wild sex with Mike Diamond. Suck on that Karen Lester!"

I roll Mike over so I can grab the buckle on his belt and my phone starts buzzing on the table; I hadn't taken it off vibrate after work. Mike looks up.

"Do you want that?" he puffs, reaching over to grab my phone.

"No!" I practically yell at him as I see in large letters on the front 'Call from Gary'.

I'm too late as Mike hands me my phone, but not without seeing the name on the front first.

"It's Gary," he says, looking puzzled.

Oh poop!

Chapter Twenty-Two

So here I am, gorgeous guy in my arms and my 'boyfriend' on the phone. Not that I've actually given Gary that badge of honour, but he did consider himself my boyfriend last week. I unravel myself from Mike's arms and apologise. I feel as though I ought to take the call, even if it's just to gain extra time to think up a reason why some bloke named Gary is calling me.

"Hi, Gary, what's up?" I start to make my way to the kitchen. For some reason, I think taking the call in my bedroom would confirm what Mike is probably thinking right now.

"Hi, babe, nothing's up; just thought I would try and catch you between clients to see if you fancy going for a drink instead of the pictures tomorrow night? One of the guys at work is having birthday drinks at Povkas."

"Oh erm yeah why not, sounds great. I'll call you later as I have someone coming in any second."

"Great stuff. Perhaps I could stay at yours as Povkas is so close, what d'ya think?"

Oh my God now what do I say?

"Of course, no problem, great idea!" I say enthusiastically. Oh well, I can always cancel, but for now I need to get off the phone and think of something to tell Mike.

I hang up and stare at my phone. Mike is standing in the doorway.

"Oh hi, you scared me."

"Sorry. You OK, you look panicked?"

"No, no I'm fine," I mutter, throwing my phone into a draw for some odd reason.

"So why is Megan's brother calling you. Is she all right?"

Oh of course, I forgot he's met Gary, that night my mum and her lesbian came over. I'm saved!

"Yeah she's fine. He's planning a surprise for her birthday and needed some help." I smile and walk towards him. He wraps his arms around me and kisses the top of my head just as his pocket starts ringing. I can feel his body slump as he sighs and gently holds me away so he can answer his phone. He looks at me disappointed "It's work. I'll have to take it."

Now I don't consider myself paranoid but I'm sure I saw the initial C for Chloe on his caller ID; I could be wrong.

***

Once again I'm conflicted. I am feeling guilty about Gary but if I'm honest, sex with Mike would have been great; especially as I'm so lean at the moment. Plus, think of all those calories! I could treat myself to a roast dinner.

"Damn!" Mike hangs up his phone. "I'm sorry I've got to get back. Some bloke is making a complaint about the changing rooms or something. Do you think we will ever get it together?" he asks, pulling me to him again.

"We do seem to get a little further every time we meet."

"You're right perhaps we should meet more often."

Mike kisses me, tucks his shirt back in and makes his way to the lounge to retrieve his shoes.

"Thanks for bringing me home again." I call after him.

"My pleasure, how about trying this again on Sunday night?"

"We could but we will have to make room for Jared and Meg on the sofa," I reply.

"No you numpty, I meant dinner."

"Oh how boring. All right then."

Mike laughs and scoops me into his brawny brown arms. He kisses me one last time and then makes his way back to his car.

As soon as he leaves, I hog the last two biscuits and make myself a coffee. I'm searching for the rest of the biscuits when I notice the lovely Jennifer Aniston staring at me from the fridge. She is certainly doing her job as I immediately shut the cupboard door and settle for a coffee.

I sit back on the sofa and pull up some magazines from the floor. The first of which is a fitness magazine hailing the virtues of blueberries and advertising their section on *How to Get a*

Beach Body in Two Weeks. Two weeks my arse! I've been starving myself and training fifteen hours a week for the last two months to look like this. Performing two sets of twelve squats twice a week is not going to get you a bottom like JLo's believe me.

I throw it on the floor and pick up a celebrity magazine showing various girls from a reality show in their bikinis at a beach party in Marbella. The interviewer in the article asks them how they keep themselves looking fabulous. The answers vary from 'I run every day at 6.00 a.m. and 'I refrain from alcohol,' to 'I drink two litres of a special green tea every day, which increases my metabolism.' Unfortunately, I've watched the entire series of the programme, following every aspect of their lives, none of which has shown them drinking green tea avoiding alcohol or participating in exercise of any sort. Actually, if I don't win this competition and have to leave the gym, I may apply to be one of their Personal Trainers.

I decide to prepare dinner for everyone as I'm home early. I'm finished with the whole detox thing but will stick to my previous diet. Actually, after eating nothing for the last few days, even chicken and brown rice sounds like heaven. It's all a matter of perspective I suppose.

I raid the fridge, freezer and cupboards, and come up with Cajun spiced chicken breasts with a tomato and onion salsa – which was in my fitness magazine – minus the fresh cilantro because I don't know what that is but I'm sure we don't have any. I find a couple of packets of lemon couscous and read the instructions. As I'm sprinkling my chicken breasts with Cajun spice, the doorbell rings. It can't be Jared or Meg as they have a key. I look through the spy hole and see a distorted version of my mother.

"Mum, how did you know I was home?" I ask as I open the door.

"I didn't, I was in town and decided to pop in and see Jared. Why are you home by the way?"

"Oh, I changed shifts."

"Is Jared not home?"

"Not yet. He's due any minute, so is Meg. Want a cup of tea or coffee?"

"Yes please. Oh my goodness Wanda Mikos are you cooking?" she asks sarcastically as she walks into the kitchen.

"Well, it's not gourmet but I'm having a go. Do you want to stay; I can get more chicken out?"

"Yes, thank you that would be lovely."

"You haven't tasted it yet."

"What are you making?"

"Cajun chicken, salsa and couscous with a green salad. Anyway, didn't you have a date this afternoon?"

"Sort of, I had coffee with Dennis."

"How did it go?"

"He's really nice. Completely different to Tony in every way. He's a bit older than me but he looks really young. I'm just hoping he doesn't go in for all that Botox-for- bloke's thing."

"You think he's had Botox?" I exclaim, turning away from cooking my couscous.

"The man doesn't have one wrinkle on his forehead! Honestly, I don't think I could put up with a man who is vainer than me."

"Maybe he's naturally young looking. He probably looks after himself."

"If that's true, then he's pretty perfect. This brings me back to the problem of which one to date."

"Why not date both of them?"

"Oh, Wanda, don't tell me you haven't sorted out your own little *ménage-a-trois*."

"Mother, I haven't slept with either of them, so technically it's still dating."

"But I thought you went away with that Gary chap."

"Yes I did. But nothing happened, I told you that."

Just as my mother is about to hit me with a stream of embarrassing questions, the front door opens and Jared walks through.

"Hi, Mum, I didn't know you were coming over," Jared says, kissing her on the cheek.

"I was just in town darling. Wanda is cooking and has invited me to stay."

"Oh my God, Wanda I can't believe you're cooking. Sorry, Mum, if I'd have known you were coming I would have cooked."

"Don't be so bloody cheeky Jared. It's going to be fab."

Jared laughs and goes to get changed out of his uniform.

I try and keep the conversation flowing on anything but my love life when I hear Meg's key in the door. She walks into the kitchen lifting her nose in the air.

"Ooh what's that smell, is Jared making dinner?"

"No, I am."

"Really? Oh hello, Nina, how are you?"

"I'm good thanks." Mum smiles, rising from her chair to kiss Meg on the cheek.

"How are you? Have you got yourself a boyfriend yet?"

"*Ermm*,"

"Mum! Give her time to get through the door for goodness sake."

Megan laughs as Mum makes a face at me.

"I'll go and get changed. It smells great Wanda, I'm starving."

I set the table in the kitchen and dish up the food on plates, except for the salad which I place in a fancy glass bowl in the middle.

"Dig in everyone."

I watch as one by one they attempt a small forkful of food.

"Oh for God's sake, just eat it will you," I exclaim, exasperated after all my efforts.

"It's wonderful, darling," Mum says eventually, still chewing her first bite of chicken.

"This couscous is lovely," enthuses Meg.

"You've overcooked the chicken," states Jared.

I give him a sarcastic grin and steer the conversation away from my dinner.

"So Jared did you hear about Mum's date. She had coffee with some guy called Dennis today."

"Oh yeah, how did it go Mum?"

"He was very nice."

"You didn't fancy him then?" Jared laughs.

"I didn't say that."

"You didn't have to."

"Anyway, Megan," Mum says turning away from Jared, "when was the last time you had a date? You could come with me on the next speed dating night if you like."

Jared and I giggle and nudge shoulders.

"Oh thanks Nina but I have had a couple of dates with Gary's friend. We all met on the same night."

"So Gary isn't Wanda's boss?"

"No, that's the gorgeous Mike Diamond."

"Have I met him?"

"No, he did turn up when you and George came over but Wanda slammed his head into the door and made him leave."

"Oh dear."

I can tell by Jared's face he's shocked that I told her about Gary and Mike.

"I didn't mean to Mum, I just had to get rid of him a bit sharpish. Actually, I've just remembered that Gary is meant to call. I'd better check my phone as I left it on silent.

"Wanda darling, can it not wait until you have finished your dinner?"

"There. Finished!" I push the last of my couscous to one side and place my knife and fork on my plate. My mother just shakes her head at me.

***

I am still in a quandary about Gary staying over tomorrow night. I just need another week to sort out whether I want to be with him or Mike. Until I actually sleep with either of them, I can feel less guilty about dating them both. Unfortunately for us girls, having sex with a bloke changes the situation. I don't know why, I'm sure most blokes wouldn't give a rat's arse if they were in the same situation. We girls are far too moralistic for our own good.

I check my phone, even though I'm not meant to hear from Gary until tomorrow and there is a text message from Mike.

Hope ur feeling better.

Would love to finish wat we started.

Did you say yes to dinner this Sat?

See you at work Friday. Xx

Oh good grief, this is getting worse. Why is it that you can spend five years swooning over someone you can never have and spending far too much on AA batteries — if you know what I mean — then two perfectly fabulous blokes come along at once! It's totally unfair. You would think that the universe would spread them out a bit. That way nobody would have to go through a 'dry spell' as it were.

I throw the phone onto my bed and make my way back to the kitchen where I can hear the others chatting. Just as I get near, the chattering changes to sudden silence. I stop to listen for just a second before slowly stepping into the kitchen.

Mum, Jared and Meg all look up at me from the table. Mum looks upset and Meg hangs her head.

"What?" I ask looking at each one in turn.

My mother is the first to speak. "Why didn't you tell me you are going to be Laura's bridesmaid?"

I shoot a look at Meg who is staring at her empty plate.

"Thank you, Megan." I pull up a chair next to Mum and place an arm around her shoulder.

"I'm sorry, Mum; I didn't know how to tell you. Laura ambushed me on the phone and I couldn't really say no."

"Don't be silly, darling, of course you had to say yes." Her watery smile not doing a very good job of hiding how devastated she feels.

Chapter Twenty-Three

Thursday 9th August

It's my day off today so I'm going to the leisure centre to work on my routine. Maybe I should ask Meg for a few more gymnastic moves. I know it's meant to be an aerobic routine but I need to up the wow factor as much as I can.

I must admit that although I feel great for having lost a few more pounds on the detox, I much prefer eating. Heading to the kitchen, I crack some eggs, keeping only one yolk and three whites. I mix them with some oats and throw them into the frying pan with a knob of coconut oil. Unfortunately, it still tastes like crap unless I cover it with tomato sauce. I take it into the lounge to eat and switch on the TV. The Morning Show is on and they are following a group of people as they try to lose weight for their holidays. The celebrity trainer is a woman called Nancy. She's about thirty-five but looks amazing. Her tiny bottom is peachy and her legs are so well defined, I'm sure she can't ever break her diet. Again, the reality dawns on me that if I want her kind of life, I'm going to have to be this strict all the time too. I look down at my plate of eggy slime and wish I desired a different career, like a chef or maybe a teacher. I swallow the last of my breakfast and get my things together.

***

I am greeted like a celebrity at the leisure centre, which is rather odd. The receptionists are usually efficient but not overly friendly, however this morning they cannot do enough for me. The manager is called and he walks out of his office to greet me.

"Wanda, hello there. Megan called to say you would be here today. The hall is set up and the audio system has been checked. Is there anything else you need?"

"No I don't think so, thanks."

"Great. I was wondering if you would mind if we took a photo of you for our posters." He grins and puts his flabby white arm around my shoulder.

"Posters, what posters?"

Trevor turns me towards the back wall. There, in large coloured letters is a poster declaring that Wanda Mikos, The Main Event competitor and TV personality, trains here.

"Oh my God, why do you have that up there?" I ask, unable to take my eyes off it.

"Well my bosses thought it was great publicity for the local council when I told them about you and the television crew. The local newspaper wants to do an article too," he says and takes a camera from his jacket pocket.

"But I haven't even been on telly yet."

"You will be. Here let's try taking one of you standing at the juice bar."

He ushers me to the café area and adjusts my fringe before stepping back and snapping two or three shots. I look a bit bewildered in all of them but he shrugs and announces 'they're fine' before taking off back to his office.

I wander back to the hall slightly dazed and begin my warm-up. My handstand hold is great until I move my legs apart to each side. I feel my back sinking and collapse to the floor. I thought that side splits would actually be a little easier but I was wrong. I suddenly have an idea about faking an injury so to avoid sleeping with Gary tonight, which would give me more time to sort my head out. Unfortunately, I may have overplayed the injury card. Time to think of a Plan B.

I continue with my routine when I suddenly notice about ten pairs of eyes watching me through the doors. I look up at the clock and realise I've been here for over three hours. The little faces at the door are a local school that are using the leisure centre for P.E whilst their gym is being refurbished.

"Sorry guys, Come in, I'm just about to pack up."

A tall skinny guy holds open the doors to let the kids through.

"OK kids, lets get set up quietly please!"

I gather up my things and walk towards him. "Hi, sorry about that, I didn't realise how late it was."

"Not a problem; the kids loved watching you. They were asking if you're Wanda."

As I look around, half of the children had stopped what they were doing to listen.

"Yes I am. How did you know?"

"They were asking me about the posters."

"Oh, how embarrassing, I didn't know about those until today."

"So when are you going to be on television? The kids want to make sure they watch. In fact, I was wondering if, after the competition, you would come and give a talk at the school. What with the Olympics last year, they are really into all sorts of sports which we are trying to encourage."

"Yes, I don't see why not."

"Great, my name's Alan by the way. Here, let me give you my number and we will sort something out. I'd better go before they kill each other."

"OK, thanks. Bye."

I must admit to feeling pleased at my new-found fame; I can't wait to tell Meg and Jared. It will be good practise for becoming a celebrity trainer in Los Angeles. Actually I have just thought of another reason why I shouldn't do the deed with Gary tonight. Do I really want to get serious with any bloke if I'm going to be moving to America within the year? I really need to consult with Meg.

***

Once home, I simultaneously peel off my sweaty training gear and gulp down a rather yummy chocolate protein shake before taking a shower. As I'm drying myself, I hear the front door bang. That is usually Jared bringing his bike up and smashing it into the door.

"Is that you Jared?" I call out through the door.

"No it's me," Meg calls back.

I throw a towel over my wet hair and meet her in the hallway.

"Meg, we need a conflab. What on earth is that?" I ask, peering into a large bag.

"It's a coffee machine, I got it from work. It's bloody heavy though."

"It's not one of those industrial ones is it?"

"No, you idiot, we've been selling them to go with our own blend coffees. This is the last one so I got it really cheap."

"Excellent."

"Anyway, what's up?" she asks, placing the box on the counter.

"I still don't know what to do about Gary staying over. Do you think I should fake an injury?"

"Another one? He'll think you're permanently incapacitated in some way."

"Then tell me what to do."

"All right, let's see, if there was no Mike Diamond, would you sleep with him?"

"Yes."

"Problem solved," Meg says, opening up the coffee machine box.

"How does that solve anything?"

"Pretend Mike doesn't exist and just enjoy yourself."

"So what do I do on Saturday when I have a date with Mike?"

"Do you want to have sex with the handsome Mike Diamond?"

"Oh yes."

"Pretend Gary doesn't exist and just enjoy yourself." Meg laughs and carries on sorting out our new coffee machine.

"Thanks Megan, very helpful," I say sarcastically, pulling my towel off my head and making my way to my bedroom.

I call Gary and we arrange a time to meet up later. He has invited Jared and Meg too, which makes me feel a little easier as I'll be meeting some of his friends for the first time. I open my wardrobe and attempt to put together an outfit.

***

It's 7.20 p.m. and we're meeting Gary at …actually we're late. Jared has changed his outfit three times and has settled on a pair of cream chinos and a light blue denim shirt.

"Jared, don't you think it's a bit hot for a long-sleeved shirt? It was really stuffy the last time we were there."

"Yeah but I look amazing." He does an Eric Morecambe eyebrow raise as he gyrates on the spot.

"You won't look quite so amazing when you are dancing around with armpit stains," Megan comments as she walks past my bedroom.

I snigger as Jared's face falls and he slopes off to change — again.

I have decided on a pair of white jeans and a bright pink posh T-shirt – this is like a normal T-shirt but costs a lot more. I think my pink sandals might be a bit matchy, matchy but they look great. Meg announces she's ready and stands at my bedroom door wearing a pair of jeans and a pink and grey polo shirt. She has made the effort to wear heels and has stolen my grey clutch.

"You look great," I tell her, looking up from my mascara brush.

"Thanks. You had better hurry up. Isn't this meant to be a surprise party?"

"Yes but I don't think it matters if we turn up a bit late."

"Why?"

"He doesn't know us, you Muppet!"

"Oh yeah," Meg says looking embarrassed.

We arrive at Povkas by 7.45 p.m. and the bar is already buzzing for a Thursday night. Meg and I look around for Gary and Luke whilst Jared goes to the bar.

"It's about time." Gary sneaks up behind me and places his arms around my waist. Luke comes over to see Meg.

"Yes, we're sorry. We would like to blame Jared as he has changed four times." I spin around to face him.

"Well I hope he doesn't look too good; my sister is here tonight. I think she wants to turn him."

"This I've got to see."

We all meet up with Jared at the bar and I decide to have a glass of wine as I have trained for three hours today.

Manny the bar owner is doing the rounds and chatting up as many of the ladies as he can. I see him head in our direction.

"Wanda, my darlings, how are you?"

"Good thanks, Manny, how are you?"

"Wonderful, but darlings I haven't seen you for so long." He holds me at arms length and looks me up and down. "What happened? You are losing the weight, yes?"

"Yes, I'm training for a competition," I announce, chuffed that he noticed.

"Well do not lose more, you had fabulous boobies. Would be a shame to lose more of them." He stares at my, now smaller, chest area and walks off.

I am sporting a bemused expression as I turn to Megan who is laughing into her glass.

Luke smiles and looks me up and down. "Don't worry Wanda, even without humongous 'boobies' you look great."

"Thanks, Luke."

We meet up with Jared who is being chatted up by Gary's sister and her friend who are both flicking their hair and touching themselves; all well-known signs of flirting. Complete waste of effort of course but Jared appears to be enjoying the attention.

By 9.00 p.m., I've had one small glass of wine and far too much sparkling water but am feeling rather zippy. We are all singing along with the 'Bander Boys' which comprises of two blokes singing to backing music on the tiny stage. Gary is giving me lots of attention and kisses, which I must admit I am enjoying. Meg and Luke seem to be 'Gettin' it on' as Zoe would say and Jared is dancing with all the single women. Luckily, I don't have to be in work until 10.00 a.m. tomorrow so we stay until midnight, then Meg, Jared, Gary and I all head back to our flat. I could kill for a bag of chips.

"I think we all need a kebab," Jared announces, as we walk up the road towards the kebab shop.

"OK, but just chicken for me," I shout.

"Don't get garlic sauce," Gary whispers in my ear whilst simultaneously squeezing my waist.

I see Meg give me a cheeky wink.

When we get back to the flat, Meg and Jared attempt a couple of fake yawns before announcing they are off to bed.

"Goodnight, see you both in the morning."

"Yeah night guys," Gary calls as he tries to figure out how to switch the television on.

"Do you want a drink?" I ask, standing in the doorway.

"Coffee would be good if you're making one."

I decide not to use the new coffee machine, as I haven't worked it out yet, so I fill the kettle. I am contemplating the events, which are about to take place, when I hear Meg coming out of the bathroom. She pokes her head around the doorway.

"Hey Wanda, don't do anything I wouldn't do."

"*Shhh*," I turn and throw the tea towel at her. "Go away."

Meg giggles and tiptoes back to her bedroom.

I finish the coffee and take them into the lounge. Gary has put football on which is not going to get me in the mood.

"Sorry," he says when he sees my face. "I was just browsing."

He switches it over to a music channel and pats the cushion on the sofa next to him. I smile, flop myself down next to him and snuggle up against his chest.

"So how do you feel about your competition?" Gary asks still keeping his eyes on the television but giving my shoulders a squeeze.

"Oh Ok I think. I would love to know what Karen is doing though. She doesn't seem to have to work as hard as me. I tried to copy her twirls and leaps but with her willowy frame she seems to make everything look effortless."

"How do you know she isn't thinking the same thing about you? Maybe she went to the Brecon Beacons camp because she's threatened by your power, strength and grace."

I shift position to look at him. "Wow, that's a really nice thing to say and you could be right. I may not be tall and slender but I am powerful and strength-wise she has nothing on me."

"So play to your strengths and stop trying to be Karen. Be the amazing athlete I know you can be and do it your way."

I think I just had an epiphany — I may be falling in love.

Gary puts his arm around my shoulder and I let out a relaxed sigh before he leans down to kiss me. I respond with enthusiasm. He really does get sexier every time I see him. We start to fool around and he eventually pulls me on top of him. I'm getting a distinct feeling of *déjà vu*.

Friday 10th August

My alarm blasts into action at 8.00 a.m. precisely. I untuck my arm from the duvet and smack the 'snooze' button. As I stretch my arms out, I suddenly remember I'm not alone this morning. Slowly, I turn my head and fully expect to see Gary sleeping soundly. But I was wrong. I am alone.

Oh my God, what did I do this time! I wrack my brain trying to remember the details of last night. The corners of my mouth turn up as I recall our bedroom gymnastics and how tender Gary was. I'm sure I didn't do anything offensive or gross to make him want to leave without saying goodbye. I heave myself up onto my elbow and look at the pillow where his head should be. Perhaps he has left me a note. I scan the left side of the bed — no note.

Flopping backward, I think some more, Coyote Ugly comes into my mind. This is where someone wakes up after sex and the person next to them is so gross, that they would rather chew off their own arm than wake them up. I pull back the covers and grab my dressing gown, which has frolicking sheep on it. I wouldn't have let Gary see it but as he's pissed off and left me it doesn't matter.

"Morning Meg, you not at work today?" I ask, rubbing my eyes and yawning.

"Yes but I'm on the late shift. I swapped with Leila so I could have a drink last night."

I grab a mug from the cupboard and look curiously at our new coffee machine.

"Here, let me," Meg says, taking my mug, "and dish the dirt about last night."

"Well," I start slowly, "it was all good and he's really sexy…"

Meg stops what she is doing and turns to face me.

"I can sense a but coming."

"Well."

"Oh my God, did he want you to do something freaky like poke his poo pipe?"

"*Eww* Meg! No he did not." I sigh and open the fridge to get some milk.

"Well what then?"

"He's gone."

"What do mean he's gone?"

"He obviously couldn't bear to stay with me for the whole night and left."

"When did he leave?"

"I have no idea. He crept out in the middle of the night for all I know."

"That doesn't seem like something he would do. Why don't you call him?"

"What, so he can tell me '*it's been great but*', I don't think so."

Meg sighs and hands me my coffee. I hear the shower finish and look up.

"Jared's up, don't mention this to him. Let's just tell him Gary had to go to work early."

"Deal," Meg says and chinks coffee mugs with me.

We chat over our coffee and Meg instructs me on how to work the new machine. We are bent over the instruction book when we hear someone clear their throat behind us.

"Morning ladies," Gary says looking rather sexy with damp hair. "Can I get one of those?"

Chapter Twenty-Four

I arrive at work happy that I wasn't dumped this morning ready to take on the day. That is until I remember that not only is Karen back today but so is the TV crew. Oh crap!

"Hi," I call out to Annie on reception. She is looking less than chipper this morning.

"Oh hello, Wanda."

"What's up? You look pissed off."

"In a word — Karen. I wish she would go back to that camp and stay there," she mumbles through gritted teeth.

"What has she done now?"

"She balled me out in front of those television people. In her words," Annie sticks her nose in the air in a haughty manner, "'This reception area is disgusting. I can't leave for five minutes before standards start slipping. Get it cleared up before the end of your shift.'"

"Oh dear. Perhaps her training camp didn't go well?"

"Couldn't give a shit. Wish she had broken her leg on the first day."

"Well I'm going to avoid her as much as possible. See you later."

I arrive in the gym and my first client Vanessa has arrived for her session. We get started straight away and I push her harder than ever between gossiping about her love life and she leaves sweaty and red-faced. An hour later, I take a yoga class and assure my members that I won't be fainting this time. Luckily, I have managed to avoid Karen and the TV crew all day, although I did notice them filming during Vanessa's training earlier. I didn't mention it to her.

By 4.00 p.m., I take a break and decide to have a run on the treadmill. Sergio and Teagan are in the gym interviewing Elliot who is fidgeting from one foot to the other. I start my treadmill and warm up for 5 minutes before running. As I'm about to increase my speed, I notice that Karen is also on a treadmill three across from me. My shoulders drop a little as I notice how amazing she looks. Plus, her stride is even and every step appears effortless for her. I am hoping that Elliot can keep the TV crew busy until we get off. I really don't want to be filmed running near her.

Unfortunately, Elliot's sparkling personality only holds them off for another 5 minutes. I can see them coming towards us out of the corner of my eye. I shoot a quick look over to Karen who smiles at me.

"You look great!" I shout to her over the music.

"Thanks," she says and nods at Sergio who is approaching her treadmill. It wouldn't have hurt her to say that I look good too. I mean it's only polite isn't it? Bitch.

Karen slows to a walk as she has a short chat with Teagan, then increases her speed to a fast-paced jog. I look across and notice that from the angle Sergio is filming, I am probably in the shot, so I increase my speed to 8mph and try to keep focused. They keep filming as Karen increases the gradient on her treadmill. It's no good the competitor in me can't be beaten by this skinny ratbag. I increase my speed to 9mph and increase the gradient again. I am now running up a steep hill and there is no sign of Sergio finishing filming. This is fine for the first few minutes but after a late night and serious bed bouncing, I could do without it.

I am thinking about reducing my speed when Mike walks over. He must have only just started work, as I haven't seen him today. I use him as an excuse to slow down to a walk as my legs are now numb and I'm in danger of wandering off the back of my treadmill onto some unsuspecting member ab crunching on the mats.

"Hey, you were going at quite a pace there," Mike says as I continue at a walking pace.

I puff, wiping my forehead with the back of my hand. "Yeah well, I need to keep up with Karen. She doesn't even look like she's breaking a sweat."

"Apparently, those training camps are pretty intense. She was telling me about it earlier."

"Really? Well I think it's cheating getting professional help."

"Are you sulking?"

"I might be."

"I've got a one-to-one meeting with her tonight so I expect I'll hear more about who the trainers were."

"Oh, you're meeting with her tonight?" I sound a bit jealous which is rich coming from someone who was shagging Gary all night.

"Yeah, she wants to go to that restaurant up the road. She says we won't get time to eat otherwise." Mike smiles knowingly.

"Have fun."

"If I didn't know any better, I would say you are jealous Miss Mikos."

"Don't be ridiculous."

"Anyway, are we still on for tomorrow night? I would like to pick up where we left off."

"Oh erm yes of course," I reply, tucking my hair behind my ear. "That will be lovely."

"Lovely? OK, I'll call you tomorrow."

I would never make a good lawyer, I always sound like a complete Muppet whenever I'm in an awkward situation. Why can't I be cool like Jared? That boy can charm his way out of a murder conviction.

I am just about to leave the treadmill for a spot of rowing, when Sergio and Teagan start to walk my way.

"Oh are you getting off Wanda?" Teagan asks.

"Yes, I was going to go change to the rower. Why would you rather I stayed on here?"

"No, no it's fine if you don't mind that we follow you and ask you a few questions about what you are going to do on it."

"No problem." I instantly begin working out a short training programme in my head. To be honest, I was just going to 'wing it' today. This is something I scold members and clients for. My mantra has always been *Know where you're going and you'll get there*. But I'm just trying to get through it today without falling over or falling asleep!

I get to the rower and strap my feet into the stirrups, put the level indicator up to 10 and start to row. I can see Sergio with his camera on his shoulder walking around the machines to get the best shot. I do a quick form check and turn my head towards Teagan who is about to ask me a question.

"So, Wanda, what sort of a workout are you going to do on this piece of equipment?" she asks squatting next to me.

"I'm going to row at a steady pace for one minute, then a fast pace for one minute. This is called Interval Training."

"And how does this type of training help you with your routine for the competition."

"It improves cardiovascular fitness. My routine requires some short bursts of power and speed and this helps train my white fast twitch muscle fibres." I smile rather smugly. I bet Karen doesn't even know about muscle fibres.

"Yeah, that's too technical, Wanda, we just need to hear it in layman's terms."

"Oh, OK."

"We'll have to cut that bit Sergio."

Shaking my head, I perform the higher intensity part of my workout and crank up my speed on the rower.

"Right, we're back." Teagan nods at Sergio who starts filming.

I keep my pace fast for another 30 seconds to make them wait. Plus, Mike is now sitting on the rower next to me chatting to the member on the end machine. As I begin to slow down, a wave of fatigue rolls over me. I need my pillow.

"You all right Wanda you look shattered?"

"I'm sorry it's probably not the best day to film me training."

"Oh yes, late night was it?" she asks, with raised eyebrows.

"Just a bit."

She slices her finger across her throat at Sergio indicating that he can cut.

"So, who was he and have we met him? Of course this is all off record," she says briefly touching my arm as I slide past her.

My eyes shoot immediately to my right. I am hoping Mike didn't hear that. Teagan takes this completely the wrong way.

"Oh my God! You were shagging Mike last night," she announces in a loud whisper.

"No!"

"Oh sorry, who was it then?"

Mike who has stopped talking, stands up and is about to walk away. Teagan has made him think I had sex with someone else, which of course I did but he doesn't need to know that.

"I was at a birthday party that's all," I shout, forcing Teagan off balance and onto the floor.

***

It's the end of my shift and I'm not sure if Mike has been avoiding me but I haven't seen him since the rower incident earlier. I decide that it's probably best if I try and bump into him and act normal.

I grab my sports bag from the gym office and make my way downstairs. As I turn towards reception, I see Mike hovering by Karen's office. I reach into my bag pretending to search for my car keys."Oh hi, Mike. I haven't seen you all night, you off to dinner with Karen?" I ask lightly once I reach Karen's office.

"Yeah, she's just finishing a phone call. Listen, are we..."

Karen appears at the doorway. "Hello, Wanda," she says, not even looking at me; her face contorted as though she is searching for a lost bit of protein bar around her gums.

"Hi Karen, how was your training camp?"

"Good thanks. Ready to go?" she says smiling at Mike.

She grabs his arm and raises her hand and smiles at me. Why is she such a bitch? I decide there and then, that if Mike still wants to see me tomorrow night, there will be sex!

When I arrive home, Jared is at work but has left me a message that Mum has called and do we want to meet her for lunch tomorrow. I poke my head around the lounge door. "Hi, Meg, I didn't think you would be home."

"I've just got in. How was work?

"Not bad, I suppose." I flop onto the comfy chair.

"So, did you see Mike?"

"Yeah but it wasn't good."

"Why, what happened?"

I spend the next 20 minutes going over the whole Teagan and Karen thing and Meg analyses it minute by minute.

"So basically, you don't know if he's pissed off at you or not," she summarises.

"No idea. As usual, Karen interrupted before he could complete his sentence." I get up out of the chair. "Anyway, I'm not going to worry about it now. I need to call my mum."

"Hi, Mum, sorry I missed your call, I was at work."

"I just called to ask if you and Jared wanted to meet me for lunch tomorrow."

"I have to work tomorrow, can we make it Sunday?"

"Yes, just let me know where you want to go. Sorry Wanda I'll have to rush as I have a date and he is at my door."

"Oh you wild woman, three men on the go."

"Could be, I'll give you the skinny tomorrow," she says with a girlie giggle.

Saturday 11th August

It's 7.30 a.m. and the rest of the flat is quiet. I turn on the shower and decide to weigh myself. Dropping my pyjama bottoms I stare at the scale; it stares back. I nod my head and dare it to give me a crappy weight reading. I take a deep breath and step confidently onto the plate. Exhaling, I look down to see the digital readout, which is showing 9stone 5 pound. Hooray, I'm skinny again. Well, maybe not skinny but it beats the post university bloat I've been sporting since I left.

I arrive at work by 8.30 a.m. and it's pretty empty except for me, Zoe, Pat on reception and a couple of enthusiastic members. I run up and ask Zoe if she minds covering me for a while so I can practise a few new moves. I don't want to take the chance of Karen watching me. I want her to think I haven't improved since the last time she saw my performance. I've taken Gary's comments about being myself and changed my routine slightly to include more strength and balance poses as opposed to flinging myself about like Karen. I must admit to feeling more confident with my new routine.

As my music starts, I unfurl like a flower, spin and then leap into the air. Even I have to admit it is an impressive start; I just need to make sure that I nail the rest of it. The routine lasts only 3 minutes but is so packed full of power jumps, strength holds and balance poses that I have to take off my top layer T-shirt and wipe my face with it when I finish.

The next 20 minutes, I spend perfecting the hardest sections of the routine and end with some stretching. I'm bent over stretching my hamstrings, when I hear a tapping sound. I look through my legs at the studio door. Zoe is jumping up and down and waving at me. Why doesn't she just open the door?

I stand up, head to the door and pull the handle. Zoe has gone. I look around puzzled, when I hear another sound.

Zoe is poking her head out of the changing rooms. "Quick, get changed, Karen's here," she hisses, gesturing me towards her.

"OK thanks, Zoe. Why didn't you just open the door?" I ask as we both creep into the ladies changing room.

"Because then she would hear your music and know that you were practising, not working."

"Good idea. Thanks again. You'd better get back to the gym."

"Right, by the way, I told her you were doing a changing room check so hurry up."

Within minutes, I'm back on the gym floor, still slightly red-faced and sweaty but at least Karen didn't see me. I join Zoe behind the gym desk and we make ourselves look busy.

The day passes without incidents. Luckily Karen only came in for an hour to catch up on some paperwork. Although, she did make a point of letting me know that her and Mike 'Had a great meal at that place up the road'. I should try it. I was so close to saying 'Actually, we're going out on a date this evening, so maybe we will'. Unfortunately, I'm not entirely sure how I stand with Mike so I hold back.

Mike hasn't turned up by midday so I decide to check my phone hoping he has left a message. He hasn't.

My shift ends at 2.00 p.m. but I'm going to stay on to get an extra weight-training workout in. By 1.45 p.m., I have checked my phone five times. He must be pissed off.

My weights programme begins with some bench presses. I keep the weight heavy enough to be able to push out ten repetitions as this helps with some of the strength moves in my competition programme. I dig my heels into the floor on my final set and hold my breath as I force the bar upward. On my last rep, I drop the bar back onto the rack and look up from the bench to see Mike's rather beautiful face smiling at me.

"Forty kilos is a heavy weight for a delicate thing like you," he says smiling; his blue eyes twinkling.

I can't believe how relieved I feel that he isn't pissed off with me.

"I've never been called 'delicate' before." I pull myself upright and tuck a stray strand of hair behind my ear.

"I think you are. Anyway, I came to check we are still on for tonight?"

"Yes I'm looking forward to it. Karen was in earlier and she went out of her way to tell me what a great time she had with you last night." Admittedly, they weren't her exact words but that was the gist of it.

"Oh did she indeed? Well the meal was nice I suppose and I did find out what went on at her training camp."

"You need to tell me everything," I say urgently and sitting back onto my bench.

"Not so fast. You owe me a date." Mike leans down to whisper in my ear. "I'll tell you at dinner. Pick you up at 7.30 p.m.?"

"Yes, fine I'll see you then." I feel all warm and fuzzy as I watch him walk out of the gym.

***

When I get home, I can hear Jared practising French in his bedroom. He's halfway through his online course and I must admit, is sounding rather good.

"*Bonjour Jared. Ca va?*" I call out as I reach his room.

"*Ca va bien, merci. Et toi?*"

"*Je suis bon, merci.*" I reply in my best French accent, and poke my head into his room. "I told Mum we would meet her for lunch or something tomorrow."

"Great. I hope she isn't going to tell us about her love life again."

"I wouldn't build your hopes up."

I spend the next few hours huffing and puffing and trying on every piece of clothing in my wardrobe. Other than stopping briefly for a cup of tea and a pot of cottage cheese and pineapple, I keep going until I have finally run out of ideas and clothes. I sit on my bed and look around at the mess.

"Did your wardrobe explode?" asks Meg, who has appeared in the doorway.

"Oh good, you're home. I need to find an outfit for tonight, please help me."

"I take it that the lovely Mike Diamond is not pissed off with the fact that you slept with Gary?"

"Megan! No he's fine. Well, not about the Gary thing but only because he doesn't know about it."

"So." she sighs, looking at the pile of clothes on the bed. "What have you come up with so far?"

"Nothing."

"Oh, well let's take a look."

We decide on my cream floaty dress, with tan wedges. Meg spends the next half an hour straightening my hair and by the time Mike arrives I am ready to go.

"Wow, you look lovely," Mike says, kissing me on the cheek.

"Thanks, come in I just need to get my bag."

Mike walks into the lounge to say hello to Jared and Meg who are playing a quick rematch on the Wii before getting ready to go out. Meg is going to the pictures with Luke and Jared is meeting Marcus at a nearby pub.

We arrive at 'The Fish Plaice, which I've never been to but I think is where my mum went with one of her dates. The sudden realisation that my mother and I are both dating two men at the same time and going to the same restaurant makes me feel rather nauseated.

A beautiful young girl wearing a black apron guides us to our seats and giggles when Mike makes a comment about the live lobsters in the tank. I grab Mike's hand as she shows us to a table in a quiet corner and takes our drinks order.

"So, what did Karen tell you about training camp then?" I ask, leaning my elbows on the table.

"Wow, you are keen aren't you?"

"Sorry, I'm just a little obsessed with this bloody competition."

"Well, she was up at 6.00 a.m. every morning to run and then do yoga before a breakfast of oatmeal and fruit — ."

"OK, I don't need to know the bloody menu," I say, sarcastically.

"Right, noted," Mike says slowly nodding his head. "She did mention that one of her trainers was Neil Whettenhall, whoever he is."

I nearly choke on the water I just sipped.

"Oh my God you're kidding! Well that's it, I may as well give up now," I exclaim, leaning back into my chair.

"Who the hell is Neil Whettenhall and why does the fact that he trained Karen make you want to give up?"

I lean forward again just as our wine arrives. I wait for the waiter to fill our glasses and take a sip before I begin.

"He's a world famous Australian fitness trainer who has completed the Iron Man Challenge ten times! He lives in Los Angeles normally but is obviously spending time over here for one reason or another. I don't think I can eat." I sigh, looking down at the tablecloth. After a few seconds of silence, I look up to see Mike trying not to laugh.

"It's not funny!"

"Wanda, you are so confident in some areas of your life and so insecure with regard to this stupid competition."

"It is not a stupid competition," I growl through gritted teeth. "It happens to be a big part of my career pathway. If I win, I'll become a Personal Trainer to some of the most famous people in the world. I could really make a difference."

"You mean you could make some actress bimbo's bum a bit higher? It's not exactly curing cancer is it? All I'm saying is..."

"Well at least I have a dream. You're running away from an ex-girlfriend to work in a local gym. It's not like you're single-handedly relieving the world of obesity related diseases!"

"Hey, Wanda, sit down. I didn't mean to belittle your dreams."

"Look, I'm sorry but this competition is making me a bit crazy. I need to focus and this ...," I wave my hands around, "whatever it is we're doing here, is not helping."

"What are you saying?"

"Listen, I think I'll just get a cab home. I'm sorry." I stand up and grab my bag off the arm of the chair. Mike just sits there looking shocked as I walk out of the restaurant. Poor Mike, he really doesn't deserve to see the lunatic in me this often. I can't wait until this competition is over.

I've only gone ten paces before I calm down and realise I may have overreacted. Pulling my bag onto my shoulder and taking a deep breath, I turn back towards the restaurant. My mind is whirring and I'm rehearsing my latest apology when I look through the window to see Mike and the good-looking waitress laughing together.

Chapter Twenty-Five

I'm feeling a bit deflated as I enter the flat. Meg and Jared are still out and it's too quiet. I can't help going over what happened in the restaurant. The more I think about it the more it occurs to me that I may have over reacted to avoid the awkward situation of spending the night with Mike. I open the fridge and look inside. There is nothing but Jared's cheese triangles, natural yoghurt and raw chicken breasts. I close the door without taking anything out and stare at Jennifer Aniston in her bikini.

"Who the hell are you looking at, skinny cow?" I rip her picture from the door and throw it into the bin.

I hear the doorbell ring and pull my head out of the cupboard, where I'm searching for Jared's biscuits. Who the hell can that be? I kick my shoes into the corner and open the door.

"Oh, Mike."

"Listen, you didn't give me time to apologise earlier," he says, holding up his hands in defence.

"I know, I'm sorry."

"Truce?"

"Truce." I step aside to allow him in.

"I don't know about you but I'm still starving. Shall we get a take-away?"

I am extremely hungry but take-away is like swearing at this crucial point in my training. I would offer to cook, but it is already 9.30 p.m. and I don't think that grilled chicken, brown rice and cheese triangles is exactly what Mike has in mind. He's already perusing the Chinese menu we keep on the fridge door. I never thought how bad that has been for poor Jennifer; she's better off in the bin.

"I'll just have plain chicken and boiled rice," I tell him, not even bothering to look at the menu. Having choices just makes things worse.

After dinner, I put a film on and we snuggle up on the sofa. For some reason, I feel really nervous. I'm not sure if it's because of Gary or because he is so gorgeous. I keep looking at him out of the corner of my eye. He could be a model with that perfect bone structure.

Just as the film ends, he catches me staring at him. He doesn't say anything, just smiles and pulls me onto his lap and plants his most perfect lips onto mine. I fall into his arms and just go with it. Thoughts of Gary are long gone.

We smooch on the sofa for half an hour before Mike suddenly stands, scoops me into his arms like he did in the gym and carries me into my bedroom. I get a twinge of guilt as I recall waking up with Gary yesterday. Oh my God, I'm a whore! What is wrong with me? Mike places me gently onto the bed and I quickly flick a pair of knickers I wore to work off the duvet and scrape them under my bedside unit with my foot. As I look up, Mike is standing at the end of my bed he grabs the bottom buttons on his shirt and rips them open! I stare in disbelief as he reveals his bare chest and amazing abs.

He grins and picks up his shirt. "Poppers," he says, pointing to the fastenings. "I thought they were buttons when I bought it. It's a bit Chippendale stripper but I thought it would make you laugh."

"Very sexy," I say laughing as he crawls towards me on all fours.

Sunday 12th August

"It's official. I'm a slut."

Meg puts a finger to her lips and closes the kitchen door. "That was really loud Wanda. Is he still here?"

"No he had to be at work early. Oh Meg I feel terrible," I moan as I dump myself into a chair.

"Why, was he rubbish?"

"No! I meant because I haven't slept with anyone in nearly two years and now I've managed to shag two blokes in two days. What the hell is wrong with me?"

"I hope you managed to change your sheets after last night."

"Megan!"

Meg sighs and goes to the kitchen draw. "OK, this is what we're going to do."

Oh good, Meg seems to have a plan for me. I wait with bated breath to see what she is getting out of the drawer. She turns to me holding a folded piece of paper and places it on the table. Meg smiles as she passes me the 'Pros' and 'Cons' list we wrote when I couldn't decide who I liked best.

"Right, we can finish this list of yours."

"What do you mean?"

"Well, you now have 'willy knowledge' of both candidates."

"Megan! This is not being helpful." I pick up a place mat and throw it at her.

"All right, well let's look at this in a practical way," she says seriously, switching on the coffee machine.

"Go on, but I'm not getting my hopes up here."

"Think of how many calories you used last night."

"Meg, you're not helping, but I did forget to tell you that I now weigh 9stone 5Ib."

"Oh, Wanda, that's great!"

"I know, I can't believe it."

"You should weigh yourself again today. You might have lost another pound after last night's bedroom aerobics."

"Don't be ridiculous. Just make the coffee."

I casually get up from my chair and slope off to the bathroom. Can't hurt to check.

***

Jared and I are meeting Mum for Sunday lunch at a pub near the park. It is a beautiful day and the garden tables are full of families and friends chatting. The entrance opens into an oldie worldly bar with a slightly sloping floor and a small restaurant to one side.

We have a table booked and I can see Mum is already here, cradling a large glass of wine. Jared and I glance at each other.

"Do you think this means she is going through some sort of drama?" Jared asks curling his lip.

"We'll soon find out."

Luckily, she smiles as we walk up to the table. We all exchange air kisses and I slide into the seat next to her.

"So, Mum, how's it all going with the dating scene?" Jared asks, nudging her hand on the table.

"Actually, it's rather fun; Dennis is refined and likes to take me to good restaurants and the theatre, and Tony is younger and likes doing fun stuff like bowling and concerts. All in all, I can't believe I have waited so long to get back out there."

"You go girl!" Jared says, and then looks up at the waitress who has just arrived.

I am dying to ask her if she has slept with either of them, but even though we have become closer recently, I don't think we are quite at that point yet.

"So, Mum." Jared leans forward after ordering our drinks, "Have you bonked any of them yet?"

I shoot a look at Mum who I'm sure is about to freak out, when she replies.

"Yes actually both of them."

I stare at her, eyes agog as she peruses the menu.

"What? Why are you staring at me Wanda darling?"

"Because Wanda has only had carnal knowledge of Gary this week and she can't believe that you are doing better than she is!" Jared says laughing into his glass.

"So you finally got to spend the night with Gary then?" she says enthusiastically.

"Yes, and Mike last night actually," I boast, unable to contain myself. Well I couldn't be out done by my own mother could I? Beating me at handstands is one thing but surely I should have the monopoly on the shagging front?

"I didn't know that." Jared says, sitting back on his chair and flinging his hands open.

"Darling, you don't have to lie to keep up with me. I just couldn't decide between them so I thought why bother? I've been on my own for long enough, why not have both."

Although I'm flabbergasted by the woman sitting next to me who I'm sure is not my mother, I cannot help but defend myself. "It's not a lie!" I protest. Jared didn't see him as he stayed over Marcus's house last night.

"Oh yes?" Mum raises her eyebrows over her wineglass.

"Yes, with about three others."

"Oh darling, we don't need details," she says screwing up her face whilst I wish we could just change the subject.

I steer the conversation to a less delicate subject, Dad's wedding. Surprisingly, Mum seems rather at ease with talking about it.

"So have you picked out a dress yet?"

"Yes, you would approve. I didn't show you because I didn't want to upset you."

"Guys, I'm sorry if I have been a bit bitchy about your step mother-to-be," she sighs and squeezes my arm. "It's just that I have never known anything but being with your father and I didn't know how to start a new life without him."

"Listen, Mum. I'm sorry we weren't as understanding as we should have been. You should have said something."

"I know darling but I needed to work it out myself."

"Well, it's about time you started enjoying yourself."

The rest of the meal was rather enjoyable and not our usual awkward lunch of trying to avoid certain subjects and not really talking about anything. We give Mum our flight details and she even says she would like to get a small wedding present for us to take from her.

"I think our mother is definitely going through a mid-life crisis," Jared whispers as we are leaving the pub.

"Well enjoy this new Nina for as long as it lasts. Let's face it; this was the most fun we've all had together since Dad left."

We promise to call Mum as soon as we arrive in Cyprus and she gives us each a big hug before getting into our cars and heading for home.

Wednesday 15th August

This week has been a little awkward at work. Mike and I have exchanged a few furtive giggles and I'm sure that Karen knows there is something going on between us. She's being even bitchier than ever and I'm really worried about what's going to happen if neither of us wins the competition, but I beat her in points. That would be like winning but without realising my dream of working in America. Actually, it would be more like winning but getting the much shittier prize of still working for someone whose life ambition is to make mine miserable, just because she can.

Luckily, I am now off work for a few days and although I freaked over it being so close to my competition date, it couldn't have come at a better time. Gary called me on Monday and asked to see me but luckily, I had to work Monday and Tuesday evening. I told him that I would be busy Wednesday so I haven't seen him since sleeping with him. It hasn't stopped him from texting me every day. Today's message read:

Hi babe, missing u this wk. Can't wait til u get back from Cyprus, Mum wants to have us over 4 BBQ. XX

Not only that, but Meg came home from a date with Luke and he told her that Gary is 'well loved-up'. Meg thinks the situation is highly hilarious. I haven't told her that yesterday Mike pulled me into the equipment cupboard and snogged me 'til my knees wobbled. It's all so confusing but I'll sort it out when I get home.

"Hi, Wand'," Jared calls as he passes my room with an armful of dirty washing.

I haven't seen him since Sunday as our shifts have clashed this week.

"Hi, Jay, I hope that isn't clothes you are taking to Dad's."

"Well, I haven't had time to wash them. Meg said she would do it but she didn't," he calls back from the kitchen.

"You lying toe-rag, Jared Mikos," Meg exclaims from the lounge, "you didn't tell me what you wanted washing. It's not like I didn't ask you ten times!"

I look at my list that I have prepared and there seems to be a lot on it. The most important is my bridesmaid dress. I can't resist trying it on, as it should fit even better now I've lost more weight. I take it off the hanger, undo the zip and pull it over my head. As I begin to zip it up, I realise that it feels quite a bit looser than before. Oh my God, where have my bosoms gone? The v-neckline was really flattering when I first tried it on, but now it just hangs off me. Originally, it was vintage chic; now it just looks like I raided my granny's wardrobe!

"Meg I need help!" I shout, staring at my reflection in the mirror.

Meg runs from the lounge and arrives with such force that she has to stop herself by swinging around my door jam.

"What's wrong?"

"Look." I open my arms to show her the dress.

"Oh dear."

"What the hell am I going to do? I can't wear this to my dad's wedding."

Meg walks around me looking pensive. "How much weight have you lost in the last couple of weeks?"

"Not much but don't forget I'm concentrating on losing body fat and gaining muscle. It doesn't show up on the scales as they counteract each other. I must have had a heavy carbohydrate day when I bought the dress."

"Let's not panic. I know what about a belt?" she suggests.

"So you think a belt is going to make my boobs big enough to fill this dress?"

"No, don't be silly, but it will pull in some of the material."

I sigh and decide that I have no choice. We are leaving tomorrow morning.

"What about this one?" Meg holds up a wide black belt.

"With natural colour wedges?"

"You could wear black shoes."

"With a blue dress? Meg you have to help me."

"Well, let's have a look at some others. This?" she holds up a thin metallic belt with tiny silver stars on it.

I make a face at her just as my phone rings. I secretly hope it isn't Gary or Mike.

"Oh hi, Mum. You OK?"

"Yes, I wanted to make sure you were in so I could pop over and drop your dad's present in."

"Yeah, no problem."

"What's wrong, darling. You sound fed up?"

"I just tried my dress on for the wedding and it looks stupid."

"Surely you tried it on when you bought it."

"Of course I did, but I've lost weight since then, all off my boobs by the look of this dress."

"Can't you get one of those bras with the chicken livers in," she suggests helpfully.

"I think you mean chicken fillets Mum and yes I could get one at the airport I suppose but that won't fix the fact that it's also swinging around my hips."

"Well I'm on my way. Don't worry, Gran taught me how to take in a dress."

"Really? Oh Mum you're a life saver."

I cannot believe the difference in my mum this year. If someone had told me last year, that she would be helping me with a bridesmaid dress that I was wearing for Laura and Dad's wedding, I would never have believed it. For the first time ever, the thought of moving to Los Angeles and leaving my mum, feels a little scary.

Chapter Twenty-Six

Thursday 16th August

"Jared I cannot believe you are still packing! You do realise we leave for the airport in half an hour." I look into Jared's room where he's standing over his luggage, most of his clothes still on the bed.

"I'll be ready, you just worry about yourself."

I double-check my flight bag; passport-check, money-check, perfume-check, camera and make-up-check. I drag my rather too large suitcase to the front door and have one last look at my list to make sure I have everything on it. Jared is still grabbing stuff out of the dryer when the doorbell rings.

"Jared, our cab is here, hurry up."

"Will you stop panicking woman? I won't let the aeroplane go without us."

"Just because you work for the airline doesn't mean you can control the take-off schedule. Now stuff that into your bag and make sure you have the tickets and your passport."

"Wanda darling, I'm never without my passport. Now let me take that and you take this one."

Jared gives me his bag, which is about two inches smaller than mine and picks up my suitcase. Meg is at work, so we leave her a note.

***

We arrive at Gatwick airport and I hear my phone ringing; it's Gary.

"Hello, you missing me already? I haven't left England yet."

"Actually I am missing you as I haven't seen you all week. Was beginning to think you were avoiding me."

"Don't be such a knumpty of course I wanted to see you but the only day I had time, you were busy."

"So you're going to miss me then?"

"Yes actually I am."

"You sound like that's a revelation."

He's right. I didn't realise it but I have missed his face this week and I would have loved him to have come to the wedding with me. "It is. And thanks for the pep talk about not trying to be Karen; it's really made a difference."

"Good, it's my job to remind you how great you are in times of doubt. Will you text me when you land so I know you arrived safely?"

"Will do. See you in a few days."

I suddenly feel very loved and protected. I wonder if Mike will ask me to let him know I arrived safely.

We check our bags in and head for Duty Free. I am standing in the perfume section sniffing various scents when I hear my phone bleep again, this time it's a text from Mike; his message reads:

Have fun at the wedding, wish I was coming with you,

we could join the mile-high club! ;-)

**

The warm air envelops me as we walk down the steps of the aeroplane onto the tarmac at Larnaca airport. Dad said he would be here to meet us so we make our way to baggage collection.

As we are waiting at the carousel, I notice a tall dark handsome guy who was sitting two rows behind us looking at me. I give him a half smile just as I feel a nudge from Jared.

"Seriously Wanda, don't you think you have enough problems?"

"Yeah all right, he smiled first."

"Oh well that's different, you must go and shag him immediately!"

"Jared!"

We both laugh and go back to watching for our luggage.

It's great to see Dad as we walk through the gate. As usual, he is wearing khaki trousers and a blue shirt; his smile bright against his tanned skin.

"Hello my darling. Ti kanete?"

"We are fine Dad, you look wonderful." I smile and give him a hug.

Jared hugs him too and they slap each other on the back. I can see the resemblance more than ever, but I don't mention it, as Jared is petrified about losing his hair; our dad is nearly bald.

"Come on," Dad says, picking up my bag, "Laura has made a special lunch for you."

My immediate reaction is panic. One of Laura's lunches probably consists of about two thousand calories. If I don't keep myself in check, I will ruin all my hard work in just three days.

The drive back to Protaras takes about half an hour or so. We take the coast road and I admire the beautiful azure blue sea whilst Dad tells me how skinny I'm looking. I feel a little sad as I notice the new hotels, shops and bars that have gone up since I was last here. Luckily, Dad and Laura live just outside the main town which has kept its traditional landscape.

By the time we arrive, wisps of hair have escaped my ponytail and formed a halo around my head; bloody humidity. Eventually, we drive up to the front of the house. The villa is large, square and whitewashed with lush hanging baskets and a 20ft pool. I can feel myself relaxing already. We are just getting our bags out of the car when Laura rushes out of the front door.

"Wanda! You look amazing. You're so skinny. Come on in you two, you must be starving." She ushers us all into the house. Laura is one of life's feeders, as far as she's concerned, everything is always fine as long as you have good food and wine.

The cool air conditioning is a relief as we step inside the front door that leads straight into the lounge.

"So Laura, are you excited about the wedding?" I ask, heaving my bag up the stairs.

"Oh yes, I can't wait. But there is just so much still to do, and of course your father is no help," she says, almost to herself.

I nod in agreement. "Yes, well men are pretty useless at that sort of thing."

Jared and I settle into our rooms whilst Dad pours some wine and Laura fusses about finishing the mammoth lunch she is preparing. Within 10 minutes, the lunch she has prepared has been laid out on the patio. It is a full Greek Mezze. There are dishes of feta salad, herby tabbouleh, lamb souvlaki, hummus and toasted flatbreads plus a pork dish, potatoes and grilled aubergines. Actually, I have forgotten how easy it is to eat really well here, it all looks fantastic.

"So, Wanda, did you manage to pick out a nice dress for the wedding?" Laura asks as she serves my dad with salad.

"Yes I did but I lost weight and Mum had to take it in for me last night."

"Oh no, did she mind?"

I notice Dad look over and wait for my reply.

"No, actually she has been really great recently."

"Yeah she's even dating two blokes at once," Jared pipes up.

I glare over at him as he scoops up more hummus with his pitta bread.

"Only joking." He laughs, trying desperately to back track.

Laura and I spend a few hours organising the flowers and going over last minute details. By 8.00

p.m. I'm shattered but I cannot allow myself to rest until I have done some form of training. I won't have time tomorrow and I can't afford too many days off at this stage, the competition is only nine days away.

"Jared, fancy a run on the beach?"

"Not really, but I need to work off lunch so I'll get changed."

We leave the villa and turn right down a man-made track for about half a mile and then take a left down the bank and onto the beach. The sun is still shining and the whole beach has an orange glow. I suddenly feel very free as we start to run along the water's edge. The feeling of euphoria grows as I gain speed. My stride increases and Jared is struggling to keep up. He glances across at me.

"Thought we were meant to be jogging not sprinting," he says gasping and trying to increase his speed.

"Race you!" I shout as I take off like I'm being pushed from behind.

Friday 17th August - THE WEDDING

It's the morning of the wedding and Laura is buzzing in the kitchen making breakfast. The actual wedding isn't until 2.00 p.m., but she decides that we should all be up by 7.00 a.m. Dad just follows along as usual and Jared just ignores the commotion and stays in bed. I feel as though I should be up helping Laura as I'm bridesmaid and pop in to remind Jared that he is best man so surely he should be up too.

By noon, the villa is full to the brim with family and friends. I'm running around organising drinks and trying to teach my cousin, Alkis, how to straighten my hair. and Jared is swanning about looking cool in his cream suit and white shirt, making all the girls laugh. I notice that the daughter of one of Laura's friends is flirting with Jared — another heart broken.

We leave for the chapel early in a convoy of eight cars. The journey from the villa to the mountains is long and bumpy, but the scenery is breathtaking. As we draw up to the chapel I cannot help but smile. It really is rather beautiful, nestling amongst the woodlands, the red wooden roof contrasting against the grey stone of the walls. There are slit windows and a small spire rising up from one end that also has a red wood roof. Laura has even organised tubs of flowers along the outside wall.

Dad and Jared arrived 10 minutes ago and we wait in the car for the rest of the guests to make their way inside.

I'm admiring the chapel, when, I notice two people in the crowd who shouldn't be here. It's Sergio and Teagan! I cannot believe what I'm seeing. I turn and look at Laura eyes agog.

"Oh my goodness, what is it. You look shocked?" she asks, panicking.

"Erm, those two people hanging around outside the chapel with the big camera. That's the TV crew that have been following me for the competition," I say slowly, still trying to figure out how the hell they got here. I am just about to apologise when Laura erupts into an explosion of tears.

"Oh Wanda how wonderful, my wedding is going to be on television." She hugs me, let's me go and hugs me again.

"Yes, well...you're welcome. Shall we get this thing started then?"

As we exit the car, Laura looks so happy. Teagan waves at me but stays behind Sergio who is filming us as we enter the chapel. I am dying to ask how they got here but it will have to wait.

The inside of the chapel is small with wooden folding chairs either side of the aisle, which is lined with, flowers in tall vases. My dad is standing at the front, wringing his hands and sweating profusely. His face relaxes into a smile when he sees Laura.

Sergio is not allowed to film the wedding inside the chapel but is waiting for us outside. After the ceremony, I leave Dad and Laura who are being congratulated by their guests and make my way over to Teagan and Sergio.

"Hello, guys. Can I just ask you a question?"

"Oh hi, Wanda you look great by the way," Teagan enthuses, placing her hand on my arm.

"Thanks, but how the hell did you get here?"

"We flew to Larnaca this morning then — ."

"No. I mean how did you know where the wedding was and why didn't you tell me you were coming?"

"But we called you a few days ago and Jared gave us all the information. Our producer thought that the wedding would film great and we could follow how you get on with the break in training so close to the competition. We did try and get here yesterday but couldn't get a flight."

Sergio wants to get some shots of the guests and wide shots of the chapel with the woodland surround, so I leave them to it and go and find Jared who is congratulating the bride and groom.

"Can I have a word?" I ask, pulling him away.

"What?"

I glance over at Sergio and Teagan who are busy filming the chapel. The penny drops and he pulls a face.

"Oh. I'm really sorry Wand' but I took a call for you and gave them the info. I thought you knew they were coming."

"Well I didn't."

"It's not my fault; I didn't see you all week. Besides, Laura is rapped about being on TV. She thought it was your idea."

"Yeah and that's great, but what is Mum going to think when she sees it?"

"Oh crap, I didn't think about that."

We make our way to the reception, which is in a nearby village where my aunt lives. It is a beautiful spot surrounded by mountains on three sides. Sergio wanders off to take some film of the area.

As soon as everyone has arrived, the women and some of the locals start setting out food and drink on the long tables which have been laid out in the town square. There is a buzz of excitement around the village that is catching and I am so glad to be here. I smile and take a deep breath as I look at my father who is trying to make sure everyone has a drink.

"It's really gorgeous here isn't it?" Teagan says as she takes in her surroundings.

"Yes it is," I reply looking around. "So, are you really going to put my dad's wedding in the show?"

"Yeah, we can splice it in with how you have to cope with your diet and training away from home so close to the competition. By the way how have you managed so far?"

I tell Teagan about my run on the beach and the wonderful lunch that Laura made yesterday.

"Sounds great, I wish we could have got here to film it. Perhaps we can do a quick interview later about what you choose to eat from all this lot." She waves her hand over the table.

"Actually, that might do me a favour as I do tend to go over the top with the old souvlaki and ouzo at these occasions."

"Great, I'll tell Sergio and we'll set it up for about 6.00 p.m., after the reception."

By 6.00 p.m., I'm pretty sure that the interview is not going to take place as Teagan has made friends with my cousins and they are all sitting around one end of the table playing drinking games. I see her wave at me as she stands up from the table and 'cheers' me with a tumbler of wine. I smile and nod my head as she makes her way towards me.

"I see you are enjoying yourself, Teagan. Hey look out!" I catch her as she walks straight into a wooden plinth that is holding the tarpaulin pole.

"Thanks Wanda. These cobblestones are a bugger aren't they?"

"Yes, and that was a big one."

"Your family are *sooo* lovely Wanda, you are very lucky. This is one of the best assignments I have ever had."

"I'm glad. Shall we do that interview in the morning?"

"Oh fuckit, I forgot about that. You know I hope you win the Main Event; you are much nicer than Karen. She has her head so far up her own bum she could eat her lunch twice!"

Teagan bends over laughing at her own joke.

"Oh and plus, you should hear what she said about you. With luck she'll fall on her skinny arse in the first minute of her routine and break it."

"What did she say about me?" I shouldn't ask but I can't help myself.

Teagan leans down to whisper in my ear and stumbles on the cobblestones. I grab her elbow to steady her.

"*Oops*, sorry, these heels aren't good on this surface."

"So what did Karen say about me then?" I try again.

"Oh yeah, she said you are built for body-building and don't really have the elegance it takes to pull off an aerobic dance routine. Plus, she said you like to party too much, so you would never be able to stay disciplined enough to be a trainer in LA."

"Oh did she really? That cow!"

"Don't worry Wand' I told her that we really like you. She backtracked after that."

As Teagan goes back to join my family, I try to decide what I'm angrier about; all that stuff Karen said about me, or the fact that maybe she's right.

Saturday 18th August

It's 9.00 a.m. and I'm up and ready for my run. The sun is already hot so I will keep it to an easy jog along the beach.

As I start down the bank, I see a figure standing on top of the dune a little way down the beach. He's in shadow as the sun is behind him. I am assuming it's a 'him' as the figure is quite sturdy looking with short hair. Unsure whether or not to continue my run, I look along the length of the beach, it's empty. I stop and look again at the figure that is now waving at me.

"Hi, Wanda, I've only been here a couple of minutes. Glad you made it," Sergio shouts from the dune. I completely forgot that I told him I would be running here about this time today. I wave back.

"Morning, Sergio. Sorry I wondered who you were."

"Just ignore me; I will get a better shot from up here. I would like to follow you back to the house afterwards if that's OK?"

"No problem." I wave back and start my run.

Luckily, Sergio and Teagan have to leave today, so after a few interviews at the house they set off back to England. I eat some left over chicken and salad from the wedding and decide to work on my tan. At least that's one thing I know I can do better than Karen; that woman looks like the aftermath of a vampire attack!

I spend the remainder of my time in Cyprus chilling out, eating healthy Mediterranean food and admiring how fabulous I look in my new bikini. The whole training and diet thing is getting easier each week, as it becomes more of a routine. Plus, seeing the results I'm getting helps too. As I sit at the edge of the pool dangling my lean muscular legs in the cool water, I start to think that maybe Karen is wrong; maybe I could cut it training celebrities in LA. I'm always telling my clients that they don't need to change themselves to get healthier, just some of their habits.

Sunday 19th August

Our flight is due to leave at 8.00 p.m., so Jared and I enjoy as much of the day as we can before packing to leave. I really hope Mum can eventually be as happy as Dad is. Laura has been really good for him.

"Well we're packed Dad." I smile and throw my arms around him as he sits in his favourite armchair.

"OK my darling. It's been lovely having you and Jared here," he says looking up at me and kissing my hand, which he is squeezing with his. "And I'm sorry that we had the wedding so close to your competition. I hope it hasn't ruined your chances."

"Actually, it couldn't have come at a better time."

"Why, what's wrong?"

"Oh nothing major, just man trouble."

"Oh, that's your mother's department," he says, making a face.

"That reminds me," I exclaim jumping up. "Mum has sent a wedding gift for you both."

Dad looks at me with a furrowed brow and scratches his head. I run up to get the gift which is a beautiful porcelain bowl big enough to hold plenty of fruit. Dad used to complain the one we had at home was always too small to hold enough fruit.

"Here." I hand it over and watch for his reaction.

He unwraps the bowl then smiles knowingly and nods his head. "Tell her thank you it's a lovely gift."

"What is?" Laura asks as she walks in from the patio.

Dad holds up the bowl. "It's from Nina. Sorry, I should have waited to open it."

"No, that's fine," she says taking the bowl, "it's lovely. Wanda, tell her thank you so much. It will be perfect for putting fruit in."

My father and I smile at each other and he hugs his new wife.

Chapter Twenty-Seven

Tuesday 21st August

I arrive at work tanned and toned to perfection. I wish Sergio and Teagan had arrived after I'd been to Cyprus so I could look buff and gorgeous in all my shots. Oh well. I spend the first hour at work telling Elliott and Zoe about the wedding and they tell me about how Karen has done nothing but recite stories of how hard it was training with the great Neil Whettenhall.

"I was a bit in awe," Elliot confesses. "I would love to train with him, but I tried my best to look bored."

"Well done Elliot." I pat him on the back as he wanders off to do a floor check.

"So Wanda, are you not seeing Mike anymore?" Zoe asks.

"I was never really 'seeing' him; why?"

"Some girl called Chloe has called him a couple of times since you went away."

"Oh. She's his ex-girlfriend or so he says."

"So, are you having a thing?"

I look at her and laugh. "To be honest Zoe I don't know what it is we're doing."

"Heads up." Zoe glances over my shoulder as Karen enters the gym. Her lips are set in a thin line and her hair is tied back revealing her skeleton-like bone structure.

"Wanda, I know you have clients this week, but I'm afraid you will have to train them outside of your shift times. We have a promotion on at the moment so the gym is going to be busy and we'll need all hands on deck."

"But what if I have already booked them in?" I protest.

"Then you will have to re-book them for another time. You can book them in your lunch break if you like," Karen announces whilst flicking through the appointment book at the desk and not even looking at me.

"Gee thanks," I mumble under my breath. She knows that I do my own training in my lunch hour. I think the competition is definitely on!

I spend the next hour trying to rearrange PT sessions with Vanessa, the Clamps and my doctors. I'm feeling decidedly unprofessional and pissed off when I make my way down to the studio where I know Karen is practising her routine. Mrs. Clamp can't change her time so I'm going to have to swallow my pride and be nice to Karen in the hope she'll let me keep her appointment.

As I peer through the window, I can't help but watch my skinny-arsed boss as she twirls effortlessly around on one very long leg, then drops into the splits. I don't want to disturb her, but I need to get back to Mrs .Clamp in the next 10 minutes as she's waiting for my call and is not a happy chicken. I slowly open the studio door; Karen doesn't see me so I walk a little way in. As she turns, she notices me and jerks with fright, loses her balance and whacks the back of her hand on the wall.

"*Jeesuus!*" she cries, hugging her hand to her chest.

"Oh my God, I'm so sorry Karen. I really need to speak to you but I didn't want to just barge in."

"Oh, so you decided to scare me to death instead. Couldn't you just knock?" She spits at me.

Her face looks even whiter than normal as she walks over to her towel and water.

"I did but you didn't hear me," I lie.

"What do want that can't wait anyway?"

So much for trying to be nice to her. "Mrs. Clamp is not happy that I can't see her at the arranged time. I think she'll want to speak to you if she can't keep it." This lying thing is coming a little too easy lately. I really must stop.

She begrudgingly agrees to let Mrs. Clamp keep her time and I go back to the gym to call her.

Karen was right, the gym is buzzing and we are all busy showing people around or teaching new members how to use the equipment. It's 5.00 p.m., before I get a chance to run downstairs to the café to grab a sandwich. I really need to get a training session in, but I can't train without having eaten all day. I'm sure this was Karen's intention all along. I really hate that girl!

After spending too long analysing the café sandwiches, I settle for a chicken salad and make my way back to the gym. Walking past Karen's office, I can hear her asking Mike if he is definitely going to the competition on Saturday.

"There is a hotel nearby if you prefer to stay over. It's quite a drive home otherwise," she says in her most girlie voice. "And I've booked a double room... you know if you need somewhere to stay"

What the hell makes her think he would want to spend the night with her? She's so rigid, I bet she would just lie there like a plank whilst he did push ups on top of her.

"I am coming. Hadn't thought about staying over but it sounds good to me," Mike says casually.

I cannot believe he said yes. What a complete wanker! I stomp my way back to the gym and struggle to eat my sandwich as it keeps getting stuck in my throat. Actually, the more I think about it the more pissed-off I become. Throwing the rest of my sandwich into the bin, I leave the gym office and head back downstairs. As I turn at the bottom of the stairs, Karen is walking toward the changing rooms. Then Mike leaves the front desk to go into her office so I take a deep breath and stride over. I walk in and Mike looks up and smiles.

"So, I hear you're going to stay over after the competition on Saturday."

"Yes, Karen did suggest — ."

"Well, I hope she's a bit less rigid in bed than she is normally. And FYI, see this?" I indicate my new colour. "It's an all over tan!"

Mike just stands there with his eyes wide and his mouth open. I turn away then stop and turn back. "And I suppose that sleeping with me was just something to do between dates with Claudia and Karen!" I shout.

Mike looks over my shoulder where Karen is standing behind me red-faced and furious. Oh poop.

"Wanda, shouldn't you be in the gym. And who the hell is Claudia?"

"Look, can we just..." Mike says throwing up his hands.

"Sorry, Karen, I meant Chloe; he's not-so-ex girlfriend." I snarl at Mike and walk out of the office.

As I'm leaving, Karen turns to Mike and I wait outside her office to hear what she says.

"So, my Health and Fitness Manager is sleeping with one of my gym staff. You do know I can have you fired for that?"

I suddenly feel bad that I may have just lost Mike his job. Karen closes the door so I have no choice but to go back up to the gym and perhaps hide in the equipment cupboard until it's time to go home.

I was intending to train before leaving tonight, but I just want to get home. As soon as my shift ends, I grab my bag and Elliot agrees to clear the gym for me. I promise to tell him tomorrow, why I'm avoiding Mike and Karen. As I get to the last step on the ground floor, I quickly check that neither of them are around and make a dash for the main doors. Unfortunately, Annie on reception calls out 'Goodnight Wanda' as I pass and Karen appears from nowhere.

"Wanda, can I see you in my office when you come in tomorrow?" She looks at me briefly before turning and striding off in the opposite direction. Great.

***

When I get back to the flat it's late but there is nobody home. I know that Meg will still be at work but I'm not sure where Jared is until I find a note to say that he is staying over at Marcus's house and Mum called.

I dump my sports bag in my room and check my phone. There is a message from Mike. I really don't think I want to read it, but I can't help myself. It reads:

What the Fuck was that all about? We need to talk. M

Oh crap. Everyone wants to talk to me and the two people I want to talk to aren't here. I open the fridge and see a piece of cheesecake covered in Clingfilm. Without even thinking, I reach for the plate, shut the door and grab a fork. Although it is a large portion, big enough for two, I hoover it up in about one minute flat. I then get some bread out and make my way through three slices of toast with peanut butter and jam.

Oh where is Ms Aniston when I need her?

Wednesday 22nd August

I open my arms to stretch and let out a relaxing yawn. Then I remember my outrageous behaviour yesterday and bury my head in my pillow. My dad has always told me that my temper would get me into trouble one day. I hate it when he's right.

There is lively chatter coming from the kitchen so I fall out of bed and pick my robe up off the floor and wrap it around me.

"Morning, guys," I manage through a yawn. "Whatever you're giggling about please tell me as I could do with a laugh."

I go to the cupboard and take out a mug for some coffee.

"I was telling Meg about a passenger we had on a flight the other day," Jared begins, "I was asking if she wanted any duty free and she kept screwing up her face and saying 'sorry?' So I repeated myself and she just looked at me and said 'I'm sorry but I can't hear a word you're saying.' So I pulled her earphones out of her ears and asked her again. She was really embarrassed as all the passengers were laughing. She forgot that she had them in; she thought she was going deaf."

I laugh and pour myself some coffee.

"Anyway, Wanda, why do you need cheering up this morning?" Meg asks.

I take a sip of coffee and relay the whole embarrassing story to Meg and Jared whilst they listen and make the appropriate noises.

"Oh, now I know what happened to my bloody cheesecake!" Jared announces as he sits up suddenly in his chair.

"Wanda you didn't?" Meg throws me a look.

"I needed it."

"But the competition is Saturday. You only need to focus for a few more days."

"No Meg! You don't understand. What if Karen was right? If I do manage to win this thing, I will have to stay this lean, like — always."

Meg looks puzzled for a moment as though she is thinking about what I just said. She looks up. "If you lived in Los Angeles, working long hours with actresses who have to watch everything they eat; plus the sun shining all the time, I think staying the way you are now would be easy. It was only university that threw you into plumpness anyway."

I chew the inside of my cheek whilst I consider this statement. "You know what Meg, you are absolutely right. Thanks babe."

"You're welcome. So, for the next few days, all you need to do is concentrate on yourself and the competition."

"Great idea, I think I'll tell Gary and Mike that I am unavailable for anything until Sunday. I won't see either of them. Well I might see Mike at work but I'll look busy and avoid him if I can."

"Ah," Meg says, looking at me and then at Jared who makes his 'oh dear' face.

"What are you two hiding from me?"

"Well, I think you ought to know in the light of recent information that Luke and Gary are going to be there Saturday as well. They wanted to surprise you."

"Oh my God, I can't believe this is happening! Bloody men ruin everything."

"I know," Jared says sympathetically, "It's not like you had a choice of whether or not to shag them both. Totally not your fault, Wand'."

I throw a place mat at his head. "Very funny, anyway I'm off to work."

***

I arrive at work and my first job is to take beginners' circuit class. Not my normal class, but I'm glad to do it as I may not get much chance to train again today. The class is mainly made up of mums and retired women who come to have some fun and feel smug that they can get through a circuit class. They rarely exit the studio soaking with sweat but love a natter and a coffee afterwards. Unfortunately, today may have to be different; I need a good workout.

"OK, ladies let's get started shall we."

After a brief warm-up, I show them what exercise they need to do at each station. Some seem to be glad of the change but others are a little miffed.

"Right, listen up. For the first circuit you will stay at each station for 30 seconds, we will eventually go up to 2 minutes on each station."

"Two minutes!" they protest in unison.

"Just do the best you can. You will never improve if you don't push yourselves."

I start the music and the fun begins.

Today, the circuit ladies leave the studio silent and heading for the showers. A couple of the young mums hang behind to tell me how much they enjoyed it. At least I have had some exercise as I took part in the whole class. As I head for the showers myself, Karen calls to me from reception.

"Wanda, don't forget that I want to see you in my office as soon as you are free."

"I haven't forgotten," I shout back and turn toward the changing rooms.

***

Karen is sitting at her computer when I arrive at her office. She doesn't look up as she tells me to sit down. Even I know that is an intimidation technique. I sit on the chair opposite her. Still she doesn't look up.

"I'll come back if you're busy," I say with a tight grin.

Karen stops what she is doing and gets up to close the door. I'm not scared of her but my heart is beating fast. I stretch my neck to one side then the other, trying to look relaxed.

"I have had a word with Mike about yesterday," she says sitting back down. "I'm not going to take any further action but you should know that any two staff members, who are in a relationship, will not be allowed to work in the same gym. One of you will have to go."

She glances away as she announces that last part and then turns her eyes back to me. I can't decide if she looks upset or constipated. Mind you, if she were constipated, she probably would be upset.

"You had better get back to work I think Elliot is really busy up there." She stands up, walks around the desk and goes to open the door.

"Karen," I start, tucking my hair behind my ear. "Sorry about my outburst yesterday. I don't normally do that sort of thing."

She holds onto the door handle and gives me a half smile. "It was very informative," she says with a nod of her head before opening the door.

"Oh OK."

Although glad to get out of there, I cannot help but wonder about her last comment. Has Mike been giving Karen the same old 'flannel' that he's been giving me?

Chapter Twenty-Eight

I wander back to the gym my brain in a whirl. What exactly has been going on between Karen and Mike? Am I stupid to think we had something more than just casual sex? I push open the gym door and am greeted by Mrs. Clamp and her daughter Fiona.

"Wanda, at last, we thought you had gone home," Mrs. Clamp says, rushing towards me.

"No, I just finished a class. Sorry if I'm a bit late. Are you ready to go?" I smile enthusiastically.

The next hour, I encourage the Clamps to push themselves beyond their comfort zone, which is more like a parking zone. They leave feeling as though they have achieved something and I give them a programme to follow for the next week.

"I can see that those two are losing tons of weight," Elliot says as I walk up to the desk.

"Really?" I ask, watching them leave.

"No!" He laughs. "Have you seen them train when you're not here? They make my nana look positively athletic!"

"*Ha ha* very funny. Oh shit," I exclaim, looking through the appointment book.

"What?"

"I forgot that I have Vanessa coming in tonight. I couldn't see her on shift so now instead of going home at 6.00 p.m.; I have to hang around until 6.30 p.m. I won't finish here until 8.00 p.m., and then I have to do my own training."

"Maybe Karen's idea was to not give you time to train or eat."

"I think you're right."

"That could be the only way she has a chance against you in the competition," Elliot says, leaning on the desk.

"*Ahh*, thanks for assuming I can beat her."

"It's a no-brainer Chicki."

The gym is throbbing with house music, the clashing of weights and friendly banter between members. This is when I love it most, being able to walk around and help people achieve their fitness goals by giving them my expert opinion. It's a fun place to work, especially with Elliot and Zoe. That is until Karen strides through the door.

"Wanda, could I see you a sec?"

Jesus, not again. What is her problem? I follow her to the gym office.

"I have a Mr Hart, who wants a personal training consultation," she starts.

Great, a bit of good news for a change.

"Unfortunately, he can only get in tonight so I told him you could probably stay on after your shift and see him."

And there it is, the bad news.

"I've already got to stay after shift to see one of my other clients I can't really..."

"Well that's perfect then. I'll call him back. He'll be here at 8.30 p.m." With that, she swings around and flounces out of the door.

I am left standing in the office dumbstruck with my mouth still open. It looks like she has won again. I won't have time to train. I really hate her. I hope her skinny legs eventually snap and go up her arse!

By 10.30 p.m., I'm home and ready for bed. I would prefer a pizza and then bed but as that's not an option, I settle for my pj's and a pillow. Checking my phone I have another missed call from my mum. I really must call her, and Gary has left me two messages. I didn't tell him I would be working late so he's probably wondering where I am. I can't be bothered to talk to anyone so I text him back.

Worked late. Can't see you til Sunday.

Sorry but need to concentrate on training and study for competition.

I am missing u though.

Wil cal u tom. X

Within seconds I get another text.

Ok but if you want a study partner I'm your man!

Miss you too. Sleep well xx

I read his message and smile before turning off my phone and flopping into bed.

Thursday 23rd August

I'm not at work until 2.00 p.m. today so can at least make get some training and studying done. I make myself some egg whites and toast for breakfast and squeeze a tiny blob of ketchup on the plate. My phone is on the table and I remember I still haven't spoken to my mum about the television crew being at the wedding, so as soon as I finish breakfast, I give her a call.

"Hi, Mum, it's me."

"Oh hello, darling, I've been trying to speak to you for days."

"Sorry, I've been working non-stop since we got back."

"Yes Jared said you were working more and trying to train in between."

"Yeah, but it hasn't been easy."

"It will soon be over. Anyway, Jared seemed to enjoy your father's wedding. Did you give Dad my gift?"

"Yes and he loved it. And Laura thought it would be great to hold lots of fruit. That made me and Dad smile."

"Well he does love his fruit. I'm glad they liked it. How was your dress?"

"Much better since you took it in. Listen Mum, I need to tell you something."

"That doesn't sound good. What's wrong?"

"I would like to point out that I didn't know and it was really Jared's fault because he should have told me and didn't."

"Wanda will you please stop rambling and tell me for goodness sake."

I take a deep breath and get ready for her to freak out.

"Dad's wedding might be on the documentary about the competition." I grit my teeth and wait.

"What do you mean; I mean, how did they know about it or where it was?"

"In a word JARED. They rang and Jared took the call. He gave them all the flight details et cetera and I didn't know a thing about it until they turned up at the chapel."

"Oh well, that will be nice won't it?"

She sounds sad as she says it and I feel terrible.

"I doubt it will feature at all. They'll probably just use the bits with me in. Anyway, how are things with you, Dennis and the other one?"

"Tony darling, they are both fine but I have had to choose as I couldn't keep up the pretence any longer. I was lying for a living! It was too much like hard work. I'll leave that to you youngsters."

"Well it isn't any easier when you're younger, believe me. So who did you pick?"

"Tony, the younger one as he's more fun and that's what I need right now. How about you?"

"Well," I sigh. "Gary is being lovely and Mike is seeing his ex-girlfriend and my boss, so I may have to go with Gary."

"Oh dear. Which one is Mike?"

"Also my boss."

"Ah, well it's probably easier if you just stick with Gary. I liked him anyway."

I spend the rest of the morning at the leisure centre where my picture is now everywhere and I am constantly stopped by staff and members who want to know how I'm getting on. It's really lovely, but I don't have time today. In fact so many people stop me, I'm convinced they've been hired by Karen to interrupt my training.

Finally, I get home in time to get showered and changed for work. I decide to take my books in to work with me. With a little luck, I can sneak in some studying behind the gym desk. I'm not sure if Mike is in today but if I see him walk through the gym door, I may hide. We still haven't spoken since my outburst. Actually, I would really like to know if anything has been going on between Mike and Karen before I speak to him. If he has been getting 'jiggy' with her, I can stand my ground and feel morally justified in my actions. If however, he professes his undying love for me and wouldn't touch Karen with a sweaty mat, I may have some crawling to do.

***

By 5.00 p.m. the gym is starting to get busy and my ducking under the desk to revise percentages of One Rep Maximums is starting to attract attention. I haven't ventured downstairs since I arrived and have not seen Mike or Karen.

"Hi, Wanda, how's your competition thingy going?" Zoe asks as she bounces up to the desk.

"Not bad. I can't wait to eat a large pizza though."

"Perhaps we can all go to a pizza place after the show. Will you know on the night if you have won?"

"Yeah, they announce the winner right at the end. If I haven't won, I may need a large bowl of ice-cream to go with that pizza."

"Stop worrying, you're gonna be great. I'll cheer really loud to keep you going."

"Thanks mate, I appreciate that." I smile and give her arm a squeeze.

"Anyway, I heard that you and Mike had a big row the other day. — so give."

I relay the sordid details to Zoe and she makes appropriate faces at the appropriate places. Just as I get to the end of my story, Mike Diamond walks into the gym. I assume he has been in some sort of meeting as he's wearing a shirt and tie with dark trousers. His dirty blond hair is framing his angular face; I really wish he wasn't quite so handsome. As I look up, he catches my eye and I debate for a second whether or not I have time to duck behind the desk. Too late, he walks towards me. I glance around hoping Zoe is still here, but she has gone over to the free weights talking to some guy.

"Hi." Mike smiles as he reaches the desk.

"Hi, I'm erm sorry I haven't replied to your text. I know I was out of line the other day," I say, suddenly feeling hot and wiping an imaginary fringe from my eyes.

"Yes, you do tend to say whatever is on your mind without thinking it through first."

"Yes, well sometimes I'm justified!" I retort, not meaning to sound quite so sarcastic.

"Well you should have got your facts straight," he says, sounding a little superior.

He is about to say something else when Zoe comes back.

"So, are you all ready for the big competition Saturday?" he says lightly, trying to change the conversation.

"I suppose so. Karen has been even more of a bitch than usual, although I suppose she has her reasons."

"I won't be able to cheer you on I'm afraid, I have to work as the guy that was covering for me has been taken ill."

Once again when it comes to Mike Diamond, I cannot decide whether or not I'm relieved or gutted.

Zoe, Mike and I just stand there and look at each other for a second or two before he excuses himself and makes his way back downstairs.

Friday 24th August

It's the day before The Main Event, and my tummy is all over the place just thinking about it. Luckily, Meg knows me so well that she has taken the day off and we're going to go to the leisure centre for a quick run through, then lunch at the Coffee Snob and a chick flick before bed.

As soon as we walk into the leisure centre, I can't help but look around to see if anyone wants to chat to me. To be honest, I could use the encouragement today.

Trevor the manager sees us as we approach the gym hall and rushes up to greet me. "Wanda, great to see you. All ready for the off tomorrow?" he says, enthusiastically grabbing my shoulders.

"Yes I think so. Just having a last run through of my routine and then I'm relaxing for the rest of the day."

"Good for you. Now, Meg did mention you might be here today so I was wondering if you would allow a few kids who are interested in what you're doing to watch?" he says, hopefully.

"Oh erm yes, I don't see why not. It'll prepare me for tomorrow."

The second I say 'yes', Trevor waves his hand to someone along the corridor and a stream of children pour out from the main hall followed by the teacher I met here before.

"Hello, good to see you again," he says as he props the door open for the children.

"Thank you so much for letting them watch you're a celebrity in our school, they may ask for your autograph."

"Oh dear; no pressure to win then."

I am slightly embarrassed by the attention but must admit to getting a buzz every time I see the posters with my name, and now face, on them.

Luckily, my routine is seamless and I get a spontaneous round of applause from the children who jump up from the floor and rush over to see me. I spin around looking at them all. I feel a bit like Fraulein Maria in *The Sound of Music*.

"Thank you guys, I appreciate you watching and I'm going to come and talk to you in your class after the competition."

"Great, will you bring your trophy?"

"I will if I win."

"You will, miss."

"Miss?"

"Yeah, you'll win miss, my brother fancies you by the way!"

"Really? How old is your brother?"

"Twelve miss. He thinks you're smokin'."

I turn to look at Meg who is laughing. "Don't even think about it Wanda, you have enough problems."

"Meg, that's sick."

The children leave the hall and I leave the leisure centre on a high and ready for the competition tomorrow.

Chapter Twenty-Nine

COMPETITION DAY

It's 8.00 a.m. and the flat is buzzing with excitement and nerves. Meg and Jared are crashing around in the kitchen trying to organize breakfast and coffee but I don't think I can eat.

I eventually force down a tiny bowl of porridge and a protein shake before doing a final check that I have everything including my music.

"Nervous, sis?" Jared asks as he sees me staring at my sports bag.

"Just a bit. I'm checking my bag."

"You've checked it ten times already. Come on; let's do a bit of yoga before we go, it'll relax you."

"Good idea, Jay."

We manage some deep cleansing breaths and a couple of Sun Salutations before Meg pokes her head around the lounge door. "Right, we'd better get going in case we hit traffic."

"It's show time!" Jared declares in his best Jack Nicholson voice.

We set off with Meg driving to The Hallop Centre where the competition is being held. It's about 90 minutes away and we plan to get there by 9.30ish. I have to be there early as the interviews; Personal Trainer session and knowledge rounds are first. The aerobic dance section doesn't start until 3.00 p.m. Mum and Tony are going to get there for 2.00 p.m.; I can't wait to meet him.

We arrive at the centre and park up. It is an old yellow brick building, with intricate details in the cornices. We walk up the wide steps to the double doors and make our way to the reception desk. The reception area was obviously plush once but the patterned carpet is now threadbare and the gold painted coving is rather dull.

"Are you here for the competition?" The woman behind the desk asks.

"Yes, my name's Wanda Mikos."

She hands me a sheet of paper. "Here, this is your schedule. Please make sure you are available at those times and make your way to the appropriate venue 5 minutes before your time."

The Knowledge

My first test is the knowledge section. We all take this part together and it's the first time today that I've seen Karen. There are about twenty competitors and I have chatted to a few, which may have been a mistake as most of them have competed in this competition before. They all have the advantage of knowing the ropes and what the judges are looking for.

The questions on the sheet are straightforward, for me anyway. I'm pretty sure that Karen won't fly through it as easily. I sneak a peek over to her when I finish and she looks troubled. After talking to the other guys, my only ambition at the moment is to beat Karen in points. I think winning this thing is just a dream for the future.

The Interview

The interview is conducted by Patsy Cosby and Rae Flynn; two of the owners of Move Makers. I'm sitting opposite them in a casual space in an office with a large window where the sun is streaming through. There is no desk between us which makes me feel a little more relaxed.

"So, Wanda, what made you want to take part in The Main Event?" Rae asks leaning forward in her chair.

"Well, I love being a Personal Trainer it's all I ever wanted to be. Apart from that time I wanted to be The Queen." I pause for laughter. There is none. "Plus, I want to live in LA where the sun shines and it's not a chore to eat salad."

Patsy laughs at last. "OK, well thank you Wanda for your honest reply. We usually get the same answer from everyone and it always sounds rehearsed."

"To be honest, I did rehearse a speech but I can't remember a word of it."

This seems to tickle both of them. They gather themselves and continue with their questions.

The rest of the interview is an easy chat about training and my future ambitions. Rae and Patsy are really easy-going and not as scary as Karen made out. What a shocker!

Personal Training Session

There is already a gym in the building, which I think they have added to, as I can see where new equipment has been squeezed in amongst the old. This section of the competition will involve taking one of the instructors for a short PT session based on the information they give us.

They have brought one of their trainers with them to help with the judging. He is tall, swarthy and very muscular; I really hope I don't get him. I look around and start to flap my elbows as I can feel the sweat starting to stick. Just as I finish my chicken impression, I turn to see Patsy walking towards me. I'm relieved that it's not the hunky bloke.

"Right, Wanda. I am going to give you a scenario and I would like you to tell me what exercises you would give me and which you would avoid. I would then like you to take me through how you would start, including the static and dynamic fitness tests. Do you understand?"

"Absolutely, no problem," I reply, discreetly raising my arms.

Patsy tells me she is a 45-year-old female who has had recent surgery on her right knee. I explain how I would take her static tests before her dynamic tests and then ask her more about her injury. She looks impressed as I note down exercises I will avoid and exercises, which will help strengthen the area around the knee.

"I'm going to start you on the recumbent bike and check your heart rate."

"Good. What programme are you going to put me on?"

I take her through a warm-up programme and check if her knee is hurting.

"That's great, Wanda. What amount of weight would you give me and how many sets and reps?"

I'm feeling more confident as I show her how to perform each exercise and test her power maximums. As she gets off the chest press machine, she writes something on her clipboard whilst nodding her head. I take this as a good sign.

"Well, you seem to be very thorough, Wanda. If you could just take me through a cool down, I think we can finish there.

As we move to the matted area to perform some cool down stretches, I notice that the hunky bloke is taking Karen for her test. She's wearing a grey top and her pit stains are creeping down to her waist! I can't help but hope she's a bit stinky by the end of her session.

I'm feeling much better since completing three quarters of the competition. And since catching Karen red-faced and sneaking a sniff of her underarms.

We've taken a break for lunch, so I'm going to make my way back to the cafeteria to meet Jared and Meg. I quickly change my top before taking the stairs with some of the other competitors to the 'The Lunch Spot'.

"OK, guys, I'll see you all back in the changing rooms at 2.00 p.m.," I say to two of the girls as I turn towards the back of the cafeteria where Meg said she would be sitting. I look around at the stark white interior with cheap prints hanging on the wall. It reminds me the café at Uni. Ugly with no atmosphere. I spot Jared who is standing to take off his jacket. He's laughing and pulling his shirt out of his jeans. It's then I notice who he's with; Gary and Luke. I didn't think they were going to turn up. Or was I hoping?

"Hi, guys," I say, standing at the end of the table, "where's Meg?"

"Getting drinks, I'll go and give her a hand," says Luke.

Gary stands and offers me his seat before kissing me on the cheek. "How's it going so far?"

"Really well I think. Unfortunately, a lot of the other competitors have entered before so they do have the advantage."

"That doesn't mean you won't win." Gary says before kissing my nose. I know you can do this Wanda, you've worked so hard to get here."

He really is the nicest guy in the world and I'm glad he's here.

***

By 2.00 p.m., the butterflies are back and I'm milling around with the other contestants in the changing rooms. I notice Karen who looks up and smiles at me. I decide to go over and wish her luck as she has been picked out of the hat to perform her routine first.

"Hi, Karen, how are you feeling?"

"Nervous as hell — you?"

"Crapping myself actually. You know how clumsy I am; I'll probably misjudge the space around me and throw myself into the crowd," I joke, taking a seat next to her on the bench.

"Do you want to hear the best tip I was given?" Karen asks as she turns towards me.

"Absolutely!" I can't believe she's being so nice to me

"Look for people you know in the audience; they'll give you a confidence boost."

"Oh, actually that is good advice. Thanks Karen."

I'm just about to say something encouraging to her when we both look up as we hear the screeching of the Tannoy. *Will contestant number one please make her way to the stage entrance?*

I look at Karen and touch her arm. "Good luck."

"Thanks, you too. What number are you?"

"Seven," I reply, nervously.

"Well I'll be back out the front by then so I'll be watching you." She smiles as she gets up and walks away.

Did she just say that to make me more nervous?

I manage to sneak around to the stage entrance to watch Karen's routine. After seeing her elegantly spin, leap and pose with such perfection, I rather wish I hadn't. The theatre erupts in an explosion of applause as she performs her final balance, which she holds perfectly. Oh poop.

I watch the next couple of contestants whose routines are so well choreographed they make mine look amateurish by comparison. By the time my turn arrives, the butterflies in my tummy have turned into angry bats and I'm sure my legs are going to give way before I even start.

***

Well who would have believed that Karen was right? — Nobody, because she lied. When you stare into the audience, the lights on the stage are so bright that not only can you not see your friends but are rendered blind for the next few seconds.

I oscillate from wide-eyed to blinking in an effort to establish where I am. It takes a few moves but I get my routine back on track and the smile back on my face. The crowd begin to cheer and a feeling of exhilaration propels me into my flick-flack with such force, I wobble on landing but instead of falling over, I perform an impromptu forward roll to standing where I raise my arms to indicate the finish of my performance.

I'm buzzing with excitement as I return to my family and friends in the audience who all come up to congratulate me.

Mum pushes through everyone to give me the biggest hug "Oh my goodness, Wanda you were wonderful. I didn't know you could do those things. I'm so proud of you."

"Thanks Mum." I smile and look across at the man she is with.

"Hello there, I'm Tony," he says, shaking my hand.

"Oh sorry darling I got carried away," Mum blubbers.

"Nice to meet you, Tony."

"You were amazing by the way," he says looking impressed.

"Thanks."

Jared and Meg are close behind with their hugs of congratulations and I notice Gary patiently waiting his turn. He eventually pushes past the chairs to get to me before scooping me up in his arms.

"Told you, you would be amazing didn't I?"

"Thanks, I really enjoyed it actually."

"Well I think you are a dead cert to win."

"You may be bias. I was good but I'm not sure I was good enough."

"We'll soon find out."

I spend the next couple of minutes with the guys from the gym who agree that my routine was so much better than Karen's. We settle back into our seats before the next contestant arrives on stage. I am sitting in the aisle seat next to Gary and look over at Karen who is texting on her phone between talking to her mother. She doesn't congratulate me. I am not sure if Karen intended to sabotage my performance with her advice but she could have at least said 'well done' even if she didn't mean it.

The next contestant falls over twice and Meg and I give each other sneaky looks which say, *ahh* that's too bad, but *hoorah*, one less competitor to beat. By the end of the show, I'm feeling great.

It is 6.00 p.m. before they are ready to announce the winner of the competition and all I can think of was how long until we hit the local pizza restaurant.

I even have my toppings all worked out; pepperoni, peppers, mushrooms and olives.

"You nervous, Wand'?" asks Meg as we fidget in our seats.

"No, not really, just hungry."

Meg laughs and nudges me. "You do know you could win this don't you?"

"Megan, I am under no illusions with regard to who is going to win this competition."

"Who?"

"Anyone but me," I say with sigh. "They are all so lean compared to me, and did you see how professional their routines were? I know Karen had help at the camp but I reckon all the other contestants had some sort of professional help too."

"Well, keep your chin up. It's not over 'til the fat lady sings."

"I'm not bloody singing as well!"

"Wanda Mikos, how can you have such confidence in Wii bowling – which you're crap at – and no confidence in this?" Meg whispers, indicating the arena. "Besides, it's not all based on the routine; don't forget the other three sections of the competition."

"You're absolutely right Meg, I *could* win this thing. In fact, the next 10 minutes could change my life. I could be leaving here with the knowledge that in two months' time; I will be off to Los Angeles."

Meg nods her head as we look up at the stage where Patsy and Rae are about to give their speech and announce the winner.

And the winner is — Karen Lester.

Chapter Thirty

"Congratulations Karen!" I smile, give her a hug and try to sound as genuine as possible. In fact, I squeeze her so tight, I have to release my grip when she starts making groaning noises and coughing.

"I thought you were going to suffocate me then," Karen says, looking slightly dazed.

"Oh I'm sorry I'm just so excited for you."

"I'm sure," she says before being whisked away by Rae to get her pictures taken.

***

By 10.00 p.m., I have managed to stuff down a whole pepperoni pizza, hot fudge sundae and about 12 units of alcohol. My mother is — what she would call — tiddly and Zoe has taken to bitching about Karen rather too loudly. Luckily, Karen is sitting at the other end of the table and hasn't noticed.

"I think we had better get you home soon," Gary says, putting his arms around my waist and kissing me on the lips.

"OK, Gary old chap, but I need to use the loo first." I stand up slowly and scan the restaurant for a 'Toilet' sign.

I'm washing my hands when I look up and see Karen in the mirror. She has just exited the toilet next to mine.

"Hi, Wanda, enjoy your pizza?"

"Yes thanks, did you?"

"Oh, I didn't have pizza, I had the chicken salad," she says through a smile.

What a bitch! Any other girl in the world would have dived headfirst into a pit of shit and chocolate after what we've been through. No wonder other girls don't like her — she's not normal.

I'm about to leave when she looks across at me from the hand dryer. "So who's that bloke you're with?"

"Who, what, what bloke?"

"The good looking tall guy with the floppy hair; the one you were kissing." She stops drying her hands and waits for my reply. Quick, Wanda think.

"Megan's brother."

"He's cute. I assumed it was over between you and Mike anyway."

I look at her puzzled before she continues.

"You know, now that he's back with Chloe."

I feel my bottom jaw drop as Megan bursts through the door.

"Wanda my girl, you need to hurry up, Gary wants to make a speech."

I'm still thinking about Karen's last comment when she stops and turns to Meg.

"So Megan, what do you think about Wanda and Gary? He seems really nice."

"Well I'd give him one." Megan blurts out before giggling to herself and backing out of the toilet.

Karen eyes widen and her lips curl at this comment. "*Eeww*, that puts a whole new meaning on brotherly love," she says before following Megan into the restaurant.

Once I am safely back in my seat, Gary stands up and taps his spoon on his beer glass to gain the attention of the table.

The clattering and chatting stops and everyone faces him. He looks slightly embarrassed and clears his throat.

"I would just like to make a toast to two great athletes who have worked their butts off to get here today," he raises his glass, "To Wanda and Karen."

Everyone joins in by cheering and banging on the table.

Gary continues. I wish he would sit down.

"I would also like to say congratulations Karen on winning the competition, I know Wanda thinks you a worthy opponent and we all wish you luck in your new adventure."

No we don't. We wish she choked on her chicken salad and nobody in the room knew how to perform the Heimlich manoeuvre.

Monday 27th August

I know I should have taken the day off today but my shift didn't start until 2.00 p.m. and I may have wanted to gloat if I'd won. Unfortunately, Karen is also in this afternoon, so I'm going to have to watch her gloat and basically suck-it-up with a smile on my face.

I'm about to leave the gym office when I am accosted on the gym floor.

"There she is, star of stage and gym...Wanda Mikos!" Mike picks me up and kisses me as he swings me around.

I can't help but look around furtively to see if anyone is watching. Karen obviously hasn't mentioned Gary to him yet. And I can't ball him out about Chloe as not only would that make me two-faced, but it could be another of Karen's lies.

"I heard you were great," he says grinning at me.

"Yeah but Karen was better."

"Well look on the bright side, she'll be gone and you can try for promotion by sleeping with the new boss."

"*Eeww*, what if it's a woman."

"I meant me you idiot." Mike looks directly into my eyes which makes my heart flip but I think it's more nerves this time. Let's face it; we are both as bad as one another. Unless, of course, he's not back with Chloe then it's just me again.

I spend the next few hours answering questions from members about the competition and trying to stop the smile on my face from becoming a grimace when we mention Karen's victory. The only thing that makes me feel better is that everyone is glad she won and not me, as they want Karen to leave the gym.

Friday 31st August

Meg and Jared have been great since the competition, they haven't mentioned it once. Gary has been calling and texting every day as he's been working in Scotland and feels bad he can't be here. I'm rather glad, as I hate people clucking around me.

Mum has invited Jared and me to dinner with her and Tony, and Mike has asked me out for dinner tonight.

So, to recap; I'm not going to fulfil my dream of working in LA, Karen has bested me like Mr Polly's Poodle — long story — and I'm now stuck in a love triangle, which is about to explode in my face. I need cheesecake.

***

As I'm not at work today, Meg and I take a trip to the leisure centre. We walk in to a very warm welcome from the staff and some of the members. They treat me like I won the competition, which is a great feeling after listening to Karen brag all week.

"There she is our conquering hero." Trevor the manager comes over to greet me in the juice bar.

"Hi, Trevor, not quite conquering but I did my best."

"You're still a hero to us young Wanda. Listen I have just been speaking to Mr. Rice, headmaster of the local school and he asked if you would be able to go and talk to the children about the competition next week?"

I look at Meg who is nodding her head at me. "Of course I can. I'll check my work schedule and give you a call later."

"Marvellous, marvellous, I'll get back to him." Trevor squeezes my shoulder and strides off to reception.

"I suppose it won't be so bad," I sigh, looking around the centre.

"What won't be?" Meg asks.

"Teaching aqua aerobics and keep fit to the over fifties."

Meg looks at me with a furrowed brow. "Wanda, what are you talking about?"

"Well this is where I'll probably end up isn't it? Whilst Karen is in America training the beautiful people and taking classes on the beach."

"OK, you know what we need?"

"What?"

"Cocktails at Povkas."

"I'm meant to be going to dinner with Mike." I sigh unenthusiastically.

"Do you want to go to dinner with Mike?"

"Not really, he probably knows about Gary by now anyway."

"Does he know that you know about Chloe?"

"Doubt it — anyway I'm not exactly Mary Poppins in this scenario and what if I go mad again and find out Karen is lying?" I rub my hands over my face and look at Meg.

"So what should I do?"

"Do what you normally do."

"What?"

"Get pissed and worry about everything tomorrow."

I try to look horrified. "OK, good plan."

"Come on, let's go home and we can decide what to wear."

Reluctantly, I finish the last of my smoothie and drag myself out of my chair. I think I'll text Mike to say I can't go out, just in case he does know about Gary.

***

By 7.00 p.m., I'm glad I decided to go out with Jared and Meg instead of Mike. I need fun and friends, not butterflies and bonking. Well, not tonight anyway.

"Wanda, have you seen my cream top?" Megan asks as she runs past my bedroom.

"It's in the ironing."

"Thanks babe."

"Phone's ringing," Jared shouts from his bedroom.

"Bloody answer it then!"

"Can't, I'm under the bed."

Although totally curious as to why Jared is under his bed, I run to answer the phone.

"Hello."

"Hello, is that Wanda Mikos?"

I'm about to say 'No she died' which is our standard answer to cold callers, when her accent stops me; she's American. "Yes, can I ask whose calling?"

"Hi there, Wanda, it's Patsy from Move Makers."

There are about a thousand things running through my head. My heart is beating so loudly that I have to press the phone hard against my ear. "Oh erm, hello." I want to ask her what she wants but I just wait for her to speak.

"I don't know if you realise this but the competition was very close; Karen won mainly based on her routine, which was excellent."

"Yes it was," I say sounding as upbeat as I can.

"After the results, both Rae and I couldn't stop talking about you. Your collective scores on the P.T tests were ninety-eight percent."

"Really?"

"Yes, we both think you're an excellent Personal Trainer. In fact, with regards to knowledge, people skills and personality, you were our favourite contestant."

"Oh, thanks."

"Well let me cut to the chase; Wanda, we are going to do something we have never done before. We are going to offer you a place with us in LA for one month. This would mean you arriving the same time as Karen, we'll show you the ropes and see how you get on. What do you think?"

"Are you serious?!"

"Absolutely — so, shall I tell Rae you're coming?"

"Hell yes!" I shout down the phone, bringing Jared and Meg into the lounge to find out what the commotion is about.

Patsy laughs on the other end of the phone. "I'll send you the details, good to have you on board Wanda."

"Thank you, thank you, thank you, I can't believe it."

"You're welcome, we'll see you soon." Patsy hangs up the phone and I turn around in shock to see two expectant faces staring at me.

"Well?" Jared and Meg shout in unison.

I speak slow and deliberate so we can all take it in. "That was Patsy from Move Makers; they love me. They want me to go to LA for one month with Karen."

"Oh my God, Wanda, that's great!" Meg runs and hugs me, followed closely by Jared.

"I'm going to be a celebrity trainer!" I scream jumping up and down. I can't wait to tell Karen.

"Wanda, you need to call Mum," Jared says when we have all calmed down.

"I know. I'll call her now. Do you think she'll be pleased?"

"Of course she will."

I feel so much closer to my mum recently that my hand shakes when I finally get enough courage to call her.

"Hi, Mum."

"Hello darling, how are you feeling now?"

"Good actually; I got a phone call from Move Makers last night."

I relay my conversation with Patsy and Mum sounds excited for me until it dawns on her that I might not come back. This dreams coming true thing could be harder than I thought.

Saturday 1st September

"Wanda, you look terrible are you alright?" Mike is behind reception when I turn up for my shift at 10.00 a.m.

"Hangover," I reply as I tap my head.

"Oh, so that's why you couldn't make dinner with me, you had to go and get pissed."

"I know it sounds bad but I was depressed and needed cheering up, then I got some news and needed to celebrate. Sorry."

My phone beeps from under the desk; it's a message from Meg, I'll look at it later.

"Let you off. So what's the good news then?"

I look up from under the peak cap I'm wearing and smile. "I'm off to work in LA for a month."

"What do you mean, I though Karen won?"

I tell Mike about the phone call from Patsy and make him promise not to tell Karen, as I want to see her face when she finds out.

"Well I'll miss you if they decide to keep you on, but it's a great opportunity; congratulations!" Mike says walking around to give me a hug.

"Thanks. Is Karen in?"

"Yeah, come on, I want to see this too."

We make our way to Karen's office.

"Wanda has some news," Mike says as we poke our heads around the door.

Karen raises her head looking puzzled. "What is it?"

"I'm coming to LA with you!"

Karen just looks more puzzled.

"What?"

"Patsy called me last night. They want me to go over with you."

Karen's face has turned from puzzled to horrified. "What? Why? How long for?"

"Only a month, not three like you but they think I'm a great trainer and want to give me a chance." I can't help grinning like a Cheshire cat.

"Oh, well that's great," she manages weakly before a smile works its way across her face. "I bet your boyfriend will miss you."

Bitch!

Chapter Thirty-One

The look on Mike's face has completely taken all the fun out of telling Karen that I'm going to LA with her. I can't believe she told him about Gary. This is going to take some fancy footwork.

"What boyfriend? Not sure who you mean. Anyway, got to get back to the gym, we can chat about America later...bye!" I exit her office at breakneck speed whilst trying to think how I'm going to get out of this one.

"Wanda, who is this boyfriend Karen, is talking about?" Damn Mike Diamond and his long legs. He is next to me in seconds. I stop and decide to tell him the truth. This is not from a sudden urge to relieve myself of burden, but the fact that I cannot think of a lie he might go for.

"His name is Gary, I met him a while ago and it's not serious. I wasn't sure if anything was going to happen between us; you know, as you still have a girlfriend," I add, trying to pass the blame.

"Wanda why didn't you tell me? Was you out with him last night?"

"No, just Meg, Jared and Marcus. Look, I'm sorry I would have broken up with him if you and I had got serious."

"You do remember we slept together?"

"Oh, yes of course, I was going to break it off with Gary but Meg had already invited him to the competition. I haven't seen him since though," I say, glad that Gary has been away this week so at least that wasn't a lie. — That is until I look up to see Gary walking through the door armed with a bunch of expensive-looking flowers.

"Oh look Wanda it's your lovely boyfriend," Karen announces with an over-the-top arm gesture.

Gary walks towards us looking rather pleased with himself.

"Hi guys," he says with a friendly nod to Karen and Mike, "I finished our project early so I thought I'd surprise you Wanda." He hands me the flowers and kisses me on the cheek.

I manage a smile before introducing him to Mike. "Gary this is my other boss, Mike."

"You're Gary, Megan's brother, aren't you?" Mike says looking puzzled.

"My name is Gary but I'm not Meg's brother," Gary says, looking equally confused then turning back to me.

I'm aware that I've adopted Meg's scary puppet face but other than that I've got nothing at this point.

"Wanda, you told me this guy was Megan's brother that night at your flat. Is he your boyfriend?"

"Well, erm…"

I catch Karen beaming from ear to ear before she casually looks away.

"Wanda, why did you tell your boss I was Meg's brother? And when was he at your flat?"

"Look, I can explain," I say whilst tucking my hair behind my ear, "It's very confusing but I met you both on the same day and nothing was really happening between any of us for a while so I was trying to make up my mind."

Mike runs his hand through his hair as though he is trying to digest this new information and Karen now has a look of pure joy on her face, surpassing the look she had when she was announced the winner of the competition.

"So our sleeping together was nothing happening?" Gary asks using air quotes on the nothing happening.

"No, no of course not…"

"And you've been seeing this guy as well?" Gary flings his arm towards Mike who is looking rather amused.

Mike shrugs his shoulders and steps back. "I didn't know about you either mate."

Gary raises his eyebrows at me. "Is there anything else you haven't told me?"

"I think there might be," Karen says behind her hand.

I jerk my head to scowl at her.

"Well go on, how many of us are there in the Wanda's Boys Club?"

"None, I mean just the two of you."

"So what other gem do you need to tell me?"

I place my flowers on a nearby chair and sigh. "I've been invited to go and work in LA for a month."

"What do you mean? But I thought Karen won the competition."

"Yes but they like me and my training methods plus I scored ninety-eight percent on all my theory and practical tests, so they want me to go with Karen in October."

Gary's shoulders fall as he exhales; he looks crestfallen. "I'm going to go, maybe we can talk later?"

I nod my head slowly. I feel sick as I watch him walk away. This was meant to be a great day but Karen had to stick her fuckin' pointy nose in and ruin it! I look across but she has high-tailed it back to her office before I can slap her bony face.

Turning to Mike, I notice he doesn't look as upset as Gary — bloody cheek — but I give him an apologetic smile. "Sorry."

"Wanda Mikos, you are indeed full of surprises. I thought you were a good girl."

"Yeah well, Mike can I ask you something; are you back with Chloe?"

Mike's mouth tightens into a guilty smile. "Not officially, but I have been to see her — sorry."

"We had fun though didn't we?" I say giving him my cheekiest grin.

"We sure did. Shame it was to be short lived."

"Yeah, I wanted to see what other stripper moves you could do."

Mike laughs as he walks over and gives me a hug. "You are an amazing girl Wanda Mikos and Gary is a lucky guy."

"Not sure about that, he deserves better."

"The way that guy looks at you I think you'll be alright. I would say give him some time and space but you're pissing off to America soon so that solves that problem."

I give him a teasing punch on the arm as we laugh and walk off in different directions.

I run up to the gym as I can't wait to tell the rest of the guys my news and when I do, their first question is 'what did Karen say?'

I relay the whole story including Karen outing me about Gary and then Gary turning up with flowers. A couple of members are sent away with insufficient information as neither Elliot nor Zoe is willing to miss a thing.

Karen is conspicuous by her absence for the remainder of my shift and I take a minute whilst tidying the weights, to reflect. This has been a funny old day with a mixture of emotions like no other I have experienced before: joy, at the news from America followed by feelings of sadness, shame and above all, the intense need to shit all over Karen's head!

Yes, it's been a funny old day.

***

I can smell lasagne when I get back to the flat and feel a twinge of fear knowing that if all goes well, I could be gone forever in four weeks. I switch from being really excited about LA to being scared stiff of leaving Meg, Jared and Mum. The thought of having to keep up the diet and exercise regime that has practically killed me is another aspect that is making me nervous.

Chapter Thirty-Two

1st October – Leaving for LA

We arrive at Heathrow at Terminal Three by 5.00 a.m. and I book my luggage in as soon as possible. Meg, Mum and Jared have insisted on seeing me off. I am grateful, but Mum keeps getting emotional and I have to remind her that I will be back in four weeks. It might just be to repack my bags if they want me but I don't dwell on that.

"It's just going to be a great experience that will help me in my career," I tell her, squeezing her shoulder.

"And what about Gary?"

I look up at her and sigh. "He hasn't returned any of my calls. I think that relationship is over. Probably for the best really."

"So it was a relationship then?" she asks gently touching my hand.

I look away as an unexpected pool of tears fills my eyes. I dare not blink or speak.

"Wanda, my darling, you are allowed to feel sad that you're leaving someone you truly care about."

I casually flick the tears away as they drop onto my cheek before turning back. "I didn't realise how much I did Mum, not until I lost him. He hates me and I can't blame him."

"Gary is a mature man who has been hurt but if he cares about you as much as I think he does, he'll come around. He probably needed time to think."

"Mum, it's been over four weeks; if he wanted to see me again he would have got in touch."

She gently strokes my hair away from my eyes and purses her lips. She knows I'm right.

"Hey Wand' is that Karen sitting in that coffee shop?" asks Jared who is making a telescope with his hands.

I look over to Karen who is wearing a suit like the ones she wears to work. I have chosen a pair of casual flared dark grey trousers with a pink t-shirt — my posh one — and a dark grey hooded jacket. Karen and her stern-looking mother are talking quietly and eating a sausage roll! A sausage roll? I need to get over there. Besides, it'll take my mind off Gary.

"Look Jay she's eating a bloody sausage roll. Shall we go over and say hello so she knows we know."

"Absolutely baby," he says before offering his hand up for a high-five.

Mum and Megan shake their heads in disapproval but follow us anyway.

Karen looks up as we approach her table and immediately drops her sausage roll and casually slide the plate to one side.

"Hi Karen, thought that was you."

"Oh hi, Wanda, this is my Mum, Carol."

"I remember you from the competition but didn't get a chance to hello; it's nice to meet you. This is my mum, Nina, my brother Jared and my friend Megan."

We exchange pleasantries for a minute but I can't help myself I have to mention it. "Having a last sausage roll before embarking on a life of salads and protein shakes again?"

"Oh," she says looking down at the plate, "that was Mum's breakfast, I just had a bite."

Jared lets out a cough and looks away. What a liar! She was hoovering that thing up like a new Dyson.

I am feeling superior and about to leave when she smiles that venomous smile of hers before she bites. "Didn't your boyfriend Gary want to see you off?"

A knot forms at the back of my throat and before I can respond my mum interjects.

"No, he wanted to but he had to work. They said their goodbyes last night; honestly, they are like two lovebirds. Now come on Jared, I thought we were going shopping."

I cannot believe my mum just said that. I give her a sneaky squeeze as we walk towards the shops.

The powerful scent of ...well everything, hits my nostrils as we enter duty free. Jared and Meg run around spraying each other with the latest perfume by some minor celebrity and I find myself taking a sneaky sniff of Davidoff. It immediately puts me back in Gary's arms when he greeted me after my performance at the competition. This is not healthy, so I move away. Unfortunately, the aroma appears to be following me out of the shop. I turn to let the others know I'll wait outside, when I see Gary standing there and smiling at me.

My knees dip and my tummy flips as I try to comprehend what's happening.

"Hi Wanda, I'm really glad I caught you before you left. I'm sorry I didn't return your calls but I needed to have a decent amount of time away from you to know for sure if I wanted to make a go of this or not; especially as you're going away for a month."

My fingertips are covering my mouth whilst he makes his speech. "And what did you decide?"

Gary flings his arm up and laughs. "Obviously I never want to see you again, which is why I have come all the way here today — you Muppet."

"Oh my God, I can't believe it, I'm so sorry," I say walking straight into his arms where I inhale the familiar smell of Davidoff once more.

"I have an idea," he says gently holding me away and looking into my eyes, "why don't we start again? Just pretend we have never met before and see where it takes us?"

"Really?"

"I'm game if you are."

A feeling of warmth begins at my feet and rises until it flushes my cheeks.

"I'm game."

Gary pulls me towards him and kisses me full on the lips.

"Oh my goodness, Gary?" Meg exclaims as they exit duty free.

We pull apart and Gary smiles. "Hi everyone."

"What are you doing here?" Jared asks

"Jared!" I respond, "He's here for me of course."

Gary smiles, pushes his fringe from his eyes and hold up a ticket. "I have this if you fancy some company on the trip."

***

By 8.00 a.m., the flight board indicates our flight is 'Now Boarding' and we say goodbye, cry a little and Meg squeezes me so hard she won't let me go. This is most unlike her and she makes me cry all over again.

Gary and I finish saying our goodbyes to everyone and recheck our gate number before moving off.

"So how long are you staying with me in LA?" I ask.

"Just a couple of days. I didn't know what your plans were so I booked into a hotel near your gym. I thought we could have a few days together but I don't want to get in the way."

I look into his grey eyes and smile. "Sounds perfect."

"Is that Karen?" he asks as we arrive at the gate.

Now I don't want to be shallow and spoil this romantic scenario but I really want to shove Gary up Karen's nose. Not literally of course and I realise it is immature and childish but my in-love smile is turning into a smarmy up-your-bum smile as we move towards her.

"Hello Karen, you remember Gary?" I present Gary like one of those girls on a prize giving show.

Her face drops and she sits back in her chair. "Oh, of course, nice to see you again."

"Gary decided to surprise me. He's flying with us to LA and staying for a few days."

"How lovely."

We make small talk before boarding the plane. Gary has managed to get a seat in the same row as me and has persuaded an old woman to swap seats so we can sit together. Karen is sitting across the aisle from me.

I tap her on the arm as the airplane engine rumbles into life. "Well, this is it," I say, noticing that Karen is looking rather green, "today is the start of a possible new life for both of us."

Karen takes a deep breath and exhales before nodding.

"Are you alright?" I ask as her face turns chalky white.

"It's just the take-off; I'll be fine once we're in the air."

"Well I just wanted to wish you luck."

"Thanks Wanda." Karen says turning to look at me. "I'd wish you luck too, but I have a feeling you're not going to need it."

THE END

About The Author

Wendy Ogilvie lives in Essex with her boyfriend Carl and their two dogs; Chinook and Storm. She has been a Personal Trainer for twenty years and has been writing training books and short stories in her spare time. The office in her new house is her favourite place to write as she can see the fish swimming in the pond and her two huskies digging up the garden!

She is currently working on the next novel in the Wanda series called Wandering Among the Stars.